# BECKONING BLOOD

*Bonds of Blood: Book I*

## DANIEL DE LORNE

*For Tracy*
*Wish you were here to see this*

## ❦ I ❧

# THIS SICK MONSTER
# WHO WORE HIS FACE

**1390**

Carcassonne, France

# I

THE PIG REFUSED TO DIE. THIERRY'S BLADE NICKED THE skin, and the animal bucked beneath him. *Stupid, squealing thing.*

"Christ's balls!" his twin brother Olivier spat. "What's the matter with you?"

Thierry ignored him and readied the knife for a clean cut, waiting for the swine to calm a little. He hugged it tighter as it tried to bolt. Its bristled hide stabbed him through the grime and blood coating his chest. The pig screamed louder.

*Why couldn't it just be silent?*

A shadow fell in front of him, as much as a shadow could form in one of Carcassonne's abattoirs, where light barely penetrated the wooden slats that penned them in.

"Are you trying to kill it or fuck it?" Olivier said.

The other slaughterers chuckled. Thierry's twin sighed, grabbed the pig's ear close to its skull, yanked the head up and plunged his knife into its neck. He sliced forward and out, blood spilling onto the stone floor as death shuddered through the pig's body. Thierry released the animal as it weakened and stood when it collapsed to the floor.

He turned to his viscera-coated brother. "I had it."

"Like hell you did." Olivier shook free the flecks of blood in his black hair and smiled a smile familiar yet so different to Thierry's own. One that said: *Admit it, you need me.*

They might have been twins, but Thierry knew *he* never smiled like that.

"Marcel, did Thierry have that pig?"

Marcel just laughed and went back to hanging the meat. The other workers snickered. Olivier smiled wider.

Thierry grabbed one of the pig's back legs and dragged it past his brother. When he got to the hooks, Marcel winked at him before going to pull in another animal. Thierry hoisted the carcass and slid a metal spike through its leg. Olivier's cut had been deep, but Thierry slit the throat wider to fully drain the animal, and then sheathed his blade by his waist.

He sensed his brother's eyes on his back, that questing gaze sliding up and down the gore and sweat on his skin. And then he felt that...*probing*...inside him. Not a gentle touch around the edges, rather the full hammering of Olivier's need to know what was going on inside his brother's mind. Deep breathing usually blocked his twin, but summer in the walled city was always bad, and here in the abattoir the air smothered. Flies buzzed around the meat or landed on the men and bit into their flesh. He tried to breathe through his brother's intrusion. The hot, heavy stink filling his lungs did nothing to prevent Olivier working the bond in deeper.

And Thierry knew, then, what he was really looking for. Or who.

He turned and glared at Olivier who stood there, eyes bright even in the gloom, a liar's smile on his face, convinced he was getting closer to Thierry's secret.

Thierry snorted and headed out the back to a yard filled with tethered beasts. The air there wasn't much fresher, but he sucked it in anyway and Olivier's presence lessened. It faded almost to nothing. Another pig screamed.

Olivier's smile didn't fool Thierry. The bond worked both ways, after all, and he was far more sensitive to it than his heavy-handed brother. As gentle as a forest stream, he travelled back up Olivier's diminishing connection and stole into his brother's thoughts and feelings. His twin boiled and Thierry boiled with him. The deeper he went, the closer to *one* he became, until finally he could see through Olivier's eyes, feel the grip of his hand on the leather hilt of the butcher's blade, and smell the blood spraying onto his brother's chest. Underneath it all, arrogant and unguarded thoughts tumbled over one another.

*Thierry. Thierry. Thierry...*

He tried to swim out of his brother's surging thoughts, but the torrent swirled and caught him. Thierry kicked to get free, panicked, and fell onto buckled legs against the outside wall of the abattoir. Sweat poured down his forehead and neck. He forced himself to breathe fully, just to prove he wasn't really trapped beneath the obsessive, greedy storm.

He didn't want to return to the abattoir, but Henri would be back soon, and he'd know, just by looking at him, that he hadn't done his share of the work. He'd be as good as unconscious after the shouting was done.

*God bless the Father.*

He pushed off the wall and turned to go inside when

the animals fell silent. All of them. No braying, no bleating. As if someone had stoppered their mouths with rags.

The silence *pressed*.

Something brushed his neck, subtle and discomfiting. Ugly enough to make him freeze when everything in him wanted to run. A feathered gaze.

He wanted to believe it was Olivier, but his brother was inside and the link between them was as quiet as the animals, as frozen as his blood.

Who watched him?

As quickly as it came, and before he could spin and peer into the shadowed recess between buildings, the sensation passed. The world breathed again, and the animals returned to their calling, louder than before.

Yet the rank darkness of the abattoir didn't feel so hostile now.

He hurried back inside, partially blinded while his eyes adjusted to the dim light. Olivier hunched over another pig, the muscles in his bare back tensing and relaxing as he sliced and gutted the animal. They had leather aprons, but in this heat, it was better not to wear them.

Thierry had another reason not to wear his. Without it, he exposed the long, pink scar on his back that stretched from shoulder to hip.

Olivier stopped butchering and looked back at Thierry. "What?"

The tension and evil of moments before—of whoever had been watching him—must have infected him because he could feel the danger of his ill-advised words even as they crossed his lips.

"Just admiring how perfect your back is." He didn't use this weapon often, knowing it would blunt. But today it was worth wielding.

Olivier threw his knife. It clanged as it struck the stone floor, blade first. The pig dropped with a sickening, wet thud and Olivier reared up to him.

"Is the Devil fiddling your prick?"

"Not at all, brother." He turned to get another pig from the pen. "I thought you liked being watched."

*Burn, my brother. B—*

Thierry lurched forward with the force of his twin's slam behind him. They crashed into the sty wall, splitting planks and spreading the foul, shit-covered straw amongst the swine. Thierry twisted under Olivier, swinging at his face, but his brother was quick and blocked his punch, grabbed his arms and pinned him.

"You use *that* against me?"

"He thought I was you," Thierry roared. "That cut was meant for you. If Aurelia hadn't—"

Olivier released him long enough to strike. His lips drew back in a snarl, his eyes glaring down like a knight's lance. "I wasn't even there."

Thierry shook his head to dispel the ringing in his ears.

"I know," he spat. "You were off fucking while father peeled the skin off my back. *Your* back."

And Henri hadn't even broken a sweat, those club hands deft with the skills of a master butcher. One effortless swipe was enough to cause Thierry's permanent disfigurement. Mercifully, Thierry was drunk, and only felt a spreading sting as his skin split like a sliced bladder. He had to thank God—or perhaps, their sister, Aurelia—that he hadn't been crippled.

"I couldn't have known."

Olivier tried to hold Thierry's arms, but they slipped in the grime. Like a whimpering puppy, his brother's remorse and sorrow nudged at Thierry's chest through the bond.

Thierry pushed it away. "Do you know what he said to me after he'd finished? 'You're a disgrace, Olivier.'" He poured his loathing into his words. "I'm sick of being mistaken for you, brother. We may look the same, but we are nothing alike. I won't be tortured for your sins."

Olivier sagged for a moment, offering enough time for Thierry to land a good punch. He fell back, dazed, away from the stall opening.

A pig bolted.

Once one escaped, the rest followed.

"Fuck!" Thierry scrambled out from under his brother's legs, out of the putrid straw, and called to the other workers. "After them."

Olivier rose, rubbing his jaw. "Take your last breath," and Olivier's mind clawed against him.

Thierry resisted as hard as he could. "Later," he grunted. "We need to catch the pigs before Henri returns."

Eight escaped, but between all of them it took only minutes to herd the trembling swine back into a secure pen. As Thierry towed the last by its tail, a silhouette filled the doorway.

Henri d'Arjou was built taller and broader than his sons, with muscles upon muscles, a closely shorn scalp. His skull, face and body sported the gouges and scars of his violent life. He never smiled but a skillful turn of his mouth showed the difference between displeasure and fury with only one result: a tirade of curses and fists.

From the doorway Henri homed in on Thierry, the only one stupid enough to still have a pig in his grasp. His hold started to give as his hands dampened. He wanted to fade into nothing.

Olivier stepped between them.

"Where have you been, Henri?"

Those cruel eyes refocused. One heavy, booted foot followed the other as he stamped his way towards Olivier. "What did you say to me, maggot?"

"I said, where the *bloody hell* have you been? We're behind on the work and—"

Only Olivier's split-second dodge avoided the fist aimed squarely at his head.

"I'll beat you until you shit blood."

"You can try, old man."

Once out from under his father's gaze, Thierry boiled with a need to fight alongside his brother. But did it come from him, or was the burning in his intestines just his brother's roused excitement?

*I will not help you.*

The pig squealed as he gripped its tail harder to prevent himself relenting then released it and followed it as it scrabbled out the door, slipping in the blood and guts of its fellows.

He grabbed a tunic off a hook beside the entrance, wiping the muck from his skin as best he could, and staggered out into the littered streets. As his brother and father brawled in the abattoir, his body flooded with the rush of fist colliding with flesh. He felt each and every blow: in his stomach, across his face, a kick to his legs. He sucked in deep breaths to calm himself and shore up the borders of his mind and body before he collapsed in the gutter. Henri rained down one final blow on Olivier's face and knocked him into unconsciousness.

Thierry leaned against a wall and retched.

THIERRY WANDERED THROUGH THE SWELTERING CITY of Carcassonne, stinking of innards and death. He weaved between the crowds as they pushed and jostled and made no effort to let one another pass. Thierry shoved back, staggering blindly until the residual nausea from Olivier's fight forced him to rest.

"Thierry? What's wrong?"

His sister ran to him through the crowd that parted for her. She placed a comforting hand on his back.

"I'm fine, Aurelia."

The words sounded more like a gurgle.

"Etienne! Can you help him?"

His head snapped up as Etienne de Balthas appeared and offered his hand. He took notice of the buildings around them and realized his blind escape had brought him straight to the apothecary.

His stomach lurched. *What was Aurelia doing with him?*

He forced himself straight before Etienne could touch him. "I'm fine. I just felt strange for a moment."

"You don't look well," Etienne said. "You should sit down."

"Thank you, but I'm better now." He turned his gaze to his sister. "What are you doing here?"

She fixed him with her brilliant, green eyes. "I was asking Etienne's advice. What are you doing here?"

Despite being younger, she spoke to him like a mother—or how he imagined a mother should sound. Theirs was long gone.

"Olivier." He needed to say nothing more.

"Ahhh."

He tried to concentrate on Aurelia but being this close to Etienne when he was ragged and hurting made it near

impossible. He stared at Etienne's hands, imagining them—
He shook his head.

"Do you feel better?" Etienne's caring, soulful eyes
filled with the concern of a healer. Or a brother. Or a
lover.

"Much." He pushed free. "I must go. Henri will be
hunting me."

Brown eyes pinned him. "So soon? I haven't seen you in
a long time. It's been nice to talk with your sister."

His skin prickled as if all of Carcassonne watched. He
pushed away from the wall. Time he was gone.

"You must visit us," Aurelia said to the healer. "You
know Father enjoys your company."

Panic roared through Thierry's body. "I'm sure Etienne
doesn't want to waste his time with us."

Etienne smiled briefly. "Not true, but I don't think
Olivier would approve. We've never really got along."

"Yes, I remember," she said, "but that's no reason why
we should be deprived of seeing you, just because of that
oaf."

"That's enough, Aurelia." And then, to his left, "She's
sorry, Etienne."

His sister held him with her emerald glare. "I have
nothing to be sorry for."

Etienne laughed. "Aurelia, stop by any time. You too,
Thierry." He nodded his head in farewell, glancing only
momentarily at Thierry's hands and departed.

"What was that about?" he growled at Aurelia as soon
as Etienne had entered his shop, gripping her elbow and
propelling her through the crowd.

"What's the matter with you? I like Etienne. You used
to like him too once, remember?"

"That was a long time ago. Things change."

"Yes, I'm aware of that. Now let go of my arm. You're hurting me."

He released her to surge ahead of him. He needed to get far from Etienne and rearrange the shields inside his mind, but as he followed Aurelia's simmering resentment through the streets, thoughts trailed behind him, catching at his heels.

He swore as they reached the abattoir. "Henri's going to be angrier than a rutting bull deprived of a cunt."

Aurelia took a deep breath. "Leave it to me."

She entered, and Thierry followed. Olivier lay passed out in the corner, left where he'd fallen. The other workers carried on as if nothing unusual had happened, every one of them knowing Henri would serve the same to any who moved to help.

The tyrant entered through the far door, dragging a wide-eyed cow behind him. He didn't acknowledge his children, but after he'd tied the keening cow to the wall, he transformed into the monster they'd lived with all their lives and stalked towards Thierry.

"Where did you go?" He raised his balled fist.

Aurelia stepped in front of their father and placed a hand gently on his chest. "Father, please, not now," she said in a soft, soothing tone.

Bile tanged at the back of Thierry's throat as hardness blanketed his body, and he crouched, ready to push her out of the way if Henri reacted. He'd been down this road so many times. So had Aurelia.

But it wasn't necessary.

Henri awoke from his berserker's fury and peered down at his daughter. "Yes, now!"

But the fire had gone.

"He's back," she smiled, "so there's no problem. Is there?"

A growl rumbled in his throat. He looked from his daughter to his son and narrowed his eyes. He lowered his fists and rolled his shoulders, turning to the next cow to die. "Get back to work."

Thierry spun her around, her green eyes slightly dulled and tired as if she'd worked through the night. "How did you do that?"

She gave him a tight smile. "Perhaps I remind him of mother." She slid out of Thierry's grasp and headed to the door. "Check Olivier isn't dead. I'll see you at home."

She left, and in her wake, above the smell of meat and sweat and shit, wafted the subtle scent of orange blossom.

II

Olivier knew Thierry itched to get away from him. His twin cowered in a corner of the inn, nursing a second tankard of ale for what had so far been a long night. His shoulders hunched. He threw hostile looks at the drunken hoard around him. He swallowed hard and beat his thumb on the wooden table.

Olivier knew Thierry had somewhere better to be.

His brother's tension sawed on Olivier's nerves as tightly as any fiddle, as if the bruises and aching bones weren't enough. The crowd pressed in on him, every laugh sharp, and every nudge a tightening on a dagger's hilt. He sipped his fifth drink. The other four had mostly ended up on the floor, or splashed into the street, or on some merry-maker. It might have been necessary, but he hated the waste of ale, even if it was as weak as child's piss.

The inn was crowded, with plenty of bodies to hide what Olivier did. The brothers wasted many evenings drinking the swill the barmaids served. Not a shadow existed in the place Olivier hadn't conquered, whether it was a fight or a fuck. And they kept coming back for more.

Tonight, he'd dragged Thierry here to guilt his brother for not helping him when Henri attacked. Olivier didn't let on how deeply that cut. He was his usual self; perhaps a little more so as he played to the crowd's desires and inspired lusty looks in the eyes of women and men alike. The stories that came out of his mouth added more fuel to an already blazing fire. They raised their drinks to him and cheered for more. He kept an eye on Thierry—one internal, one external—but it became difficult as the night wore on and the numbers grew.

*Let this play out. Let Thierry go where he wants. But he won't go alone.*

"Enjoying yourself?" Olivier slurred at Thierry as he took a seat. His brother smiled meanly and lowered his eyes, intent on his cup. Around them, the din suddenly turned off-key. The atmosphere in the inn charged, ready for a fight. Olivier knew if Thierry was going to avoid trouble, he had to make his exit soon.

Thierry faded, just for a moment, a flicker, as his clothes and body turned as see-through as gossamer. Olivier's heart sank. Thierry used this little trick whenever Henri was handing out the shit jobs at the abattoir.

Tonight he used it on him.

He banished the hurt for the weakness it was and steeled himself for what he must do. He'd find whom Thierry was fucking and slice him from groin to sternum. Thank God one of them was strong enough to do what was necessary.

Summoning all his good cheer, he slapped on a drunken smile and lurched from the table. He spilled his drink across the table, splashing it in his brother's face. "Sorry about that."

A whore ducked under his flailing arm and hugged her

warm body against him, her swine tits half exposed in her low-cut dress. Olivier guffawed and staggered away with her into the crowd. Once out of Thierry's view, he unfurled himself from her grimy, grasping hands and stumbled to a table, jolting another reveler and spewing false apologies. Muddled with ale, the drunk accepted it—just—and got out of his way. Someone else would have to start a fight.

He grabbed a stool, sat down and leaned against the wall. From here he could keep a check on his brother and the door. He closed his eyes and pretended to sleep. Barely a minute passed before he stole a glance through half-closed lids. Thierry's chair was empty, and the door just closing.

Bitterness scored his gullet. He'd been left behind again, and his brother had thought him so dumb that he wouldn't notice. He pitched the tankard across the room, the ale pouring out in an arc the color of river water. He growled to subdue his temper so Thierry wouldn't suspect anything through the bond.

Pushing people out of the way, Olivier burst onto the dark street. The sound of crashing chairs and shouting welled up behind him, but he didn't care. In the distance, Thierry hurried away from home. He'd set his course for the gates.

Olivier followed as Thierry slipped out of the town and down the road to the forest. His step was quick, almost a jog. Olivier hung back, giving him some distance.

Out of the confines of the town, the night was warm. Cicadas heralded him. The moon and stars lit the way as he focused on his step, timing each one carefully.

*Breathe in, two, three, four.*

Who knew what and whom he might find?

*Breathe out, two, three, four.*

So it went, one measured step after another, one wall

going up after another, blocking out his worry of who had seen them leave, anger over what Thierry was doing, jealousy over whom he was meeting.

Ahead, forest shadows swallowed his brother. Keeping his emotions under control was made even more difficult when he ran to catch up. A deep grunt galloped from his throat as Thierry's need and excitement burst through his blood. Too late, he clamped his hand over his mouth. Thierry was nearer to his lover than Olivier expected, and with each passing moment Thierry's desire bubbled up like thick molasses, coating his insides and dragging him down. Olivier stumbled, the gravel crunching beneath his feet, and his knee hit the ground. He hadn't felt anything like this before, not from Thierry.

*Breathe in, two, three, four.*

Perhaps it was his closeness. Little light pierced the canopy. The darkness helped focus him on the beacon of Thierry's lust-filled blood. It throbbed stronger now Olivier had caught up and pulled him deeper into the ancient wood. He tripped on roots grown to catch his feet and bashed his shins on sharp rocks.

*Breathe out, two, three, four.*

He had to go on. The leaves whispered, beckoned, enticed him to come inside, to penetrate the dark places, to discover the source of his brother's pleasure.

Thierry's desire drenched him like a wall of scalding water. He put out a hand and scraped it over the ridged bark of a gnarled tree. He felt nothing, and it did little to distract him from his twin's desire. He tried to fight it, but as it battered him and stirred his own, he lost his resolve. He closed his eyes, breathed in and succumbed to Thierry's ecstasy.

Feeling it was so much more vivid than seeing it. Yet he

could do both, despite the darkness. Despite the distance. As though he'd become his twin. Feeling his emotions, smelling, seeing, touching, tasting. All Thierry's.

All gloriously vivid. All horrifyingly real.

His cock raged to furious life, and his balls tightened.

Tongues met, pressed, hungry kisses underscored with a deep warm affection. Olivier staggered at the force of the underlying love.

"Etienne." It had to be a thought, not a word, since Thierry's lips were occupied.

*Etienne de Balthas.*

*Bastard!*

Thierry fumbled in his haste to release his cock, every part of him blazing more than the savage kiss of the fire behind them, which popped and crackled as it consumed the wood and the two men devoured each other. Thierry moaned as Etienne kissed down his body and flicked his tongue on his cock's head. He thumped the ground with his hand as his lover took him in his eager mouth and drew back hard.

Olivier dropped to the forest floor, quivering.

Afire with ecstatic agony, Thierry ripped at Etienne's hair. He wanted him. Hard and now.

"Fuck me."

Etienne licked swollen lips and spat on his hand, rubbing saliva on his own throbbing cock as Thierry turned his screaming body onto all fours. Etienne positioned himself in between Thierry's legs, one hand on Thierry's hip, one around his shaft, easing into him

Olivier's mouth filled with the sweet sting of blood as he bit into his own lip.

"Don't stop," Thierry grunted somewhere out in the darkness.

OLIVIER WATCHED IT ALL. LIVED IT ALL. HE'D DRAGGED closer on his belly like a submissive dog until he lay, ignored and unseen, just out of the fire's light. His eyes burned from forcing them open, absorbing every carnal moment. Spying as Thierry impaled himself on Etienne. Feeling every ragged second as skin slapped on skin. His own cries were disguised beneath the guttural grunts and wails of lust coming from the two men, sounds that would have shamed whores.

Betrayal and hate polluted his veins, stronger than he'd ever experienced, uglier than he'd thought possible, but still barely surfacing above the frantic pull of Thierry's base lust and blazing love.

He'd experienced every bile-boiling moment until the lovers came with shouts and collapsed to hold each other.

He staggered away.

*Never again.*

He could creep up on the two of them and beat Etienne to death with a rock. But that would be too easy. For once, he needed to be subtle.

He stoked this idea as he headed back the way he'd come. He kicked at the ground. A fight in the tavern would do him for now. The sooner he could bust his knuckles on someone's face the better. Already he could feel Thierry's need rekindle, slow, but determined.

He stopped and looked at the unfamiliar shapes in the shadows.

Any hint of firelight had long since faded, and his senses were dulled from overuse. Even if he could see, he didn't know which way to go. He remembered stories of people lost in the woods who were torn apart by monsters—though his common sense said it was most likely wolves—or of the Devil taking their souls and feasting on their flesh. He wasn't scared, just lost. He wiped sweat from the back of his neck.

He listened for familiar sounds. He strained for the music of Carcassonne floating on the wind, but nothing guided him. There was only the soft sashaying of the trees above, and his breath growing louder with each footfall.

His heart, bruised from its earlier pounding, kicked up a heavy rhythm. As he rampaged through the undergrowth, leaves and twigs crunching beneath his feet, wings beat the air. The noise grew louder, as if flocks of birds joined the flight and coursed towards him. Only his raspy breathing rivalled that awful sound.

He peered through darkness, barely making out trees which, seeing them too late, he bumped against. Giants grew in an instant and blocked his path, and all the time the fluttering kept on as he cut a jagged path. The noise was too big for one bird, or many birds.

*Whump, whump, whump.*

A cape, that's what it was. The sound of a heavy leather cape billowing in the wind behind him.

Then above him.

But capes belonged to men, not birds, and so what followed him? And where was the edge of the damned forest?

*Shit, Thierry, this is your fault.*

A fox screamed nearby. Olivier turned his head to look behind, look up, but formless shadows loomed. His stride slowed as fear anchored in his muscles. The wings circled him, descended until he thought he could feel them at his back. A light twinkled in the distance. Hope surged. His legs shook off their burden, and he ran faster. He laughed. He was going to make it.

"You're mine."

He screamed at the closeness of the serpentine voice. His foot hooked over a raised root, and he pitched forward into the black and a waiting tree. His head hit the trunk, and he collapsed on the ground. Darkness scoured his vision and unconsciousness dragged him down.

He woke. Not at home. Not at the tavern. Not at the abattoir. His eyes sought the dim light, but they wouldn't focus. The more he tried, the more his head throbbed. And any small movement made his neck sting. He had no strength to lift his body, just his hand, which quaked on the way to his throat. He took a sharp intake of breath as he touched the wet skin and held his fingers in front of his face.

Blood.

Too much blood for a small gash. Where had it come from? How did he get here? This wasn't the forest. There was firelight. He'd hit a tree. Screaming. Thierry and Etienne. Something. Flying. Lost. He was lost. Hurt. And bleeding. He breathed fast and shallow. He rushed to feel his neck again and sucked air through his teeth. With more care than before, he felt around the wound. Flesh was missing. The skin was frayed and gaping. No tree could do that.

Might this kill him? But he dismissed the thought with the sheer force of his will. Not Olivier d'Arjou.

"It'll heal."

A man's voice, low and breathy, came from his right,

and he remembered the it murmured into his ear before he fell. He tried to shift his head, but his nerves screamed at the strain on the ruined skin and muscle at his neck. He stopped moving, instead seeking the voice's owner with his eyes. He saw the fire and, behind that, a shadow. He blinked.

When he reopened his lids, the man was close to him, over him, and he quivered at the speed with which he'd moved. He had brown, thinning hair, and was at least his father's age. A greasy shine glistened over his skin, matching the bloated stomach and wispy hair. Fat hands spiked with stubby fingers stroked at his chin beneath a gash of a mouth. He looked like a simpleton, someone who had no purpose in life except to eat, shovel shit in the stables, and die. His eyes glowed in the flickering light, preventing him from guessing their real color. What had this man done to him? Who was it and what did he want?

The man smiled, his mouth opening wide to long, pointed canines dripping with saliva. Terror as sharp as the monster's fangs sank into Olivier's heart and forced the screams into his throat. He wanted to disappear into the safety of the earth, but he couldn't move. He couldn't feel anything, not the ground at his back nor the dirt under his hands. Surely this was death. And he welcomed it.

"I've watched you in the forest with that lover of yours," the monster said.

Olivier shivered. Had he felt cold before? No, it had been warm when he'd followed Thierry into the forest. Would Thierry look for him?

"He doesn't hold my interest, but you? Well, you're exactly what I'm looking for."

The thing bit into its own wrist, blood welling up

around its grotesque mouth before putting it to Olivier's lips. Blood streamed into his mouth and he gagged as it coated his tongue and wormed its way down his throat. He resisted but blood filled his mouth and he had to swallow or else he'd suffocate. The panic subsided with the first gulp, and his taste buds lit with the richness greater than that of wine and a bouquet stronger than a field of roses. Light flooded his eyes, seeing colors he had no name for. He struggled to remain conscious as his senses drowned in more life than he'd ever known. He sucked at the monster's wrist like a pig in a trough, gorging himself on the bounty to ensure he got his fill, guzzling mouthful after mouthful before it was taken away. He tried to hold on, but he was still weak and couldn't stop its removal.

Olivier growled. With his sharpened vision, he watched the wound heal without a trace. He watched as the monster ripped his flesh anew and press it back to Olivier's lips.

This time, when it returned, Olivier had the strength to grip it with both hands and crush it to his mouth. More of the stranger's blood coursed through his system, reaching to the farthest ends of his body, to the tips of his hair and tingling through every inch of skin. Strength swam through his limbs. He could lift his head again.

The life-giver sat and pulled Olivier close. He drew more, licked at the wound, marveling at its healing before he tore into it himself to feed. He cared not if he caused pain. The blood was all. The bland fare they had at home, the cheap ale in the tavern, they had never come close. He craved the thickness of it as it came into his mouth, and it reminded him of a similar texture, a similar pleasure. There was force, life in abundance.

The flow slowed but he drank until the wrist was

wrenched from him. The man, whatever he was, lay back, staring, smiling at him.

Olivier looked at his hands. His palms hummed; they seemed to glow. They were changing in front of him, but he didn't know how. He ran those luminous hands across the rest of his body and the wound in his neck. It had healed, with no trace of having ever been.

He sighed happily and closed his eyes to breathe in this miracle.

Thierry was gone.

The realization shocked him out of his reverie. Shock turned to panic prickling at the back of neck. Thierry couldn't be gone. He searched desperately for some feeling from his brother. But there was nothing.

"What have you done to me?" he snarled at the monster. Fangs dropped from his jaw and stopped thoughts of Thierry dead. He used his tongue to circle one tooth, pressing against the point, and punctured the flesh. He hissed, the surprise throwing him backwards like a frightened cat, and found he was on the far side of this—what was it, a cave? Yes, they were in a cave. He pressed his fingers to the fangs, cutting them open too, but they healed by the time he brought them away from his mouth. At the sight of the residue blood, he stuck his fingers in his mouth. Greedily. It wasn't the same taste. Disappointment swamped him.

The reclining man laughed.

"What in God's name are you?"

He continued to laugh. Olivier roared, and the sound made him snap his mouth shut, cut off mid-scream, as it reverberated against the stone. Was that him? That inhuman sound? That sound that could kill a man where he stood?

He looked again at the beast. Lying prone on the

ground, he was a much less impressive figure. Olivier raced to him, unsteady when he stopped. The speed would take some getting used to.

"What are you?"

"You mean, 'we'," the man whispered. "We are the Undead."

"What does that mean?"

"We feed on the blood of humans and in turn we will never get sick and we will never die. I have given you a great gift."

Immortality? He groped again for any scrap of his brother that remained, but he was empty. Immortality without Thierry? With each passing minute, strength galloped through his limbs. It hardened him, but without his twin he would always be weak.

Olivier helped him stand. "Why me?"

"Because I saw you in the forest with that other man and had to have you for myself."

Olivier sneered. Look how the mighty crumbled under the weight of loneliness. "That was Thierry, my brother."

The Undead growled and lashed out at Olivier, but he just let him go. Still weak from Olivier's excess, he slumped to the ground in a shameful heap. Olivier's heightened mind was already working faster. Better. Honed for survival. If he was going to live forever, he wasn't going to do it with a pot-bellied, greasy-skinned eunuch.

"Sorry to disappoint you but it's not all bad. You can have both of us." Olivier knelt down, moved close to his ear and murmured hotly: "We're twins."

He flicked the yellowed ear with his tongue, kissed along his pudgy neck and around to his mouth. He paused and looked into those golden eyes, wondering what color his own would now be. Would they be this otherworldly? Someone could go mad for those eyes.

"Imagine the possibilities."

He kissed him and rocked his hips against the growing hardness of the Undead's choked erection.

"But there's something we have to do first."

# III

THEY LINGERED LONGER THAN THEY SHOULD, BUT neither Thierry nor Etienne wanted to leave the forest. They walked in silence, hands clasped, until they neared the edge. Thierry refused to go further.

"No one can see us," Etienne coaxed. "Don't worry."

"I'm..." Normally he'd be too anxious to break the quiet, but this time it wasn't fear of other people that made him stop. He knew it was just him and Etienne. That was the problem.

"I can't feel Olivier." At all. Not one part of his body registered his brother's existence, and his stomach clenched with the absence.

Etienne let go. "He's probably passed out."

Thierry held his hands on his belly as if he could fill the loss. But whatever the connection was, Olivier had vanished and, in his place, left a slick of grease. "No. This is different."

"I thought you'd welcome the solitude. I know I would." Etienne muttered the last under his breath and turned away. He was quickly lost in the darkness, his only trail the sound of crisp leaves crunching under foot.

*Olivier's fine. He'll return, and then you'll be sorry you wasted this moment.*

Thierry chased after Etienne. When he reached him, he spun him around and kissed him hard. He blocked his concerns for Olivier, focusing only on Etienne's strong but soft lips, the warmth of his body, and the safety of his touch. Etienne withdrew.

"How long can we keep doing this? The secrecy is too much. That charade with your sister was nearly more than I could bear."

"You know it has to be this way. One day—"

"We won't have to hide?" The sarcasm in his voice stung but not as much as the truth behind them.

His body tensed, willing him not to speak, but he forced the words from his mouth. "It will have to stop." They came out in a harsh whisper, but they were loud enough to be heard. They hung in the air between them like stripped carcasses.

"Why?"

"We'll be caught."

"Then why not end it now?"

"Because..." He knew they would die for what they had done. He wanted to keep that day far away, and so they'd chosen the path of denial. As far as everyone else was concerned, Thierry d'Arjou and Etienne de Balthas were strangers.

But there had to be a balance, and now they met nearly every evening, spouting one excuse after another to justify their absence from their families. Their lies would spin a hangman's noose. The forest had provided a safe place for so long, but it, too, wouldn't last.

"Because..." He knew why. He'd said it many times before, but now, faced with a moment when he might have the chance to save Etienne, he couldn't utter those words.

Etienne didn't speak. In that moment of Thierry's hesitation, he disappeared into the night. Fear turned Thierry's feet into iron weights. The risk was too high.

Soon, Etienne was lost to his clouded vision, and those three whispered words, which he finally uttered with a reverence saints would envy, went unheard.

IV

THE SUN BLOOMED FROM BEHIND THE FOREST TO LIGHT the walls of Carcassonne and stir its inhabitants from their slumber. Death followed sharply on its approach. Olivier hadn't returned home overnight. He'd spent the hours with Rellius, that pathetic corpse, learning all he could. The more knowledge he absorbed, the more intoxicated he became with his newfound power. Strength, speed, invincibility—all his. Forever. Dawn stirred his hunger, and he was ready to make the town his hunting ground.

But first there was someone he had to find.

Olivier knew Etienne de Balthas. They had briefly been friends—of sorts—when he and Thierry were boys and had never suspected Etienne's tastes favored men. If he'd known, he would have offered. He couldn't fault his brother's admiring eye, but he could hold it against him.

He travelled faster than he'd ever thought possible, the fields a yellow blur as he sped towards Carcassonne's formidable walls. He scaled them easily, just to see if he could, and dropped into the cesspit that was once his town. A rank and rich stench assaulted his nostrils. He slumped against a wall and let the smells infiltrate him. Human and animal waste mixed with the odors of diseased and dank citizens. He filled himself with their scent until he could discern pig from sweating man, or cured meat from dying crone. Under it all wafted the aroma of blood, and he shivered.

He considered finding Thierry at the abattoir, just to check that he still lived. The emptiness of losing the bond with his twin had passed, and now his body felt filled with sand, its walls shored against letting anything in. He pressed his mind against them and found no crack. His body held him prisoner. If he saw Thierry now, he didn't know if he could restrain himself. He couldn't let Thierry see him, not yet. They would be together again. Once Etienne was dealt with.

He raced through the winding streets to Etienne's home, arriving in time to watch him depart for the apothecary. Olivier remembered Etienne as an annoyingly good boy, and the little he'd heard of him after they'd grown told him he hadn't changed. He was always willing to help and only too keen to show the boys the path of righteousness. No fun; that's how the memories were tainted.

Today, there was no smug smile on Etienne's face, no puffed-up chest. Olivier's fangs extended over his broad grin, and he trailed his brother's lover.

It took an age before Etienne arrived. He stopped and talked to an endless string of people on the way—men mostly—who called out and asked his advice. Etienne: always obliging, always so eager to please, even now with sorrow darkening his face. He was the only boy the brothers knew who Henri spoke well of. Henri thought he was something special, something good, something better than his two waste-of-flesh sons.

By the time Etienne entered the shop and got to work, Olivier was ready to destroy something, the bloodier the better.

First, he killed a maid. He snatched her off the street and pulled her into an alley. A squeak broke from between her pale, thin lips as he crushed her beneath him and drove his teeth into her. He was quick, brutal and unforgiving. He drained her blood in minutes, her life force spilling out of his mouth as he struggled to swallow fast enough. Gasping, he nearly passed out from the rush as her essence flowed through him and drowned any thought of Etienne or Henri.

He moaned over her dying body. Her feeble struggles added to the dizzying effect of her blood as he consumed her. He hungrily licked whatever remaining drops he could from around his lips and the wound in her neck before wiping his face and hands on the hem of her dirty skirt. Smears of blood stained his clothes, but no one would think anything about it, not on him. He left her empty where she fell and stumbled back into the crowd.

His first real kill. His first drink from a human. He giggled at the deliciousness of her blood and the ease at which she'd been dispatched. He needed another.

Wandering amongst the crowd, he eyed the people, sizing them up as he would a cow or pig for the slaughter. Who would be next? He recognized faces he knew and recalled wrongs they had done him. Perhaps they would suffer the most. He would try them all, from biggest to smallest, testing out his strength, his agility, his delicacy. So many to—

Someone bumped into him from behind. He reared around as fluidly as a snake and homed in on the culprit. He was a boy, about fourteen, already a broad-shouldered lad but barely bearded. Fearful recognition entered his eyes.

Olivier didn't know the boy, but Olivier's reputation was always ahead of him.

"I'm so-so-sorry. I didn't mean to." The boy looked down, as if expecting Olivier to strike.

"I know how you can make it up to me." Olivier's voice dripped with honey and spice, and allowed his eyes to burn with golden light, the same as Rellius's. The boy's fear faded as threat became enticement. Olivier held out his hand, and the boy took it without hesitation and followed into the gloom between cramped and crooked houses.

Olivier had always been good at seduction. When he was human, both sexes were drawn to him without much persuasion, for better or worse, but now it radiated from him with the force of the sun. His voice, his eyes, his whole body was irresistible.

The boy struggled less than the maid. Olivier groped him while he sucked out his life, enjoying the feel of a young cock in his palm. With his other hand, he gripped one of the boy's arms. His bones splintered, and he died whimpering.

Olivier swam his tongue through the last mouthful of blood. The difference between the blood of the boy, the maid, and his maker was unmistakable. Rellius's blood would always be something special, his first taste of the magical elixir, and filled with a depth of flavor that stirred all his senses. Rellius' blood tasted of history and all its horrors.

In contrast, the humans' blood was young. Potent. Fresh. Even then, they each had their own characteristics. He got the impression of lemon with rosemary for the boy. For the girl, it was lavender and carrots. When he thought about it, he wondered how they could incite such greed, but they were just hints. The blood carried the strength of the taste. But why would they have their own notes? Perhaps it was because one was male, one was female. Perhaps their ages. Could it be what they'd last eaten? Where they'd slept? What about the time of day? He had to know more.

He found the blacksmith next, then another maid, one of the carpenter's sons, his cousin who was heavy with child (such a lucky find) and finally—before the light started to fade, and Etienne was due to close the shop and head home —a soldier, who died while they fucked.

That had been the high point of his day.

Olivier emerged from his last kill like some sated pig, the blood of seven warming his body, and his tongue over-sensitive from the taste of so many lives. Each one had been unique, and each had something to savor. Not one flavor repeated on his tastebuds, and he regretted their loss as they slipped away. The possibilities of more snuffed out any sadness. With the urge to feed quelled, he returned to watch Etienne depart from his shop.

But instead of heading home, Etienne hastened to the east gate. He'd shaken off his earlier misery, and his step seemed almost light. There was no doubt where he was going or whom he was meeting. Jealousy reawakened the desire for blood, and its barbs stung. Olivier stalked him to the gates and spied him as he walked toward the forest.

Even in the fading light, he could make out every detail of Etienne's clothes: the tear behind his right knee, the stain across his back. When he disappeared into the under-growth, Olivier followed.

V

"WHERE'S YOUR BASTARD SON-OF-A-WHORE BROTHER?"
Henri shouted for the tenth time. His skin glowed a violent
shade of people, and froth collected in the corner of his
mouth. It had been a knife-throwing day. Thierry weath-
ered it and kept quiet. If he knew the answer, he would
have told him.

The night had come and gone without Olivier's return.
Normally that wouldn't be so odd, but every time Henri
cursed his brother's name, Thierry's belly twisted, and his
blood reached for something no longer there. He didn't
want to think about his twin. He tried to push Olivier out,
but his ghost haunted the abattoir.

Henri left around midday to find a meal, and Thierry
wasn't far behind. He should have been thinking about
Etienne, not worrying about his brother. There had to be
some reason he felt the way he did, some explanation that
made sense. Perhaps the link had just broken, worn out with
all the fighting. Perhaps he'd been granted his wish to be a
separate being. Perhaps Olivier had just eaten something

that made him sick. But if that was the case, where was he now?

Etienne had to nearly knock him down to get his attention. He'd wandered not far from the abattoir and woken from his reverie as Etienne grabbed him. The guilt almost made him groan. He'd been thinking of Olivier again.

"Meet me tonight," Etienne whispered and slipped away.

Contact had been brief but worth it as warmth flooded Thierry's body. The barest of touches, the slightest of smiles and Etienne had him completely. Maybe it would be all right after all. He returned to the abattoir and worked until evening. Not even Henri's foul mood tarnished his hope.

The sun had barely set before Thierry faded from sight and slipped out of the abattoir behind Henri's back as he finished off the last cow.

Outside the city, he trod a well-worn path and entered the soothing coolness of the forest. Memories gamboled around him of the many times they'd made love beneath the boughs of ancient oaks. His step quickened at the thought of seeing Etienne again, all to himself.

He had to make this right. He'd been wrong to speak those words and fill their time with dark portents of things that may not come. He'd been worried about Olivier, that's why he'd acted the way he did. No, he wouldn't mention Olivier, not by name. He had already caused them too much heartache.

Fantasies filled his head until they smothered all concerns for his twin. He and Etienne would survive. They would love forever, together, without fear of discovery, reprisal or the stake. To survive, he would have to find a way, even if it took a lifetime. He wouldn't give up, even under the promise of death, because to do that would be to throw ash in the face of the man who loved him above all others.

He reached the grove, guided by a fire. His eyes drifted up to see the rug spread on the ground. He held his breath in anticipation of seeing Etienne, but when he did, he halted, horror dawning on him.

Etienne sat against the tree's trunk, his legs cast out beneath his limp form. His head bent back, his perfect mouth gaping. Firelight reflected off the whites of his eyes as they stared unmoving at the heavens. Dark stains coated his neck and ran down the front of his once-white shirt.

"Etienne! Please no, Etienne."

Thierry ran towards him. Maybe if he touched him it would all be a lie. Maybe this was a joke, to teach him a lesson for being so cold to him. Yes, he would accept this punishment, and worse, if it was all just a joke, some trick, some fun.

But he didn't get to touch him.

A hand stopped him, gripped the back of his neck and held him mid-air. He scrambled to break free, but it was no use.

"I've waited so long for you, Thierry," the voice behind him said. An arm reached around, pulled him closer to his captor, increasing the distance between him and the unmoving Etienne. Thin hair brushed against his skin.

"He hoped you wouldn't come. He begged me to let you live. 'Take my life,' he said, 'just let him live.' I had to oblige."

"Murderer. If I get free, I'll tear you into so many pieces they won't recognize you." He knew how feeble his words sounded but he'd fight to the death.

The voice shushed him as it would sooth an angry child.

Thierry shouted and strained to loosen the hold, but all for naught.

His head was forced to the right. Then, the pain, a sting that sliced through his neck and emblazoned his nerves.

Bitten. Fangs. Two long, sharp fangs puncturing his skin. Soft lips created a seal over the holes. Blood flowed from his neck. The agony made him kick. The fear made him scream. It only made this depraved demon latch on harder, deeper and rip the flesh to drink his blood all the faster.

His vision wavered and his strength faded until he hung in the man's grasp. His life ebbed, just as Etienne's must have. He fixed his eyes on his lover's lifeless body, now devoid of the gentle strength that made Etienne so beautiful. There was no reassuring smile, no understanding gaze. He may as well have been a stone. That was not Etienne. His soul had fled.

Thierry cried, death running freely down his cheeks. He tried to find solace in the hope that he would soon be with Etienne forever and that they were going to a better life. He could see Etienne's soul shimmer in the shadows next to the tree behind his empty shell. Etienne waited for him.

Death would come soon.

The grip loosened, and he plummeted to the ground. Sharp rocks tore his side. He lay in a crumpled heap. The pain dulled as darkness drew near. His breathing slowed.

He flinched as thick liquid covered his eyes and blocked out everything around him: the face of his attacker, the shadow of the trees as they danced with the firelight. But from behind closed eyelids he saw a world colored red. Blood coated his face and blinded him. Was it his blood? It kept coming, in a thick and steady stream, as if it were cream poured from a jug. It coursed down his cheeks and around his nostrils before finally dripping into his slack mouth. He swallowed against his will and spluttered.

A wrist stoppered his mouth and the blood snaked down his throat. He blinked and made out shapes, the outline of someone large over him. He wanted to see Etienne. He wanted to see if Etienne still waited for him and would take him away from the desecration of their place.

But Etienne didn't come.

And Thierry didn't die.

He wiped his vision clear with one hand, surprised at the vitality regained, and looked up into the hideous face of this creature. Its eyes bulged, a greedy and ecstatic grin stretched his face, like Thierry was found treasure.

The blood flowed, slathered Thierry's tongue with rich flavors of sweet fruit and bitter wine. He gripped the wrist, glaring at this abomination above him. The more he drank, the more the blood sizzled inside him as it struck the hot stones of his fury. His strength grew as he was pulled back from the edge of blissful death, and with it came a familiar sensation, almost unnoticed at first as his hunger for the blood grew, but then, in between his strengthening heart-beats, he felt it once more, the thing thought lost.

*Olivier.*

He was here. He was close. Thierry twisted his head around to find him, wrenching the wrist with him like some infant sucking on bread and distracted by flying things. Where was he? Was he safe? Was he alive? What if this ghoul attacked him? Thierry couldn't save Etienne, but maybe he could save Olivier. He wouldn't have much time, but he'd fight. He'd kill this monster.

*There.*

Olivier emerged from the shadows next to Etienne's crumpled form. He was so close, so near Etienne. Didn't he see him? Couldn't he see Etienne was dead? He was so calm, so at ease with this strange scene before him. Why didn't he run and try to save himself? Instead, his smile was serene as he watched his twin tearing into the man's wrist.

Thierry understood and gagged. Olivier had known about him and Etienne, and now his lover was dead. What had Olivier given to make that happen? He'd sacrificed Etienne to this fiend and forsworn his own brother to drink this fetid blood. Had he been tricked, or had the opportunity just been too good to let it pass? Power, a thirst for blood, the regained connection: that's what Olivier had traded for Etienne's life.

*He did this so no one else could have me.*

The blood hammered inside his body and steeled him for what he had to do. His pulse beat faster as he grappled with his rage. He shook with the effort. Olivier would not survive this night.

With each step Olivier took, Thierry strengthened. He felt the monster weaken as the wrist hung limply at his lips. The blood slowed, but the fire continued to burn. Now was his chance.

Thierry threw the arm away and launched at Olivier, barreling into his brother and knocking him off his feet. They rolled into the shadows. Thierry straddled his brother, gripped his shirtfront, and punched his face. He was strong, so strong, and power flowed through his muscles, full of a force he'd never possessed. But that barely mattered. He wanted to bloody Olivier's face, tear him apart, and leave him for the crows and maggots. Once and for all he'd be rid of this worthless brother.

He rained down blow after blow.

Olivier didn't resist, but he didn't pass out either. "Wait, wait, listen to me," he pleaded in between the rapid strikes.

Thierry growled at him, a horrifying sound rumbling from his body to shatter the still night. He could peel flesh from bone with that sound. But it didn't shut Olivier up. He wouldn't break, even though there was enough force in his fist to shatter mountains. He just kept on, asking him to stop, to listen, after every crushing blow.

"Listen to me."

*Crack.*

"I didn't kill him."

*Crack.*

"Thierry, it wasn't me."

*Crack.*

"I don't believe you." Thierry didn't want to speak, but the frustration at Olivier's indestructibility forced him. He flexed his hand and felt nothing. No tiredness, no pain. What had happened to him?

"It's the truth. It wasn't me. It was him." Olivier lay there. Conscious but not breathing. "I swear, brother."

Thierry snarled, and the fangs appeared. He gasped, and his fingers shot to his mouth to feel around these deadly additions.

Olivier grabbed his shirt and pulled him close to whisper. "It wasn't me. It was the one who turned you."

"Liar," he hissed.

"Trust me, please. I'm sorry for what happened, I really am, brother, but this was inevitable, believe me when I say so." Thierry struggled to break free, but Olivier refused to release him. "But if you want vengeance, we have to be quick. I tried to stop him from killing Etienne, but he wouldn't listen. He only wanted you. He didn't even want me. He wanted you, understand? We have to act now if we're to use our new power to get revenge. For Etienne."

"What are you talking about?"

"Don't be a fool, Thierry. Feel those fangs in your mouth. See with new eyes. He's weak. Now is our only chance. Don't shrink from this. You have to do what is right or we'll never be free."

His mind worked fast. Until then, every thought he'd ever had felt like it had existed underwater but now they were in the crisp, clear air. Olivier he could deal with later, but the murderer, the monster, would have to be annihilated now.

He vaulted off his brother, taking briefly to the air. He was quick, nimble, a falcon—and he aimed straight for his prey. He landed on top of the killer and, now that he was closer, saw him with different eyes and a fanatic disgust. The man was fat, sallow; he had sparse, wispy hair. How could this thing have taken Etienne's life and changed him so much? He seemed so wretched.

"Thank you for this strength." He leaned close to rub his body against this pitiful creature. His voice dripped with spice and suggestion. "Allow me to repay the kindness."

Thierry raised his head, extended his fangs and, with a loud roar into the night, buried his mouth in the creature's neck. He retched against the feeling of cold flesh against his teeth and tongue but denied his disgust. Slicing through the skin, he pulled against the meat, and the screams began. Thierry rode him as he thrashed like a dying steer, but Thierry overpowered him. He chewed the flesh and spat it out, bit his windpipe to kill the cries. The creature didn't bleed a lot but something residual remained. Thierry gnawed, scratched and clawed at the body, but it continued to fight. He withdrew just enough to call for his brother.

Olivier appeared in front of him, as if he'd expected the invitation. He smiled at him and caressed the side of his face. Thierry reared back out of his touch.

Olivier shrugged and gripped the monster's arms. "Bear down."

Thierry pushed his weight through to the ground as Olivier pulled and ripped its arms from its body. The sounds of flesh being torn and bones crunching almost made him heave. But when he looked into the crazed, unbelieving eyes beneath him, he had to fight the urge to gouge them out with teeth. He wanted to hurt and desperation glowing in them while they tore this enemy apart and ground him out of existence.

They rent flesh, broke and smashed bones, and opened the body up to be devoured like some roasted boar at a banquet. Each slippery sinew, each quivering organ slid into their mouths and down their throats. Thierry had never tasted anything like it before. No animal held this much flavor, held this much potency. His anger simmered beneath his hungry grunting as he dipped into the body again and again to wolf down all he could. They chewed through heart and liver, stomach and spleen, sucked on brains and lungs. They covered themselves with gore and blood until there was nothing left but bones. Exposed to the air, they soon turned to powder. Whatever power had resided in this dark father was now in them or vanished on the wind.

They sat back and looked at each other, covered with blood like painted warriors of ancient Gaul. The afterglow of the kill coursed through him, enlivening his senses so that he could see better into the darkness, feel the heat of the fire whipped by the slight breeze, hear every rustle and scrunch. It charged him. He'd spent years in the abattoir slitting the throats of countless beasts and never felt anything like this thrill to taste blood.

He swooped on his blood-soaked brother and licked him, ran his tongue up and down his neck, kissed his face, sucked at the angry veins in his throat and across his forehead as they throbbed with the maker's essence. Olivier whimpered. His brother's lust broke into him, pleading with him, wanting him.

And Thierry wanted him too.

He ripped Olivier's clothes, then his own, before forcing his brother to lie back on the ground. He kissed him deeply, kissed the unsheathed fangs, cutting his tongue and tasting blood once more. Olivier sucked at his throbbing jugular and Thierry grunted with the pleasure. He turned his head so his twin could draw harder on the skin.

Etienne hadn't moved. Though his dead eyes weren't on him, Thierry felt he was being watched. Like *they* were being watched. That silent sentinel was enough to bring him back to the horror of what had happened. His stomach soured, along with his desire. He sat back. Olivier reached out, desperate to keep his lips on his skin, but Thierry held him down. He looked at his stained hands on Olivier's naked chest, felt Olivier's erection against his slick stomach. The blood coated everything. It reeked with his guilt. He rose from his brother and sneered down at him.

"Get up."

Olivier grasped for him, but Thierry was too quick. He had to be to stop his overwhelming disgust.

"Go find us some clothes." Thierry turned from his brother and slipped out of the fire light, past Etienne's body, and set to digging a grave. His hands gouged into the rich earth but no matter how deep the hole became it could not rival the emptiness that Etienne had left behind.

# VI

Dawn of the first day without Etienne. Thierry and Olivier returned home as light began to filter down the streets. Etienne's body lay beneath a mound of dirt, and the place that had been so sacred to them was now sacred for another reason. Olivier brought them simple, peasant clothes to wear. They bore bloodstains. He would have to get used to it. They'd decided to leave Carcassonne, but Olivier insisted they go home and rescue Aurelia. Thierry followed in a fugue.

When he walked through the door, Aurelia was sitting at the table, a vacant look in her eyes as she ran her fingers through her hair and pulled at the ends. Such a familiar sight, the way she worried. She blinked hard as they stepped into the room before rising and backing away, putting the table between them and her.

"She's not happy to see us." Olivier chuckled.

"Aurelia, it's us." Thierry didn't understand her fear at first. He thought briefly it was because they had surprised her, but her hard, sad eyes revealed she knew exactly who they were—and what they had become. He'd already lost

Etienne, now he looked to be losing Aurelia as well. Thierry edged towards her.

"Keep your distance. Both of you."

"But we've come for you," he said.

"I'll be fine, just...just go. Please."

Olivier snorted. "You know what, brother? I think she's frightened of us. Her own flesh and *blood*."

She fixed her gaze on Olivier and narrowed her eyes. "You'd like that, wouldn't you, Oli? Poor little Aurelia, scared and frightened of her big, bad brother. You're pathetic." Her fear crumbled, and she glared at Olivier with the majesty of a queen.

"Careful. There's only so much I'll take from you."

"Just try it. You're nothing but a leech, a blood-sucking worm..." She looked left. "But you, Thierry. I didn't expect you to fall for this."

How could she believe he'd actually want to live like *this*? Did she understand what had been taken from him? "I wasn't given a choice."

She turned on Olivier. "You heartless bastard! How could you do this to your own brother?"

"Olivier didn't do this to me." Even as he said it, he doubted his words. So did Aurelia.

She didn't so much as blink. "Don't be so sure about that."

"I'm warning you, Aurelia," Olivier snarled. "We're only here because Thierry wanted to see you."

Thierry spun at the lie. It had been Olivier's idea to return. He would have preferred Aurelia to never see him like this, but Olivier had persuaded him that this was the right thing to do. See her, let her know they weren't dead, and ask her to come away with them. It had been Olivier's...

The realization smacked him across the face as Henri appeared in the doorway to his room. His malevolence filled the room. He took in the scene in one look. "I'm going to beat you worthless whelps to within an inch of your lives for waking me."

"Speak of the dead." Olivier's fangs appeared and he launched himself at Henri.

Aurelia screamed, the sound rushing from the depths of her body. She threw her arms open. Bright blue light shot from her hands at Olivier and propelled him across the room, away from Henri, who looked at his daughter with violent disbelief.

Olivier didn't stay down for long. Back on his feet he roared at Aurelia and charged her, but she was ready. The blue light, that fiery magic, flew from her again. This time, it didn't relent, and Olivier couldn't push through it, even with all his strength.

Thierry stared in awe at the power his little sister commanded. "Witch," he whispered.

"Filthy whore!" Henri, that crazed lunatic who'd spent far too much time slaughtering pigs and goats and cows, ran at his daughter and punched her in the face. She collapsed to the ground, and the light vanished.

Thierry leapt at his father and forced him to the floor. He had never been able to protect Aurelia before, but now he had the strength to return the bruises Henri had given her over the years. Henri fought back, wrapping his big hands around Thierry's arms to throw him off but Henri might as well have been a child.

"You are nothing, Henri."

Thierry bared his fangs. Henri flinched. He reared his head for the killing bite. It would be so worth it to snuff out this man's life, to taste the blood of someone so vile and repellent. No one would mourn his passing. They'd probably hold a feast day.

He closed in on his throat.

"No!" Aurelia and Olivier's voices mixed.

A stinging force hit Thierry in the chest. He catapulted him across the room and slammed into the wall. Her magic allowed him to rise to his feet but though he fought she did not unleash him, just like Olivier who snarled and raged like a tethered lion against Aurelia's power. Henri lay immobile. The house glowed with her magic.

"Aurelia, why?" Thierry asked.

"You need to leave."

"But you can't stay here with him, not now, not after this."

"I have to stay, and he has to live. Go!"

"We're not going anywhere until I rip Henri's head from his shoulders," Olivier shouted. "You can't keep me like this forever."

Apart from a slight tightening around her jaw, there was no sign that this taxed her.

"Listen to me, brother," she said. "I can do a lot worse, so believe me when I say you have no power here, and you're going to leave without harming Henri." She spoke as if ordering an army.

"I'll be in Hell before that happens."

She barely moved. She simply raised an eyebrow and twitched a couple of her fingers. Their bodies absorbed the blue light, and for the barest moment they were free.

Then it hit them.

Fire consumed them and Thierry fell to the ground, clawing at his stomach. Flames scorched his veins, along his arms and legs, and erupted into his skull. He slammed his eyes shut but that didn't stop the heat from incinerating them. He tried to scream but he could only belch smoke. His throat, his tongue, the roof of his mouth seared with her unleashed fury. When she was done, there'd be nothing left of them but ash. Distantly, Olivier screamed.

As suddenly as it appeared, the fire extinguished, and he lay on his back, the after-burn smoldering in the pit of his belly.

Aurelia knelt beside him and combed her fingers through his hair. "I'm sorry, Thierry. You have to know what I'm capable of as well."

He tried to laugh, but it came out mangled between his gritted teeth. "I would have understood if you'd just done it to Oli."

"Perhaps." She smiled.

With a coldness that hurt more than fire, he understood then to what lengths Aurelia would go to have her way, whether or not she had a favorite brother.

All of them staggered to their feet, and Thierry felt the last streak of pain sputter and die. He looked at Henri, who crouched, ready to attack anyone who came near him. He seemed diminished now. They had all bested him in some way, Aurelia more than the brothers. Even with a knife in his hand, Thierry doubted Henri could intimidate them again.

Aurelia watched Olivier to see if he'd be stupid enough to make a move for Henri or her. Though his fangs were extended, and his mouth stretched open, he went with his instincts instead of his nature.

"If you ever do that to me again, I will kill you." His voice rumbled, which was all he could do to threaten her.

"Shut up, Oli," Thierry barked, then turned to his sister. "So, this is farewell?" The anger at his brother sank under the knowledge that they were leaving Carcassonne and her. At least he'd get a goodbye. He hadn't with Etienne.

"Who knows?" Her stare held mischief that sparked hope in his chest.

Olivier growled at them. "It's time to go." He stalked to the door, ripped it off its hinges and hurled it at Henri. Aurelia watched its arc calmly as it sailed towards Henri who jumped out of the way and skidded across the floor unharmed. Olivier chuckled as he exited.

With Olivier gone, Aurelia stepped closer to Thierry. He smelled that familiar orange scent around her, in her hair, on her skin, so much richer than before. He remembered all the times she'd brought the scent with her. The scent of magic. His hand went to his shoulder to touch the old scar. *I thought they were crushed herbs.* How long had she been a witch? Perhaps it was best he didn't know.

"Thierry, please watch yourself with Oli and try to keep him out of trouble."

"That's all he's good for."

"I know but now that he's stronger he'll think he can do whatever he wants. He's wrong. There will be consequences."

The night's blood feast congealed like cold lard in Thierry's gut. He wanted to say Olivier wasn't his problem. Etienne was gone and he'd planned to escape from Olivier at the first opportunity. Either that or kill him. All he wanted was to be free of this sick monster who wore his face and Aurelia telling him to look after him. He'd been granted freedom from death, but not from duty.

"I'll do my best." He glanced at their father huddled in the corner. "Will you be able to handle Henri?"

"To some extent."

"What do you mean?"

"Nothing. Go. But be careful."

He hugged her and breathed in that wonderful aroma that would stay with him always, a reminder there were good things in this world. Especially now he could not claim to be one of them.

A woman screamed out in the street, chased by Olivier's cackle.

Thierry's nostrils flared. It was time they were gone.

## ❧ II ❧
# WINE, BLOOD AND LOOSE TALK

**1792**
Near Neulehn, Saxony

# I

THIERRY TUGGED AT THE STIFF COLLAR THROTTLING his neck. Thankfully, he didn't have to breathe, or otherwise he would have done away with these ridiculous clothes long ago. Still, they itched.

"Stop. You'll undo it all."

He growled at Olivier but complied.

His brother sat frozen, a painting of the perfect man at court. Seated upright, his blue cravat in the right shape and fold matched his expensive embroidered coat. The shirt was pressed, his shoes polished. He enjoyed the clothes and the status they brought. He moved with the sway of the carriage as the horses sped them towards the castle that would be their new home for however long it took them to grow restless. Thierry's patience had already tattered. The garments were a necessity for their frivolity, but he didn't appreciate their rigidity or complexity. Only his face was devoid of some covering. If he could, he'd wear nothing at all and sleep in the woods.

"Who invited us?" he asked to take his mind off his

body and the pleasurable thought of running naked, free and alone.

"An old baroness married to an old baron that we met at a ball in Dresden. Her name is Liesel. It should be pleasant."

Thierry snorted at the suggestion. Forced to play the fawning nobleman was no such thing. True, the charade was easy, but it was dull. Being surrounded by people with nothing better to do than sit in parlors and play cards, or go shooting in the woods, chipped away at his fragile calm.

In contrast, Olivier could barely conceal his excitement, obvious from the broad grin on his face as he looked out the carriage window. He rode his violent tendencies with a firm hand, each act of cruelty carefully meted out. Being alone with these people was not going to end well.

The castle nestled amidst a forest on a hill, some distance from the nearest village. It was grandiose. Reaching high into the sky, it dwarfed the trees around it. There were plenty of windows, indicating no end of rooms to accommodate the throng of guests that would fill its interior.

Their carriage rambled through an archway and into the courtyard. Olivier leapt out first. Sunlight beamed down onto his brilliant blue coat. He flounced up the steps to the castle door. Thierry followed shortly after.

The entrance hall swam with color. Scent bled off the milling strangers. He and his brother were clearly not the only guests to stay that summer. A few of the noblemen and women looked at them, gave a polite nod, but continued on. None seemed of much interest. A harpsichord played in another room and each tinny note throbbed in his retracted fangs.

"My dear Orlando." A woman came towards them, her

ample arms outstretched, swathed in yards of fabric. "I am so glad that you and your charming brother could visit us."

"Baroness." His brother bowed low. "You remember Tomas."

Thierry remembered his assumed name as vaguely as the Baroness's. How many names had he used over the centuries?

She nodded to Thierry. "I hope you had a pleasant journey."

"Splendid, Baroness," Olivier said. "Thank you for inviting us to stay. I hope we have not been an imposition." His voice oozed charm, and the woman blushed.

"Hush. It is just too nice to have such fine young men visit. I shall accompany you to your rooms, if I may be so bold." She led Olivier away without waiting for a response. They ascended the grand staircase and disappeared from sight.

Thierry stayed behind, scanning the hall, casting his unsophisticated eye over paintings of spying paintings of mountain and forest landscapes with gold frames, white marble plinths with bronze sculpted heads, chestnut side tables: opulence in every corner. About to withdraw outside, where he preferred to be dazzled by real things, he felt a touch on his shoulder and a subtle scent from the past assailed him.

*Aurelia.*

He shouldn't have been surprised, but he was. He hadn't seen her for nearly forty years. Before that, it had been about twenty years. Before then? Olivier said she dogged them through the centuries. Thierry didn't mind, a welcome reminder of another time, not always happy but simpler. Whenever he looked in a mirror, he was reminded of that other life, and Aurelia looked almost as unchanged as he did. The same glorious flow of coal-black hair. The lithe figure of a young maid. Those intelligent, hard eyes. She'd been frozen as that beautiful young woman, yet she still breathed. That was an important difference.

"What are—?"

She cut across him. "Allow me to introduce myself, I am the Marquise de Villiers." She held out a gloved hand for him to kiss.

*So we are all here to play games.* "My name is Tomas." The rare spike of pleasure at seeing her again didn't quell his unease. He didn't like to think she would get caught in their games or even witness them. There was also the question of why she was there at all. They had very rarely seen each other by pure chance.

"May I join you on your walk in the gardens?" Aurelia held out her hand for his arm.

"I'd be honored." He led her down the stairs and around the courtyard until they came to the garden. Valets and guards milled about, and other guests walked through from one place to another, so they were forced to keep the charade in place. "Have you been here long?"

"I arrived only yesterday. I had been in Berlin and then, without warning, I was overcome with an urgent need to visit the Baroness." She eyed him.

He half-grunted, half-laughed. "Have you known her long?"

"Long enough to count her as one of my friends, and to be very upset if something happened to her."

Walking into the sunlit gardens they found a bench to sit on. Thierry looked once around the grounds to make sure they were alone and dropped the benign smile.

"An explanation, please, Aurelia. Why are you here?"

"I could ask you the same."

"It's been close to forty years and not a word, and now here you are. Why?"

"I go where I am needed. And I meant what I said, about the Baroness. Let Olivier know as well."

"He doesn't like being told what to do."

"I don't care what he likes. He'd do well to take heed."

"I thought you would have softened in your old age."

"Do I look like I've softened?"

Thierry had to admit she didn't. She'd grown since the night she'd revealed her power, though she remained the same distinguished young woman. He could smell a touch of fate about the three of them, locked in their eternal bodies. He smiled at her clenched jaw and glaring eyes. She relaxed.

"How long do you intend to stay?" Her tone had softened.

"I don't know. It depends on Oli, and how quickly he gets bored. Seeing how isolated this place is, and how few people there are, I don't think we'll be here long."

"Please be discreet."

"You'll have to talk to our dear brother about that. He's the messy one."

It was a strange habit of Aurelia's that she insisted keeping certain people safe, but for most others she overlooked her brothers' actions. No doubt, if she truly cared about the horrors they committed, she would have exterminated them years ago.

"My beloved sister, how lovely it is to see you again." Olivier strode across the lawn towards his seated siblings. He grinned brightly at them, almost as if he truly was happy to see her. "You two made a lovely figure as I watched from my bedroom window, when Baroness Liesel finally left me in peace."

Sincerity laced his words but didn't descend beneath the surface.

She stiffened as he bent and kissed her cheek. "Marquise de Villiers, if you please. And I am not your sister." Hardness returned to her voice, as if she admonished a spoilt child. "No more than you are Olivier, son of Henri d'Arjou."

He snarled. He always fell for that one.

"And what is your name?" she asked.

"Orlando." He bowed.

Her teeth barely separated. "Charmed."

II

Sometime later, one by one, they re-entered the castle. Thierry was the last, preferring to watch the sun descend behind the distant hills and turn the sky from blue to pink to burnished orange and finally black. Servants lit lamps, warding off anything that might be afoot in the woods. The night was pleasantly warm, but a chill rattled through his body. The lack of blood did that to him. He'd refrained for more than a week. He considered it a triumph, but it didn't stop his teeth from grinding. He'd have to drink soon; if not to quiet the beast, then to protect himself from Olivier. Without the blood, his brother's thoughts and emotions overran him.

Olivier had no inkling the connection still existed. After all, his appetite seemed limitless. He rarely went a moment without a bellyful of blood, so he knew no different.

But Thierry kept and cultivated this secret.

There was a balance; he just had to be comfortable with it. On one hand, he could feed until his skin swelled and that would keep Olivier out. On the other, he was losing his thirst for cruelty and for the kill. It hadn't gone completely, but it had faded.

"My Lord," a servant called out and broke his musing.

Thierry turned his head slightly.

"Dinner will be served shortly in the banquet hall."

He barely nodded. The servant left.

Thierry stood and looked once more at the thick forest in front of him. A breeze flowed through the trees, bringing with it the scent of earth and wood and rich decay. He breathed it in, held it, savored it. It stirred thoughts of another forest in another time, like dried leaves skittering across a stone path. He let them fly away, steadied himself, exhaled, and returned to the fold of the castle.

The chandeliers had been lit and the hall sparkled with the tawdry showiness of the baron's wealth. Guests moved from the drawing room on the right to the banquet hall on the left. Olivier had already surrounded himself with two women, one man. All besotted.

"Of course, the duchess never knew what hit her," he said loudly, and the trio laughed raucously. The women who walked on his sides laid a hand each on his forearms. One caressed his bicep. She raised her eyebrows in pleasant surprise and bit her lip at finding such strength beneath his refined clothes. Then she laughed again, the moment passed, and the group entered the dining room.

He sighed. Eating food was never enjoyable for him or Olivier. Everything was tasteless and he found pretending to like the muck he shoveled in tiresome. He was about to pivot and leave to enjoy the night, but the Baroness appeared and held his eye. Behind her trailed a young man. *Good Lord, was she sniffing around nurseries now?* Yet his body understood the attraction even as his mind rejected it.

"Tomas, may I introduce my nephew?"

"Reiner." The boy extended his hand formally. "I'm pleased to make your acquaintance."

But no, not a boy at all. Young, perhaps twenty-one, but Thierry was uncertain, thrown by his gentle, full lips, hazel eyes and smooth skin. There was the touch of the cherub about him: innocent, yet endearing, calm.

But most certainly a man.

He took his hand. Something sparked in their handshake. It coursed up his arm and burst in his chest. He gritted his teeth to try to keep his face smooth. Reiner looked straight into his eyes.

The breath he didn't need to take caught in his dry throat.

The lights around him seemed to dim, leaving only the two of them illuminated. His muddled mind tried to understand what was happening, but as he groped for answers, he found nothing to hold. Like trying to catch water. As each thought, each understanding slipped away, sadness and a dull ache filled its place. The more he tried to grasp what this meant, the greater the pain and the grief.

He fought back tears of longing.

Reiner blinked.

The moment passed.

He cleared his throat and kneaded his chest with his free hand. "A pleasure to meet you, Reiner." Letting go of his hand was harder than starving himself of blood. He rearranged his features so they resembled more his brother's smiling, enchanting mask. "If the Baroness doesn't have another place for you at dinner this evening, I wonder if you would care to sit beside me?"

"By all means, there are still some places, and we can

rearrange a few things." She waved over the butler and gave orders for Thierry and Reiner to be seated together.

Either Reiner was too polite to refuse or he'd somehow overlooked Thierry's moment of oddness.

"Have you known my aunt long?" Reiner asked as they took their seats.

"No. My brother made the connection when we were in Dresden a few months ago. I think she finds it novel to have twins in her home. I'm afraid my brother is more willing to be put on show than I am."

"If I may say, Tomas, my aunt is kind-hearted, and no doubt prefers your company more than the spectacle you imagine you provide."

He cursed his cavalier tongue. "Forgive me, I did not mean to question your aunt's hospitality."

Reiner excused himself as he greeted the person sitting on his left. Jealousy slithered through Thierry's veins as the boy's attention was taken elsewhere. He fought it for its irrationality and only just gained control. His fingers unfurled.

With what should have been a simple exchange, Reiner talked to the woman beside him as if they were close friends. He asked how her family was and remembered her children's names, enquiring after each one individually. The woman—whoever she was—appeared relaxed and leaned close to him.

Before he did something he regretted, Thierry looked down to the far end of the table. Olivier smiled at him and raised his glass. He almost appeared human, but that was probably because he fed on the attention lavished upon him. Thierry smiled tightly and wondered which of the guests would be his first meal.

"He's not going to cause trouble. I won't let him."

Thierry hadn't noticed he'd been seated next to Aurelia. Reiner had fuddled his mind so quickly that even a child could have snuck up on him. *So much for being a natural predator.* "He will find a way."

She took a sip of wine but said nothing.

"So where are you from, Tomas?"

Thierry turned back to that enticing voice, chagrined at the happiness he felt as Reiner looked on him. What had happened to him? Centuries filled with feeding on the weak and innocent, yet one look from this man and he was ready to pledge allegiance like a conquered queen. A warning chimed at the back of his head. Aurelia's presence reminded him there were other things afoot in the world just as manipulative and depraved as a vampire. His focus sharpened.

He launched into the story he and Olivier had agreed to but, whenever he could, he threw the questions back onto his newfound companion. Reiner's voice dragged him closer to some shared bond, but the stories of Reiner's life didn't strike a chord. If anything, they created a disharmony.

"Do you speak any languages, Tomas?"

"A number." This was an easy way for him to say nearly every one in Europe, thanks to their constant relocations. "Yourself?"

"Yes, it is expected these days, I suppose."

"Do you have a favorite?"

Reiner lowered his voice, and his eyes darted around. "Well, I would have to say, even if it may be unpopular, that it is French."

Thierry smiled. "It is my favorite as well. In fact, sometimes I think I speak it better than German."

Aurelia laughed beside him, but he ignored her.

"That is wonderful to hear." Reiner's eyes sparkled. "If you are willing, perhaps we could converse in French instead? I try never to miss an opportunity if it arises."

"It would be my pleasure."

Then Reiner started to speak.

He spoke beautifully, his accent delivered with the finesse of a native speaker, and his grammar technically brilliant, but Thierry didn't hear what he talked about. The language had changed since he'd first spoken it, especially as a gruff dialect, but the words were like notes played on a finely tuned violin, rich and full. He fell into the lyrical French that flowed from Reiner's mouth. Chords vibrated throughout his body. His scalp tingled from awakening memories. They dragged him back to a time, centuries ago, when he was mortal, and making love to a mortal man in the forest around Carcassonne. A time when mortal eyes looked on him with love.

These eyes.

*Etienne* looked at him, called to him, wanted him.

Reiner blushed and looked down at his plate. "Is my accent that bad?" he said in German.

Thierry had sat there, dumb, while Reiner spoke with Etienne's tongue. Back in the present, his hands gripped his thighs, his arms tensed. Base need threatened to force him to take Reiner's face between his hands and stare into those hazel eyes. He craved another look, another remembrance. What if he'd been mistaken? What if this was all a trick? Taunted with a vision of Etienne...

Even Olivier couldn't imagine something so cruel.

Reiner looked at him expectantly. What language was he supposed to talk in? He grasped for something to say and forced them out of his mouth.

"It was beautiful."

Reiner smiled humbly.

Etienne reborn. Did he dare believe it? Was it some horrible trick of the mind? There was no recognition on Reiner's part. A noise at the door to the dining hall broke the moment and forced Thierry to follow Reiner's gaze.

# III

"My lords and ladies, the Duke of Saxony and his son."

The assemblage rose to bow at the two men, and Olivier reluctantly pushed from his seat. The Duke nodded his greeting to the room, but otherwise didn't smile. He was a grim man, broad of shoulder, with a broken nose, and a wide stance. He'd seen war, that was certain, and he'd enjoyed it. His bearing gave away no signs of weakness other than his own pride. He only made eye contact with people to stare them down. The men and women couldn't hold his bold gaze for more than a few seconds.

Olivier willed him to turn his way so that he could prove the exception.

His son stood slightly behind him. He was not as big as his father, built strong, yes, but lithe. His rich clothes accentuated the muscular curves of his body. His jaw was square, defined, and his lips were full, the kind Olivier liked to force down on himself. He took a moment to imagine staring down onto the top of his blonde hair, tilting those storm-grey eyes to his.

The Baron and Baroness hurried to meet their new guests. Everyone else sat down and returned to their meals. The conversation buzz recommenced, interspersed with glances at the Duke and his delicious son. One of the women didn't look away. She sat with her chin resting on her right palm, staring at the son with the look of a cat sizing up a mouse. The son returned her regard with a quick smile.

After some urgent shuffling by the servants, the Baron led the Duke to the head of the table while the Baroness directed the Duke's son to the empty seat beside Olivier. The staring woman returned to her meal, smiling to herself as if she and the male were the only ones to share the secret.

Here was opportunity for sport.

"Good evening, everyone." The son stood behind the chair, both hands on its back and his strong, thick fingers wrapping over the varnished wood. "I hope you don't mind me interrupting your dinner. Father and I have just come from Wildenau." He spoke as if these people were his equals, and for each one he had a warm smile. He pulled out the chair and sat down.

"I don't think we've met," he said, turning to Olivier. "My name is Wolf."

Until that point Olivier had remained quiet and content to watch the reactions of those around him as they took Wolf's offered hand. Christine, the one who'd explored his own arm so appreciatively earlier in the night, blushed. It went unnoticed by Wolf, but obvious to Olivier, and would have been even if he were blind. He smelled the fertile flush. Perhaps the boy didn't have a full understanding of the power his body held for those around him.

Perhaps he could enlighten him.

"Orlando." He took Wolf's hand, looked into his eyes

and released the full power of his gaze. Olivier's eyes changed from their usual earth-brown to amber, stimulating thoughts of warm fires and hearing the gasps and grit of passion. It had taken two centuries to perfect the art of stirring emotion with his eyes, overriding sense and habit to bend others to his will. Wolf took two seconds to capitulate and licked his lips.

Olivier broke the contact suddenly, but the spell lingered. "Wildenau? I find it such a captivating place."

Wolf shook his head and wiped the sweat from his brow. "Not so right now. There was trouble there recently. The townsfolk spoke of demons and monsters and other superstitious nonsense. Father's presence calmed them."

"He is an impressive man."

"He is modest and..." Wolf paused, stared down the table, then brought his stunned gaze back to Olivier.

He knew that look. He kept his eyes locked on Wolf. "My brother, Tomas."

"I have never seen two people so alike."

"We hear that often. Tell me about yourself, Wolf. Are you like your father? A strong leader? A great warrior?"

It was best if Wolf didn't linger on Thierry too much. The sight of the twins unsettled some people. If they stood together, it became even more obvious how similar they really were. Olivier injected soothing deep blue into his eyes.

Wolf sighed and relaxed into his chair. "I hope to live up to my father's expectations and become as great a man as he. I am honored to be his son."

"Do you have any siblings?"

"No, my mother died soon after giving birth to a stillborn girl."

"How old were you when she died?"

"Ten."

"At least your father has you to carry on his name. Where are my manners? I must let you eat. You must be starving after your journey."

Olivier poured Wolf a glass of claret, and he ate. Peering down the table, Olivier caught the young woman staring at the Duke's son. She averted her questioning eyes back to her plate. Olivier smiled and glanced around the rest of the table. His meddling sister glared at him and he raised a glass to her. Thierry was...attentive...to the young man next to him. There was little of note about the human, yet there was something curious about the way Thierry looked at him. It was like he *didn't* want to kill him. True, he was handsome but... Jealousy pinpricked his jaw. He yawned to dispel the sensation. Thierry would kill him in the end. Meanwhile Olivier had other people to deal with.

He closed his eyes, letting the chatter form a senseless cacophony around him. He needed to feed; it had been more than a day. Hunger scraped the walls of his veins. Who would be first? Not one of the guests, not yet. There would be the Duke, of course, and Wolf. And the enamored woman. But that would come later. For now, it would have to be someone invisible, maybe one of the kitchen hands or stable boys. There was a village nearby. He could hunt there if he wanted to stretch his legs.

His brother needed to feed, too. His skin was bleached and hollow. Too much time had passed since Thierry had gorged. He'd never abstained this long before, and Olivier worried he might cause himself lasting damage. They had encountered no vampires since Rellius so they did not know their limits. This was both a comfort and a curse.

"Are you tired, Orlando?" Wolf asked.

Olivier opened his eyes. Wolf had finished his food, the plate clean except for the bare bone of a chicken leg.

"No, I was enjoying the sound of so many people. How long are you staying?"

"That really depends on Father; however, I think we plan to be here a while. Tell me, do you like to hunt?"

Olivier laughed; a hearty bark that startled the woman next to him into dropping her fork. He felt eyes on him. Aurelia's eyes. Perhaps Thierry's. Their disapproval added to his mirth. "I love to hunt. Perhaps I can accompany you and your father, if he allows it. I am eager to learn from a master such as he."

Wolf smiled at another mention of his father's prowess. A sneer threatened to break across Olivier's face. He fought it but his lips couldn't help but purse as if he'd tasted dead blood. His features dissolved into something more neutral as he picked up his glass and pretended to drink. He turned his head to the Duke's end of the table where he conversed with the Baron.

His big arms rested on the table; his elbows bent to position his fist in front of his face. He towered over his subordinate.

Perhaps all fathers were overbearing.

Olivier focused on the pair's moving mouths, and the surrounding chatter faded to a hum. Their words were as clear as if the room were empty.

"So, what happened in Wildenau?"

"Hard to say, but the fear on their faces was no trick. Something terrorized them, but no one could tell me what. No one saw it—no one alive anyway." The Duke spoke without a quiver in his voice. "Enough of this. Tell me, how long has Anna been here?" The Duke gestured to the woman who'd blushed at the sight of Wolf. She conversed with the middle-aged woman next to her.

"She arrived a few days ago."

"Alone?"

"For the time being."

The Duke continued to stare at the girl's porcelain features, and the Baron's eyes widened. The Duke nodded at the Baron's unasked question. "We shall speak after dinner."

"Most certainly." The Baron blustered, his smile uncon-strained, and joy lighting his features. The absence of greed struck Olivier as curious.

He tired of the two men and returned to the various conversations swilling around him, growing strong on the scent of wine and blood and loose talk. Anna's eyes again sought Wolf and pinned him like a hound on a wounded pheasant.

But if she was the dog, Olivier was the hunter.

# IV

After they'd dined, Thierry and Reiner retired to the garden and sat on a bench beneath the torchlight. Reiner clenched his fists on his knees and avoided meeting Thierry's eyes directly. Instead, he scanned the other guests as they wandered the grounds in the warm night, or else turned his attention to the forest stretched out in front of them.

Thierry couldn't help but stare at the young man. Perhaps if he did it long enough, Etienne would reveal himself again. Of course, it wouldn't be that simple, but until he was sure, absolutely certain that this was Etienne, he didn't want to look away. Being this close to him, after these many centuries, was a torture more exquisite than even Olivier could devise. He clasped his hands in his lap so he wouldn't try to touch him. His mouth clamped shut against what he wanted to say, the words once spoken that he yearned to repeat. Unable to speak, unable to move, he felt trapped beneath hard earth.

In the uneasy silence, memories of their short human lives together stirred. He'd denied them for so long, lost in the grey fog that clouded his mind as he travelled through this timeless existence. But now, the air was clearing, and a shared history shone through.

Recollections welled up of cool days and warm nights spent in the forest. Then further back to their childhood— young boys, the three of them, up to mischief in the streets, getting into trouble with Henri, with Etienne's parents, the fun they'd had. And then, of course, the night everything changed.

He groaned. Some memories weren't welcome.

"Is something the matter?" Reiner looked at him with concern.

Four hundred years. That's how long he'd had to endure this cursed half-life without Etienne. No wonder he'd tried to forget. In the beginning he'd felt the pain so keenly, especially stuck with Olivier and unable to die—not that he hadn't tried. But time was an effective drug. And now, he'd been delivered what he'd most hoped for. But what next? He longed to spirit Reiner away, but how foolish!

And how would he explain the fangs?

The thought roused his lust. He had to feed, if only to keep himself from hurting Reiner. He adopted a smile. "I'm sorry. My mind wandered to unhappy things."

"Are you not enjoying your time here?"

"Nothing could be further from the truth. At first, I was apprehensive, but now I can think of no place I'd rather be."

"I'm glad. I have visited often over the years. It is my second home."

Reiner leaned back, the hard set of his shoulders faded, and he was once more the companionable person Thierry had first met.

"I think it is the forest I love the best," Reiner continued. "I've spent many hours in it, in the hope of finding things once lost."

A knife of hope ran up his spine. Reiner's words mirrored his own musings so closely that perhaps Etienne signaled to him. "This one certainly entices. I'll explore it during my stay."

"May I join you?"

He nodded. He didn't trust himself to speak. Alone with Reiner in the forest... How many days and nights had he and Etienne spent beneath twisted oaks? The air shifted and brushed against his face, reminding him of Etienne's gentle touch and whispers meant for his ears only. He tightened the grip on his hands until his bones creaked.

Reiner smiled. Thierry ached to press his cold lips to Reiner's warm ones.

"Will your brother join us?" Reiner asked. For a moment, creased lines appeared between his eyes. His face smoothed again, but Thierry had seen the glimmer of disapproval and heard the hammer in his voice. Did Reiner notice his reaction? Had he formed his distaste from a few glances Olivier's way, or was it some fragment from another life?

"I hope not. From his behavior at dinner, it looks as if he has made new friends already."

"Wolf is a good companion. As long as your brother doesn't upset the Duke." He made it sound inevitable.

Of course, it was. Thierry wasn't blind. He could see the resemblance to their long-dead father, like so many other men Olivier had torn apart because of their similarities to Henri. They had all been such small men in the end: peasants, merchants, some courtly types, and, of course, butchers. But the Duke stood out, and Thierry guessed that was his way—proud and grand. Olivier wouldn't be able to resist. *Couldn't.* How much damage would Aurelia permit?

"Orlando has enough charm to woo even his strongest critics. It is amazing how many of his sins have been forgiven."

"Something tells me there are plenty that have passed unrepented." His jaw barely moved.

"Ha! You are lucky I have a realistic opinion of my brother, or I would be offended. We are twins, after all."

"You and your brother aren't alike as you think." The words were almost spat.

"I am thankful for the differences."

"There is a...gentleness to you that your brother lacks."

"You see this, and you haven't even spoken to him."

"In the short time we have spent together I already feel like I know you, and by knowing you, I know your brother as well." When he finished, he blinked hard, and his eyes flitted from side to side as if he searched for an answer. A quick jerk of his head cleared it, and he gave Thierry an uncertain smile.

He paused a moment, knowing he was about to play a dangerous game. If he spent time with Reiner, Olivier would notice him—if he hadn't already. He could try to keep Reiner a secret, but no matter how covert he was, Olivier would grow suspicious, and withdraw his attention from the Duke and his son.

If he were open about it, and made Olivier believe Reiner was his mark for their time at the castle, they might be left alone. Olivier might recognize Etienne, but it was unlikely. There was no choice but to take a risk. Olivier could stain the castle's stones red, as long as Thierry had time with Reiner.

"Would you like to meet him? Properly, I mean, as

opposed to across a crowded room when he is—how shall I put it?—on display."

"If you would prefer it." He almost sighed with weariness. "He is your brother, after all, and I would not be so rude as to ignore him."

"That is probably wise. He can be temperamental and a little jealous."

Reiner shivered, despite the lack of a chill. "Something tells me you speak too kindly of him."

"With all this talk of Orlando, I'm anxious to see that he hasn't offended anyone that has the power to throw him in a dungeon. Shall we return?"

They entered the castle and joined a large number of the guests in the parlor. Olivier's maniacal laughter filled the room and drew their gaze. He and Wolf were surrounded by a circle of the Baroness's guests. The Baron, the Duke, and many of the older gentlemen were absent. Four matrons, including Baroness Liesel, sat playing cards by a window and listened with one ear to the stories told by the two young men and the other to the calls of the other women.

"He seems quite at ease." Reiner kept his voice low and close, his breath hot against Thierry's skin. A river of cold rippled through his body and mingled with the warm, bubbling excitement coming from Olivier, a sign of his thrill at the hunt. Thierry almost felt sorry for Wolf and the Duke, but he was grateful for the distraction. He had freedom to reawaken Etienne and rekindle a fire that had been lost for centuries. Now it had a chance of burning bright, he didn't want to feel Olivier inside him again.

He'd visit the village tonight.

And drown Olivier.

"Yes, it's one of the things he does best." People were

drawn to Olivier, definitely more than him. Even alive, he'd always known what to say and how best to ensorcel his admirers. Being a vampire had only enhanced his power.

Tears ran down Wolf's face as he gripped his sides, his loud laughter rising above the others' guffaws.

"Though I think Anna is not pleased." Reiner pointed covertly to the young woman who sat in the circle. She was the only one to maintain her decorum, barely letting a sound slip from her lips. Her calculating eyes shifted from Olivier to Wolf.

"Do you know her?"

"Anna is my cousin. She is venomous, despite the saintly expression."

"I am shocked to hear you speak so, Reiner," Aurelia said in French as she glided into view beside Thierry.

Reiner bit his lip, but he gave her a conspiratorial grin. "I had no idea the Marquise held my cousin in such high regard."

*Etienne had shared jokes with Aurelia, too.* The jealousy stung him like a switch to the back.

Aurelia laughed. "In about as much esteem as a Jacobin. She has yet to provide me with a reason not to wish her ill."

"The Marquise certainly speaks her mind," Thierry said stiffly.

"I am something of an anomaly among women."

"Excuse me a moment. The Baroness wants to see me." Thierry and Aurelia looked over at the Baroness playing cards as she waved to Reiner. He put his hand on Thierry's arm and squeezed it in a way that most men did. Though no skin touched, a shock passed through him. He gasped, Reiner's brow twitching in a question. Thierry quickly smiled back to let him know everything was all right. His heart throbbed.

Reiner bowed, a fond look for them both, and left to join his aunt.

"Confirm something for me," Thierry said softly, struggling to calm himself after Reiner's touch. "Is it possible for a person to be reborn in another's body?"

Her eyes sharpened. "It's a certainty."

He frowned, surprised at her straightforward answer. He'd expected a long dissertation on why such questions were forbidden and why they were not for his contemplation. But he found no subterfuge, just a simple response—one that was both welcome and frightening.

"Why the question?"

He suspected she already knew, but he wasn't ready to voice his theory, lest unfriendly ears listened. "Curiosity."

"Could it be that young Reiner reminds you of someone?"

"Keep your voice down," he snarled, nodding his head in Olivier's direction. "So it is possible?" He spoke to himself, uttering the question like he'd just heard the word of God. His skin buzzed as if sunlight surged beneath the surface. He had found Etienne, and Aurelia's confirmation nearly brought him to his knees. He blinked away the tears that threatened to stain his eyes. He wouldn't be able to hide the blood that poured from them. Even so, a slight red haze covered his vision. He wiped his eyes with the back of his hand, the pink smear stark against his pale skin. He rubbed the color away.

"Yes. It's haphazard usually, and it's hard to know when they'll reappear, but Reiner is who you think he is."

"How do *you* know this?" Even as he asked, he knew she wouldn't answer. The slight turn at the corner of her mouth confirmed it. No matter. Etienne lived.

"You'd be surprised at what I know. I've seen Henri no

less than seven times in the past four hundred years." Her eyes lingered on Olivier as she spoke.

"If you tell Oli, he'd help you exterminate him permanently," he said coolly. Olivier had the obsession, not him. Henri had died centuries ago, and that's how he liked it. Of course, he still had the scar. "How long have you known Reiner is...who he is?"

"That doesn't matter." She faced him. "You need to understand that the soul is the same, and some similarities are carried over, but each life is different. Each one has its own story. No two are ever alike and that requires...delicacy."

"But which part transfers?"

Though he waited, she didn't answer, and Reiner's reappearance meant he'd be given no satisfaction.

V

A servant glided into the room and stood beside Wolf, waiting for a lull in the laughter in which to interrupt. He spoke when the gaggle of nobles paused. "Sir, your father wishes to see you. He asked me to take you to him."

Wolf rose without hesitation, bowing and flashing his brilliant smile at the party before following the servant into the hall and up the stairs. The planets sighed at the loss of their sun but soon returned to their stories and talked amongst themselves.

Olivier tracked Anna's gaze as she followed Wolf with her eyes. They blazed with hunger. Thierry, Aurelia and the young man who had been sitting with his brother at the meal watched him. There was the usual cool contempt on the part of his siblings, but the unknown man startled at catching Olivier's eye and looked away.

"If you will excuse me, I must speak with my brother." He did not wait for the reaction to his half-hearted apology. Anna followed behind and passed Olivier as she left the room.

"A word, Tomas?" Olivier led him into the hall as Anna

ascended the stairs. Over Thierry's shoulder, he watched her keep a distance behind Wolf, but there was no doubt she meant to follow them. She looked as bendable as a statue. She held herself better than many nobles he'd met. Her spine long and rod straight, her upturned face, the sure grip on her skirts. But even statues break.

"What is it?" Thierry snapped.

"Are you enjoying yourself?" Wolf disappeared from view, and Anna was soon at the top of the stairs.

"Thrilled." Sarcasm dripped from his tongue. "And you?"

"Immensely. Now, if you'll excuse me."

Thierry grabbed his arm like a trap. "I thought you had something important to say."

He regarded his brother's hand before raising an enquiring eyebrow. Thierry released him.

"Have you ever known me to say anything important?"

Thierry narrowed his eyes and stalked back into the room, muttering under his breath. Olivier allowed himself a grin at seeing his brother so riled, even after all this time.

Anna was on the first floor landing now. He pursued without her knowing, scenting his way on the musky trail of her desire. He'd seen the look on her face when Wolf first arrived, a heady mix of longing and determination. Her emotions were irresistible; a sign that the stakes were high. And the higher they were, the more torment Olivier could inflict.

When he caught up to her, she was poised outside a slightly ajar door. The voices of the Duke, the Baron and Wolf drifted through the opening. She held a hand against her mouth, quivering with excitement, only just able to hold herself to the spot and refrain from bursting into the room.

Olivier opened a nearby door and closed it loud enough

to startle her. She spun round, a moment's fear on her face before she realized who it was. Her glare would have withered lesser men.

He smiled knowingly and advanced towards her. "Spying, Anna?"

She hitched up her skirts as if gathering the dignity he'd frightened out of her. With her chin high in the air, she strutted past him, silent.

"It's not spying if it's about you," he said.

She paused, her brow knit in question. "How did you —?" But she stopped herself and made to leave.

Olivier reached out his hand and stroked her bare forearm.

She pulled her arm away as if his touch burned her. "How dare you touch me."

"I've been watching you since I arrived, Anna, and I can see where your affections lie."

She backed away from him, but the wall hampered her retreat.

Olivier closed what little distance there was between them and shifted the color of his eyes from brown to deep red. "I wonder if I would not be better suited than the young Wolf." His voice dripped with musk. It encircled her, weighing down on her, laden with heat and dark promises.

She breathed shallow, her skin releasing the rich scent of a ripe woman. Whatever her defiant eyes said, her body bent to his presence.

"After all, am I not just as young, but no doubt stronger?" He pressed against her. Slowly, achingly, her body gave small acceptance to his. He whispered in her ear. "Wouldn't I be better at *everything*?" He licked her earlobe.

She closed her eyes and whimpered like a bitch on heat.

Voices down the hall disturbed them, and he vanished

before she opened her eyes. Olivier watched through the chink in a bedroom door as she cast her gaze around for him while touching where his tongue had been.

The three men emerged but didn't see her. She hurried downstairs. He bit his lip in wicked sport. *Yes, here was fun.*

# VI

THE LAST GUESTS RETIRED TO THEIR ROOMS A LITTLE after midnight, and the servants hastened to extinguish the candles. Thierry bid his brother good night at his door, though he suspected Olivier would not remain in his room. As long as he was left alone, he didn't care. He had to feed.

After Thierry asserted three times that he needed no assistance, the servant reluctantly left. He stripped off the binding clothes and stretched. Being free of the garments was like waking from a long sleep. Nothing bound him, rasped against him, suffocated him. He smoothed one hand down his body, along his arms and his stomach, wiping away the last remaining sensations of the threads he was forced to wear. It was a body perfect without adornment: hard, muscular, sculpted, and lacking in flaws and vulnerabilities. When he was human, he'd been proud of the body he had, even more when Etienne worshipped it. Now, if there was anything to be thankful for in this cursed existence, it was this body.

He extinguished the lamps and opened the drapes and the window, letting in the light of the stars and moon. The room's stuffiness cleared quickly, chased away by a cold breeze.

Before him lay the forest and the mountains. There were no human habitations as far as he could see. In some ways he preferred it, so he wouldn't be tempted every time he looked out. Tonight, however, he needed the blood.

Olivier throbbed in his veins, and not feeding put Reiner at risk. His own hunger mixed with Olivier's madness meant Reiner's throat would be too alluring for the wrong reasons. A descent into the wilderness would help dispel some of it; the blood would drown the rest.

He stood on the windowsill, invisible to any who might look up, his naked form caressed by the gentle wind. He raised his arms and dove into emptiness, cutting the air, and landing lightly in the forest. He sprang into the welcoming darkness.

Weaving around the primeval trees, he set a course for the village. The distance was nothing. He'd be there in a matter of minutes, but he slowed when he came across a clearing bathed in moonbeams. Oaks stood guard over this undisturbed place, waiting for one such as he to step into their midst and remember. He recalled nights spent in Etienne's embrace, devoted lips on his uncovered skin.

A stick snapped.

He vaulted into the limbs of a towering tree and waited for someone to appear, but no one emerged. Who had he expected? Olivier? He checked inside for his brother, but his twin remained at the castle. Rellius? He shook his head to expel that phantom. If anything approached, he need not fear it. And the memories were simply that. Their maker was long since devoured.

He dropped to the ground and ran to the village. The stench of human waste and livestock assaulted him before he'd reached its boundary. Villages were all the same. He kept to the shadows and began his search for someone to slake his thirst.

Beside one of the houses, a man slept off the night's ale. He would be quick. It would be painless, half-sedated as he was by drink. He dashed from the shadow of a tree to that of the building and carefully cradled the man. The liquor permeated his clothes, hanging on his breath and seeping out of his pores. He wasn't going to wake.

He carried the drunk into the forest, murmuring gentle words as he snuffled and farted in his sleep. When they were far enough away, Thierry lay him down, undid the laces on his shirt and pulled it wide to reveal his paunch. He smoothed a hand over his bulging gut and felt the softness of middle age. A weak heart pumped blood around his failing body.

Faint, yet it beckoned.

Thierry smelled death on him. A poisoned liver, yellow skin, yet no matter his ill health, Thierry wanted to drink his fill. It would still be the same, glorious liquid ecstasy on his tongue. He bent nearer and bit into the yielding flesh. The blood flowed. The man squirmed a little but didn't open his eyes.

The vital fluid coated Thierry's eager tongue and coursed down his gullet. His stomach accepted it into his ancient body, suffusing his muscles and organs, awakening his senses once more. With each greedy gulp, Thierry wanted another. How he had missed this. How abstinence had made him suffer. He sucked hard on the dying man's neck, extracting all he could.

It ended too quickly. When the fount stopped, he withdrew his fangs and sat back. He wiped his mouth with his hands and licked his fingers and palms.

He reclined, resting his head on the dead man's belly, and looked at the sky. He bathed in the after-effects of the blood's magic and sighed. His hands slid down his hard chest, his stomach and to his groin. He buzzed with nourishment. His sight sharpened, he heard with greater clarity, and he shivered with the pleasure of the wind on his naked flesh. He searched for Olivier and found only a flutter of his twin.

No emotion, no thoughts. Merely an awareness.

If he fed again, even that would go.

While in the frenzy, he longed for more, but now he could see reason to refrain. He did not want the village suspicious. One missing drunk was acceptable, two raised concerns. And if he surrendered to his appetite, could he be certain to spare Reiner? He rose, grabbed the carcass by an arm and dragged it along behind him. Halfway to the castle, he let go. The carrion feeders would find it soon enough.

He turned to the sound of running water, sprinted to a small lake and slipped in. He washed away the gore and emerged cleansed from the night's feeding, ready to join again the civilized life of the castle. He scaled the wall, climbed in through the window and settled into his large bed.

He would sleep to pass the time until tomorrow when he could continue his pursuit without fear of ripping out Reiner's throat.

# VII

A HUNT WAS CALLED THE NEXT DAY. MANY OF THE MEN gathered in the courtyard as servants rushed to bring horses, rifles and hounds. The Baron and the Duke took the lead. Wolf kept close to his father. They would go south, setting a course for a field to hunt fox and pheasant.

Olivier enjoyed the feel of the beast between his legs, the strength of its flesh and bones as it bore him forward. He waved at Thierry standing on the steps, his arms folded in front of him, his expression disapproving.

*Nothing new there.* Olivier smiled and rounded his horse to come alongside Wolf.

"A fine day for a hunt, don't you think, Orlando?"

"Indeed." The sky was clear, and a gentle breeze kept the morning heat at bay. An attendant attached a rifle to his saddle.

A horn sounded and they set off through the castle gates. They rode slow to preserve the animals. The men formed groups and continued their conversations from the previous night or from breakfast. Wolf, however, seemed lost in his own thoughts.

"Are you troubled?"

Wolf smiled coyly. "No, just some news my father gave me last night. It has given me a lot to think on."

"Care to talk about it? I find talking through something with a friend has a way of revealing solutions."

Wolf paused as if unsure he should speak, but Olivier could see he itched to reveal all. He was eager to play confidante.

"Very well." Wolf looked around to make sure they weren't overheard. "My father has found me a bride."

"Ah, the beautiful Anna," Olivier said, a little louder than necessary.

"Shhh, lower your voice. How did you know?"

"I'm observant."

"Hmm. Anyway, it is not yet finalized."

"I should hope not."

"Pardon?" he asked.

"Forgive me, but I believe that when it comes to marriage, one should at least have a say in the matter."

"I am very grateful for my father arranging this union," he replied darkly, squaring his shoulders and straightening his back. He looked like a soldier defending the Emperor's honor. "It has not been easy for him, and he has to make the best arrangement for his position."

"Of course. I do not presume this is something you do not welcome. I just wonder if Anna is exactly the right choice." He let his eyes wander to give the impression he actually cared about their alliances.

"What do you mean?" Wolf leaned towards him.

He nearly sneered at how easily Wolf surrendered. "Nothing, my dear Wolf. I am simply teasing. Congratulations on your betrothal. You make a fine match."

Wolf resumed his brooding. Olivier watched the Duke

whose attention was on the Baron. He suspected they continued their discussions of dowry and marriage. The Duke's stern face betrayed nothing of the supposed joy of the occasion, even if it did involve his beloved son. As he spoke, he stroked his black stallion's mane, caressed it and twisted his fingers through the fine hair.

Trackers signaled for silence as the party approached the field. Metal buckles chinked against each other, leaves crunched under foot or paw or hoof, but the men held their tongues. Through the trees on the edge of the field, a stag raised its crowned head. It sniffed the air and sprinted away.

*Not quiet enough. These men know nothing of hunting.*

They raised the alarm and gave chase.

Olivier and Wolf spurred their horses to join the Duke at the head of the pack. They broke cover, sprinted across the field in close pursuit of their prey and plunged into the shady forest, the stag still within sight. All too soon the other men fell away yet these three spurred on. The Duke and Wolf focused only on running the animal until it tired and collapsed.

The stag darted between the trees with grace and agility, turning easier than the three horses that pursued it. Seeing the chance for mischief, Olivier took up the rifle and fired.

The animal's skull burst open from the shot and it collapsed in a heavy mess.

They drew up to a hard halt at its fallen corpse. The Duke spun in his saddle to glare at Olivier. Wolf looked at him with an open mouth. The rest of the party came from behind, calling out as they cantered to the three riders.

"That was some chase you gave." The Baron nudged his horse forward to the dead animal. "You are an impressive shot, Orlando. Please don't be offended, but I am surprised."

"I prefer to hide certain talents until required." Olivier bowed his head in thanks.

"You have robbed me of a kill," the Duke said, his voice flat and low.

"My apologies, Duke, but I saw a shot and took it. The animal would tire after a while, and its meat turn stringy. Forgive me, but I thought only of my stomach."

Everyone except the Duke laughed. He barked at one of the attendants. "You! Hitch up the carcass and take it out to the clearing. If anyone else cares to join me, I intend to hunt again." The Duke's eyes didn't leave Olivier's as he spoke, ensuring he lost no meaning. He was not invited this time, nor ever again. It took all his effort not to laugh in the man's face. He turned to leave.

"Where are you going?"

Olivier swiveled to see the Duke hadn't snapped at him but at Wolf, whose horse had taken a few steps after Olivier. Wolf looked after him but couldn't defy his father. Olivier chuckled and departed. No one else followed.

Once in the clearing, he tethered the horse to a tree and ran into the forest after the riders. Leaping from limb to limb and becoming a blur of shadows, he ran faster than any horse or deer as he followed the scent of the steeds and men. As much as he liked riding, he preferred the strength and speed in his own legs.

Ahead, the men fanned out. The Duke was far in the lead. The rest straggled behind, finding it difficult to keep pace with him and his son. Olivier waited for one to abandon the race. One kill would be acceptable. He could make it look like an accident. He had contemplated not killing here, but he needed to feed, and feasting on a noble thrilled him more than finding some filthy peasant in the nearby village.

Then came his chance.

But it was just an attendant. He wore the cheap but functional clothes of a worker and was mounted on a poorer horse, built for burdens, not for show or war. The man had given up hope of remaining with the hunt, content to sit back, avoiding notice and the need to push himself or his horse. He'd run when his masters called. He studied the forest, the trees, the shrubs, listened for birds and the calls of the group to hear if they made a shot.

Olivier sprang from the ground and knocked him from his saddle. He pressed the attendant down and clamped a hand over his mouth to stop his shouting. The pitiful creature looked up at him and, as Olivier bared his fangs, confusion morphed into terror. The man screamed into his immovable palm, kicked against the ground and tore at Olivier's arm, but nothing he did could set him free.

Olivier relished the sight of the terrified man. He loved the feeling of pressing down on this human, his arms strong enough to hold him in place without a thought, without the technical knowledge required to fire a gun, the precision with which to look, to measure the wind and the angle and to pre-empt the intentions of his prey. In comparison, this was blunt and primal, but far more pleasurable.

He bent down and delicately pierced the man's carotid artery. He took care not to cause too much visible damage. He fought the urge to open his throat wide and soak in the glorious font. This time, he had to be restrained.

The man thrashed until he grew too weak, and his heart buckled like a cow with its throat slit. Olivier withdrew his hand. The man had bitten his lips in his attempts at freedom. Olivier licked the puncture wound and cleaned it of blood. Some remained in the attendant's veins, enough so he wouldn't appear desiccated, but his heart had stopped, his soul flown, and Olivier's thirst calmed.

He stood, lifting the body into the air. He faced the nearest low-hanging branch and threw it at the tree with such force that bones snapped. It fell to the ground, twisted, lifeless and the victim of an unfortunate riding accident.

Hunting was such a dangerous sport.

# VIII

REINER'S EYES BRIGHTENED WHEN THIERRY'S OFFER TO join him for a walk in the forest came. Olivier rode with the hunting party so there was little worry about him sneaking up on them. As they left the castle, he caught his sister's eye and saw her benevolent smile.

*Aurelia and her damn secrets.*

They were silent as they entered the trees. Thierry paused once across the threshold, breathed in the natural air, and said a prayer for this place. A moment was enough to stir his senses and reawaken all he had thought lost. In the daylight, when times had been happier, he recalled the endless shades of green, the strength of the trees around him, the sound of the breeze shuffling through leaves and limbs.

"This feels like home." Reiner sighed. He set off into the forest, the course decided. Thierry jogged to catch up.

"Tell me something about yourself, Tomas," Reiner said. "You have heard so much about me already, it seems hardly fair that all I really know is your name, and that you have a twin."

Thierry smiled. "There is not much to tell."

"There must be something. Where does your family come from?"

"Leisnig. Have you heard of it?"

"The name sounds familiar, but I haven't been there. Is it beautiful?"

"It used to be, a long time ago, according to our parents, but now it has lost its charm. Hence why we are rarely there. My brother and I prefer to travel and see the world." At least he could tell some truth amongst the lies. From experience, he knew it got easier, to make the facts rub against the falsities and so he could be free to talk as if he talked of life in Carcassonne.

"I am jealous. I have hardly been anywhere. My parents are rather unschooled when it comes to discovering new places and experiences. My aunt is more accommodating. I think it's because she doesn't have children of her own, and she dotes on us."

"You and Anna?"

"Yes, although Anna doesn't deserve it. Not really."

"Please don't think me rude, but why this antagonism towards your cousin?"

Reiner sighed. "It is a long-standing childhood rivalry inflamed more so by the feuds between our parents. My aunt is the only common ground, the safe haven, as it were. I have tried to talk Anna out of it, to make amends for our parents' misdeeds—whatever they were—but she will have none of it. So I have grown tired of trying to win her favor. The Duke's son will be in for a nasty shock when they marry."

"Are they betrothed?"

"Decided yesterday, I believe."

*What would Olivier make of that?*

Thierry watched him move as he placed a hand to steady himself or swing from a branch for fun. There was strength in the young man. He saw it in the straining of his clothes, the raising of veins and muscles in his hand. He didn't stumble. Each footfall was certain. Thierry longed to see Reiner's bare chest or sweat drip down his back and disappear below his belt.

Thierry removed his jacket in encouragement, exclaiming about the heat. He untied the knot around his throat and opened his shirt a few buttons to expose his skin.

"Good idea," Reiner said, innocently enough, and followed suit. Thierry was right. Although covered, Reiner's muscles now made themselves known. Underneath the folds of his shirt, his arms filled the sleeves, the fabric contoured his chest.

*So like Etienne.*

They walked on and found a river leading into a lake. Sweat dampened Reiner's back, whereas Thierry remained untouched by the heat. Reiner seized the chance to cool himself in the water, undressing without reserve, pausing briefly to shoot Thierry an encouraging look. Thierry slipped out of his shirt. Reiner smiled and removed the rest of his clothes, turning his back to Thierry. Thierry's hands halted over his belt buckle as he drank in the sight of Reiner's broad shoulders and ropey muscles. His groin stirred. Reiner's slick skin was darker than he'd expected. Thierry looked at his own chest and saw how white he was by comparison. He hurried to undress.

After dropping his pants, he took a long time to rise. Starting at Reiner's naked feet, his eyes traveled up his muscular and lightly haired legs.

"Are you swimming in those?" Reiner asked.

Thierry snapped upright, stopped from continuing his

feast of Reiner's body. He casually absorbed the rest of him, his cock hanging limp amidst a nest of dark, coarse hair, a stomach ridged and bare, a proud chest with dark nipples. Behind closed lips, his fangs extended, and he bit his tongue. He tasted cold silver.

"Take them off."

It sounded like an order, and he had to fight the lust crashing inside him. Withdrawing his fangs into his jaw, he slipped his thumbs underneath the waist of the remaining vestiges of cloth. Reiner smiled as if in triumph before turning to the water.

His back, its lines and curves, proved that Reiner was every bit the man Etienne had been. His body heralded strength and power. Thierry's hands burned to smooth their way over his skin, around the rise of his buttocks, and along that sensitive line between his legs. His cock twitched. He could feel it grow and rub against the cloth. Quickly he slid the undergarments down and raced after Reiner.

Reiner dove into the water, and Thierry was in before he resurfaced. He swam behind and tackled him. Reiner laughed before sliding beneath the water, twisting in Thierry's grip, his legs thrashing as he tried to break free. Thierry let him go. Gasping for air, Reiner breached the surface. After wiping the water from his eyes, he splashed Thierry and laughed again at the game.

Diving, he swam for Reiner's legs and pulled him under. They fought again, and Thierry allowed Reiner to hold him down. At that point he resisted no more and became still. He felt safe in the watery cocoon, held by Reiner. Bare palm on naked flesh. There was a connection, and he would do anything to keep it. But before Reiner became too suspicious, he pushed back and resurfaced. He could stay down there forever.

"You won't beat me again." Thierry chuckled. They stood apart from each other, the water lapping against their chests. Water dripped from Reiner's hair, hanging over his forehead. His wet body echoed Etienne's sweaty one.

Thierry's desire could have boiled the lake.

"That's what you think." Reiner's voice was thick with temptation. He bit his bottom lip and eyed Thierry like he wanted him. The look on his face, the way he stood with his hands ready to grab, his rising chest; Thierry recognized that hunger. His mind went cold and he dissected every touch and grasp that he'd just felt, every glance and every word since they'd been introduced to indicate Reiner had wanted him all along.

Reiner splashed towards him, and Thierry dropped. He squirmed like an eel and no bubbles gave him away. He peered through the murky water at Reiner, stopping and searching. Then Reiner sank. When he opened his eyes, Thierry was ready for him. Reiner's eyes widened, and he floundered. Thierry shot forward, collected him in his arms and dragged him deeper.

With his arms wrapped around Reiner, he held him close, the shimmer of a heartbeat against his skin, the warmth of his human form. Reiner squirmed in his hold as they sank to the bottom and the disturbed silt rose. His hand brushed against Thierry's face, pushed against it, then harder, then both hands. Then his attempts to free himself stopped. Thierry had his eyes closed, focused on Reiner's touch, but when he opened them, he realized he'd got it wrong.

He grabbed Reiner's wrist and vaulted to the surface. The speed of his kicks propelled him above the water, and he flew to the bank. He laid Reiner down, his chest not rising, his eyes closed. He didn't know what to do. Was he going to lose his lover again? And at his own hand this time? He took hold of his shoulders. Forcing him to sit, he shook him and shouted his name.

"Reiner! Breathe!"

He gripped his shoulders and rattled him again. Water came out of Reiner's mouth with a spluttering cough. He drew breath. Thierry lay him back down, and Reiner opened his eyes.

"God in heaven!" Thierry swore. Reiner laughed. "Don't ever do that again!"

Reiner almost choked. "Me? You're the one who nearly drowned me. You must have enormous lungs."

The panic had gone, but guilt whipped him. A four-hundred-year-old wound torn open by a simple fact. Thierry was nothing but danger to those he loved, whether he was human or vampire. He clambered to his feet and walked away to put his clothes back on. He picked up his shirt, ready to put it over his head. He looked at the cloth and sighed.

"We should get back."

Reiner's wet body soon pressed against his back. Arms circled his waist and locked around him. "Don't feel bad, Tomas. I'm fine," he murmured. "It takes a lot more than that to hurt me." Reiner's fingers traced a slow circle around his nipple.

He froze. Reiner's hot breath danced across his skin. It teased him into breaking his resolve. This had all been foolishness. He'd come so close to killing Reiner—to killing Etienne—and now he was willing to do it all again.

But Reiner wanted him. He could feel him, the warm flesh against his back, the rising heat and friction. He closed his eyes to fight for what he knew he should do, but that only made him more aware of the arms around him. He leaned back. He felt safe.

"We don't have to go anywhere," Reiner whispered but the words might as well have come from a fire pit. His touch sent waves of heat through him, coursing up and down his body, a firestorm obliterating his shaky resistance. Reiner's hands slid down his body and took hold of his hardening shaft.

Thierry dropped the shirt as he groaned. Not only from the feel of his strong grip, but also the relief as the last remnant of his defiance withered. His thoughts might have warned him away from Reiner, but in his heart, there had been no alternative. Reiner would be his, whatever it took. And he should have known that Reiner would be the seducer.

As had Etienne.

He turned and searched Reiner's eyes for anything other than willingness. He didn't flinch, and all he showed was desire.

Thierry kissed him and crushed his lips with his own. He lifted Reiner and laid him on the grassy bank. As their tongues met, his hand slid down Reiner's muscled body, his chest, his stomach, the soft side of his abdomen, then down where leg met groin. He didn't need to look where his fingers went; Reiner's rapid breathing was all the guide he needed.

Had Reiner done this before, or did Thierry's touch unlock buried memories? The first time with Etienne had been so rushed but it still left him with a feeling of deep satisfaction. Now he had the time to explore, and it would be something he savored.

Reiner's skin hardened as Thierry drew his fingers lightly across it and cupped Reiner's sac. He gently squeezed his balls, forcing short exhalations. Warm. Soft. Wherever his hand went he could feel the heat from Reiner's body, as if he was filled with fire. Thierry thought, compared to Reiner, he must feel like ice. Reiner's skin responded just the same, and Thierry purred. His hand traced along his perineum to his hole and then his fingers rubbed against the puckered skin. He skirted around it with one finger, teasing, caressing, exciting. Part of him wanted to delay and draw this out as long as possible, but another bigger part of Thierry was sick of denial. When Reiner was open enough, Thierry worked a finger in. Reiner's hand gripped his wrist and guided him. His hips bore down.

Thierry inched deeper. Watching Reiner writhe made his cock throb even harder. He felt like the master while Reiner was the pupil. Etienne had been the one to awaken him and guide him, but as he watched Reiner's back arch, he read the experience in each movement and gasp. There was no trepidation. He knew what he liked, and Thierry was going to make sure he gave it to him. Briefly he wondered who had shown him, but he drowned the thought. Thierry would show him there was no need for anyone else.

Reiner's hungry eyes found his, and a grunt broke from his lips. "More," he begged.

Thierry pressed his lips down hard and slipped a second finger into him. Reiner welcomed him. Slowly, Thierry moved his fingers in and out, rubbing the warm wall of muscle, each time working deeper until he finally touched the spot where Reiner cried out. His fingers stroked it.

"I want you," Reiner said, shuddering.

Thierry burned. Slowly, achingly slowly, he withdrew. Reiner caught his breath and closed his eyes, a dreamy smile

across his lips. Thierry rubbed saliva along his shaft, his
body hunching from his own touch. Christ, would he be
able to withstand the feel of Reiner encasing him? His cock
leaked. He lifted Reiner's legs and exposed him, resting his
swollen, wet head against his waiting hole. Reiner reached
for one of Thierry's hands, and when he made the connection, the flickering flames of his desire changed into something softer and blanketed his body with gentle warmth.

Reiner encouraged him forward, and he pushed against
the barrier. Reiner's muscles relaxed, allowing Thierry to
enter. With each clench and release, Thierry pushed
further. Every small advance increased the heat rolling
through his body, each moment satisfying but always
holding the promise of more. Reiner grabbed his cheek and
urged him deeper, gripping his hip if it hurt, guiding him
forward when it felt good. Thierry started a gentle rhythm,
sliding in and out.

He wanted it to be how it had been with Etienne, but
that was impossible. They were different people, him
included. But there was no denying he and Reiner ached
for each other. Every stroke and movement spoke of how
perfect their bodies were suited. His thrusts gathered speed,
eager to be as close to Reiner as possible.

He buried his face in Reiner's neck, smelled the hot
blood beneath as it raced through his body.

*Drink! Drink!*

He opened his mouth ready to bite, wanting it but not
wanting it, but as he hesitated Reiner grunted, screwed his
eyes shut, and clawed into Thierry's back in climax.
Thierry slammed his mouth closed but Reiner's muscles
crushed him and forced a gasp out of his mouth. He tried
to push through the pleasure so he could pull back his
fangs, but Reiner shot over their chests and the way his

body racked kept Thierry in his thrall. He thrust again while fighting to slip his bared teeth back into their sheath. He wrung every last drop out of Reiner, and soft whimpers replaced his grunts. Even though the sticky mess was warm, it was cooler than his own burning skin, and it gave him enough control to wrestle his fangs into his head.

And not a moment too soon.

Reiner's eyes fluttered open, a smoldering smile on his face. One of his legs twisted around Thierry's waist and pulled him closer. Reiner held his gaze with enough force to draw Thierry near until their faces were barely an inch apart. Locked together, Thierry thrust faster, seeing the encouragement in Reiner's eyes. That look drilled deep, cutting through the outer layers of this false life to see who he used to be. His history laid bare, all good deeds and bad, but Reiner seemed to look through that and find the boy Etienne had once loved.

Thierry released into him, but he didn't shout or cry. Apart from Reiner's breathing, there was barely a sound. Deep thrusts, a quaking in his hips, but it may as well have happened to someone else. There were only those penetrating, all-seeing eyes. There was only him and Reiner. And he never wanted anything else again.

Reiner blinked.

The contact was lost.

The world flooded in, and Thierry could hear the lapping water, songbirds in nearby trees, and overhead, a raven's cry. He slipped out and lay next to Reiner. The cold emptiness that started in his mind when Reiner looked away filtered down to the base of his spine and mingled with the feeling of death in his groin. It only muted when Reiner rested his head in the crease between his arm and torso. He brushed a hand across Reiner's chest. Wherever skin touched skin, he felt a bond.

"It's been a long time since I've done anything like that," Reiner said.

There was a glint of envy, but after what they'd just been through, he extinguished it. Not even a trail of smoke remained. He hugged Reiner closer and kissed his crown, inhaling his warm, spicy scent. He chuckled.

"But it pales to what we just did," Reiner hurried to say. "What about you? I know I'm not your first."

"No one that compares with you." Thierry couldn't stop the sigh. How many bodies had he attempted to sate himself on?

After being turned, years had passed before he could bed anyone, and when he did, he tried his best to not think of Etienne for fear of staining the memory. Eventually he locked Etienne away to keep him safe and stop himself from feeling anything close to love. Then it became just another way to feed.

He'd draw them out, arouse them until they begged for him, and afterwards, they'd paw at him as he drained their blood. Reiner was the first since becoming a vampire that he'd ever felt anything for. Being with the real thing—the subtle way he tensed his muscles, the sheen of desire in his eyes, the rawness of sex and the relief of completion—was almost enough to bring him to tears.

Reiner rolled over to look down on him. "Why so sad?"

Thierry gave him a weak half-smile. "We have to go back."

"They'll be hunting a while yet. We don't have to go anywhere." Reiner climbed on top of him and leaned down. He kissed him lightly along his neck and down his collar-bone. Thierry tipped his head back to allow Reiner's tongue to trail up his throat. Reaching his chin, it left his skin and didn't return. He tilted his head back down and looked at Reiner. "Unless you *want* to return," he said with a delicious smile.

Thierry grabbed Reiner and pulled him into a ferocious kiss. He wasn't going to let him go any time soon.

———

THEY RETURNED TO THE CASTLE AS DUSK FELL, AND the hunting party entered the courtyard. They were a lively crowd and spoke of the day's hunt in loud, happy voices. They paraded their prizes—a stag, three boars, rabbits and pheasant—in front of the assembled onlookers on their way to the castle stores.

Thierry saw the empty horse. Olivier smiled at him.

"Has anyone seen Franz?" one of the party called to a waiting stable-hand.

They all said no. Olivier's grin grew. Thierry glowered and went inside, leaving Reiner with the other guests. He hadn't wanted to leave, but on the walk back they'd both decided a little distance at first would be best. Safer. They each had their reasons. In Carcassonne, they'd had their reasons, too. Thierry felt the past try to snare him and lead him like a captive toward a cauldron of boiling oil.

*No, it won't be like that. I'll find a way.*

He hammered out the oath with each foot on the stairs. On the first floor he found the drawing room, which looked onto the courtyard below. He would try to keep watch over Reiner, especially whenever Olivier was around, but to do that he couldn't always be by his side. Outside, the guests gathered and congratulated the men on their successes with hearty slaps on the back. Knowing a nobleman's appetite, they were probably happier to find out what had been brought back for their feast.

He spied Olivier talking to Reiner, and a vice tightened around his guts. Would Olivier suspect that he was talking to Etienne? Or worse, did his scent linger on Reiner's body? He thought back to the brief moments he'd stood with his rediscovered lover and searched for anything to suggest he had fallen for this mortal. Olivier's jealousy knew no limits. He stopped himself from running down and whisking Reiner away. This was necessary. He needed to see if Olivier suspected.

His senses strained to hear what they said, but it was useless. Everything looked innocent. Olivier was smiling, but that was always something to be wary of. Reiner stood his ground, even though Thierry knew his heart must be working hard. If they talked much longer, he wouldn't be able to stop himself from going down. But if he did, wouldn't that make his brother suspicious?

Fortunately, the decision was made for him. Olivier bowed to Reiner and entered the castle. The danger passed.

A hand touched his back. He spun round and grasped it roughly. He looked into Anna's startled eyes.

"I...I...I have been awaiting your return," she stammered. "You...you're hurting my arm, Orlando." She pulled back, trying to break free.

Of course. Olivier. It was always Olivier. He opened his hand, and she stumbled back.

"My dear, I believe you were looking for me instead." Olivier entered the room and walked towards them. Anna looked from him to Olivier and back again, a crease lining her otherwise pretty brow.

Thierry rearranged the expression on his face to something near pleasant. How had Olivier known to find them there? Had he seen him spying? Or had he followed Anna's scent? Olivier's attention was fixed solely on Anna, and a quick dip into the bond, though muted, offered no swell of jealousy. Could he trust it? Even so, he wanted to return to Reiner, and the last thing he needed was to get embroiled in one of Olivier's trysts.

"Please forgive me, my lady. I am not myself today. I was startled."

She rubbed her wrist, but her face changed from hard indignation to impish playfulness. "Of course," she tittered. "How foolish of me. I mistook one brother for the other."

"No need to apologize," Olivier said. "What can I do for you, Anna?" His voice took on that dangerously calm tone.

"Oh." Her eyes danced at Thierry. "Oh, nothing. Something silly." She lifted her skirts off the ground in readiness to depart, her courage failing her—or intelligence saving her.

Olivier gently took her hand. "I would still love to hear it, however silly you think it might be. My brother, on the other hand, is needed elsewhere. Reiner was asking about you."

Olivier stayed fixed on Anna so he couldn't see Thierry's jaw stiffen. No threat skulked behind his words. For a moment he wished he hadn't fed last night and could feel the full brunt of Olivier's emotions. Knowing what he thought could make all the difference to his own happiness —and Reiner's survival. Not trusting himself to speak, he bowed and headed for the door.

"Do not fear, my darling Anna. My brother is trustworthy. He will not mention our meeting to anyone."

She could count on that. Anna wasn't his concern, Reiner was. Now, more than ever.

IX

OLIVIER SOUGHT THE DUKE LATER THAT EVENING. Their meal was another extravagant affair with plenty of courses and wine to keep the guests entertained and in good humor. New people arrived during the day, and others prepared to leave in the morning. When everyone withdrew from the table to follow other pursuits, he trailed the Duke and waited until he was alone before approaching.

He was impressed by the size of the man. Taller, heavier and thicker than himself, he cut an imposing figure. He seemed immovable, both in physicality and in attitude. His certainty and sense of entitlement hung around him like a thick, poisonous gas. When people spoke of the Duke, they did so in breathy, hushed tones, eager to discuss and praise him, but not willing to be overheard doing so. Olivier had enjoyed listening to the stories of him, the ones told around the table or in the parlor—and those told by the peasants of Wildenau.

"Excuse me, my lord. I seek your forgiveness for today's misfortune in the woods."

The Duke glared and drank his brandy. As he swal-

lowed, his jaw clenched and an artery in his forehead
throbbed. Olivier wanted to play with this lifeline, open it
and follow it along the skin and into the body to the heart.

"It was a lucky shot," he continued. "I only sought to
turn the animal a different course so you might have a
greater chance of bringing it down."

"You are right," the Duke said after a while.

"I am?"

"Yes. It was a lucky shot."

The Duke made to walk past him but he wouldn't get
away so easily. "Your son tells me you visited Wildenau. We
were there when the...problems happened. Maybe I could
be of assistance."

The Duke took a measured sip. "How much do you
know?"

Olivier wanted to jump like some court jester, pleased
that his line had caught. "All of it."

The Duke said nothing, but Olivier took this to mean he
could continue. "We only intended to spend a night there,
but then people began to disappear, only to later turn up in
pieces."

"You didn't think to leave?" Condescension slid off his
words. The Duke thought he was talking to an inferior. A
tang pricked at the back of Olivier's throat.

"Intrigue. Curiosity. Macabre fascination. Who can say
why we do certain things?"

Olivier led the Duke to a pair of chairs by the window.
He caught Anna looking at him and the Duke, wringing a
handkerchief in her lap before dabbing her neck. Her eyes
shifted from one man to the other. He wasn't surprised she
looked so tense. The things she had said while Olivier
ploughed her had almost made *him* blush. He had spurned
her the moment he was through and taunted her with a

nonchalant maybe-I-will-maybe-I-won't response when she'd asked for his word that he would never mention it to anyone, let alone her betrothed or his father. Her pleas had made him hard again, and he'd claimed her once more. When they were done, she could barely form the thought to ask for another assurance.

He made a point of looking at her as he spoke to the Duke, striking a balance between a wicked smile and a cheeky grin. He performed for an audience of two who had come to see different plays.

"Tell me exactly what happened."

Olivier leaned closer to the Duke and spoke in almost a whisper. The Duke couldn't help but come into his confidence. "Screams came from one of the villagers the first night we were there. People left their houses to investigate. We didn't think much of it. It may have been just an ordinary fight. So we retired.

"The next morning, however, the people looked deathly afraid. We asked the innkeeper's wife what had happened, but she just lowered her head and walked away. The innkeeper later told us that one of the merchants, no, I think he was a tailor, had been found lying outside his house in a pool of blood, and his head nowhere to be seen."

The Duke's eyes narrowed like an archer looking down an arrow, and for a moment Olivier saw his father's malevolence glaring at him. How Henri had looked at him with menace when he'd turned the tables and learned to enjoy his father's game of subjugation. All it had taken was a playful moan like someone enjoying a sweet treat, and Henri retracted. His son's smile had been enough to change the punishment from buggery to beating. Blood rang in his ears, and the noise of the parlor clanged inside his head. He fought every urge to attack the Duke and tear him apart where he sat with his smug self-righteousness. Olivier had to gain control of himself, to behave as civilized men do, and destroy by device. He wanted to draw out the Duke's demise and make it more painful than a quick evisceration. That thought alone—of slow, burning agony—stayed his hand.

He returned the Duke's level look with a quick smile.

"The head turned up later that day, sitting in a haystack at the back of a cowshed. It disturbed the town, yet a murder only strengthened our resolve to stay. Would we see the culprit caught? Would there be another?"

The Duke stood.

"Don't you want to hear what else I have to say?" he said loudly, for Anna's benefit.

"You are a fiend."

"I will leave out the description if you prefer."

The Duke looked towards the hallway but resumed his seat. Olivier cast a glance at Anna. Her skin was even paler than usual. Her aunt came to her side, but she shooed her away, more brusquely than her carefully constructed prim exterior would normally allow.

"The number of deaths grew from one the first night, to two the next, then three, then five. One family decided to leave, thinking the evil wouldn't follow them, but the next morning they were found on the side of the road, torn apart. They lay where they fell, two on the road, the rest scattered in pieces as they tried to run."

Olivier couldn't suppress a flutter of delight at the delicious memory.

"The town changed. They barred their doors, and no one ventured out at night, but it was no use. They were killed in their beds. Fights erupted in the streets as they eyed each other with suspicion."

"And yet you stayed." Olivier could see that the massacre of his people didn't upset him nearly as much as having to hear it from Olivier's lips. He inched closer to the Duke, keeping low. He chafed against the chains of subservience but held the façade. Promises of bloody vengeance soothed him and allowed him to continue.

"Strange though it sounds, if we left, then we would have been accused. That didn't stop them wondering about us. After all, we had unfortunately arrived the night of the first murder. But then, just as suddenly as it started, it stopped. A fortnight had passed with the bodies piling up, and then nothing. We left soon after. The place wasn't the same. They were still frightened. You could see it as we left the town."

"I wonder why you two were not targeted," he said, in a way that sounded as if he'd quite happily see Olivier lying in pieces.

The grit of the story over, Olivier felt he could relax. His shoulders slipped. His expression was that of a carefree cad. "Wildenau is a large town. Who are we, anyway? We are of no importance."

"But neither was the tailor, nor the blacksmith, nor the doctor, the teacher, nor the children."

"Who is to say they weren't someone to somebody? They were part of the town. We were not."

At that moment, Wolf appeared at his father's side. "I see you have forgiven Orlando, father."

The Duke grunted. "Thank you for the information." He stalked away.

Olivier shouted after him. "Duke, if we could keep this to ourselves, it would be most appreciated." He avoided Anna's furtive attempts to gain his attention.

The Duke didn't respond, exiting the room like a

battalion going off to war. Anna gathered her skirts and left. Wolf watched after her and sighed.

"Is something the matter, Wolf?" Olivier leaned back into the chair, pleased.

"No, nothing." He sat down opposite. "Tell me how you shot that stag."

———

ANNA LEFT THE NEXT DAY. SHE TOLD HER AUNT AND the Baron she needed to return home to talk with her parents about her impending marriage. The Duke hadn't yet brought down any terrible judgment on her, but that didn't stop her sweating every time Olivier got within five feet of him or Wolf. Olivier was impressed by her fortitude, that she would prefer to keep out of his way than stay and wait for the secret to emerge. Perhaps she was too afraid she might succumb to him again. She had nothing to fear there. She'd been conquered.

She avoided him throughout the morning as the coach was prepared and her luggage loaded. She spoke to Wolf but, as Olivier advanced, she quickly tumbled out a farewell and a curtsy before disappearing out the door and into the carriage. It pulled out of the gates and began the journey back to her home in Dresden.

In the shadow of the doorway, Olivier stood behind Wolf. "She didn't seem sad to say goodbye."

"No. Most odd. I wonder..." Wolf's eyes tracked the carriage.

"Yes?"

"Nothing."

Olivier couldn't allow the thought in Wolf's head to dissipate. "You do not seem too sad to see her go, either."

Wolf faced Olivier, leaned against the door and folded his arms. He tried to assume some stern look, but it failed him. He was certainly not the formidable type. "I would be insulted with your observation...if it weren't correct."

Olivier laughed and clapped him on the back. "Let's talk in my rooms."

Wolf accepted the invitation. They climbed the stairs together and entered Olivier's bedchambers. Wolf took a seat at the table by the window.

Sitting opposite, Olivier turned on his most consuming smile and let his eyes shine. He thought of the sounds he would draw from Wolf and wondered if he could take pain as well. He'd served at his father's heels long enough; Olivier was sure Wolf would be a natural at following commands.

His eyes fixated Wolf, drew him in, and stripped him of his inhibitions. It wasn't long before he felt compelled to talk about his betrothal.

"Since I first met Anna, I have always thought of her as the one for me. We have known each other for so long that it seemed almost inevitable we would marry. And then, of course, there is her rank. She is highly eligible and a perfect match for me—rich and noble born. The whole ride to the castle, all I could think of was finally seeing her again." Wolf pumped out a feeble smile, but it deflated almost immediately.

He was quiet for a while, his face taking on a sad hue as he looked at Olivier. Wolf was within death's power now and wouldn't escape until it claimed him. He watched as the last residue of resistance faded, and Anna winked out of his gleaming eye. Olivier cared not that Anna had been beaten, nor that Wolf was set on a path of destruction. All he saw was the Duke's pride sitting in front of him, locked in chains. All the promises of a bright future with grandsons to carry his name, of an alliance that would only strengthen his hold on Saxony, the conceit of a king, all beholden unto Olivier's whim. Henri had evaded retribution at his son's hand; the Duke would not be so fortunate.

The words Wolf spoke next came as no surprise.

"I blame you."

"For what?" Olivier didn't bother with any attempt at looking surprised or affronted. It would help his cause better if Wolf believed he wanted him.

Wolf stood and leaned into Olivier. There was a moment of hesitation before he kissed him on the lips. It was weak, uncertain. Wolf withdrew slightly, paused, then kissed him again, lightly, like he kissed some woman grateful for the tenderness.

In his mind, Olivier scorned the gentle way Wolf pressed against his lips. Olivier thrived on pain and pressure, on ravishment and brutality. Even Anna had shown more passion. He wanted to crush Wolf's throat for the insult. But he wasn't ready to die. Not yet. And he was not the prize. Olivier would have to go slow. He would have to be sensitive, approach with timidity. He would have to take Wolf gently lest he frighten. Then Olivier might get some physical satisfaction from this conquest.

He led Wolf to the bed. They lay together, one soft kiss after another, a slow exploration of hands over clothed bodies. He recalled nights of sex, blood and exquisite pain to make himself hard. Fortunately, he had plenty to choose from.

"Insolence!" The Duke stormed into the castle with the Baron and Baroness scuttling swiftly behind.

"Please, Duke. Let us go somewhere private and we can talk about it."

"How dare she leave like that?"

The trio hurried up the stairs and shut themselves away in one of the rooms.

Thierry passed them, the Duke casting him a dirty look, forgetting or perhaps not caring that there was another like him and he had eyeballed the wrong brother. Regardless, he kept his pace steady and sure. One movement, and the Duke would be dead. It was a comforting thought.

But the Duke was the least of his worries as Aurelia charged from the parlor room towards him.

"What is he up to?"

Thierry lowered his voice and spoke through his teeth. "Calm yourself. Outside."

His sister tried to reopen the conversation, but he shut her down until they were in the gardens. He led her deep into them, away from the guests. He waved and smiled, and they did the same in return. When he was sure they were out of earshot and unobserved, he allowed her to continue.

"What is he trying to do?"

"How should I know?"

"Don't give me that horse-shit, *Tomas*. You know him better than anyone."

Her fists clenched by her sides, her jaw primed and ready to bark. The air crackled around them, and he smelled sweet spice on the air. "Settle." He knew well what she could do to him, but that didn't stop him taking a firm tone. After all, she was the younger sister, and there were times he couldn't help playing the older brother. "This is what happens. This is what he does. If you don't like it, leave."

"It's sick. It's evil." She said it almost to herself, wearing away at the grass beneath her feet.

He took hold of her shoulders and held her tight, forcing her to look at him. "What the hell do you think we are?"

"But you're not like this. You're not like him."

He laughed, hard. "You have no idea what I have done to pass the time and find a reason for existence. When it comes to cruelty, Oli and I are well matched."

She tried to speak, but he cut across her. "And you're not so innocent yourself." He released her, and she rubbed her shoulders. "Can you honestly tell me you haven't caused harm? You're as old as I am, Aurelia. I know you have plans. Perhaps they are important, perhaps not, but why should your acts of cruelty be forgiven and ours not?"

The air returned to normal, and the scent of magic dissipated. His raised voice had drawn unwanted attention. He realized he'd used her real name. Maybe they'd noticed. *To hell with it.* He took Aurelia's hand and led her down a new path.

"If you don't like it," he said, "do something about it. You're more powerful than either of us. You always have been."

She muttered something.

"What?"

"I can't." Until then she'd kept her eyes downcast, but now she fixed them on him and they flared.

He'd seen that look before, when they were children and her demands for them to play with her had met with laughter. Olivier always made sure she cried before leaving her behind. Sometimes, Thierry had been the one to do it. The memory drilled a hole in his chest and the sharpness out of his voice. But he retained his suspicion.

"What do you mean?"

"It's forbidden. I can't interfere with what happens here."

"Forbidden? By whom?"

She bit her lip—too late—and glared at him.

He sighed roughly. "What's so damn important that you, of all people, can't protect the ones you hold dear?"

They had always skirted around Aurelia's plans and her life's mission. She kept her secrets close. He should have questioned her more when they'd first arrived and she'd stepped out of the shadows, but he'd thought it was only her sentimentality. Now there was a purpose for her visit. And perhaps for theirs, too.

He crossed his arms. "Why are you here?" The iciness in his voice would have made any mortal freeze. But this was Aurelia. The look she gave him held less warmth than an Arctic winter.

"I can't tell you."

"I don't like being some piece on your chessboard, sister dear. It makes me *very* anxious." He let his fangs protrude from beneath his top lip, enough for her to see.

"And what are you two up to?" A blizzard churned in her eyes. "Isn't all this just another one of your petty games? At least what I'm doing is for a higher purpose."

He fired a short laugh. "You expect me to believe that manipulating two vampires benefits anyone other than yourself?"

She folded her arms and glared at him. He knew that look. She made mules look pliable.

"Are you going to help with Olivier or not?"

He snorted at her request. If she thought he'd help her out now, she was deluded. "It's impossible. It's always been impossible. Not once, since you foolishly thought I could contain him, has he done what I wanted him to do."

"You will let people get hurt?"

"They're not my responsibility." He'd been freed from mortal concerns when Etienne had died; his brother and sister remaining his only ties to the world. Without them, he might have found peace.

"While he's amusing himself with Wolf and the Duke, he's not sticking his fangs in my business."

"Reiner."

"Exactly." Even in his defiance, guilt nipped at his heels; no one deserved to die at their hands. And now, there was Reiner. All their lives, Aurelia had had a purpose, a reason for her everlasting existence. In comparison, he had been just a free-floating parasite, blundering from one bloody mess to another. Until now.

"Even if I could do anything about Oli, I don't want to. I've accepted responsibility for him for far too long. Now I have found the one person who ever brought me happiness, and I don't intend to let him go again."

Aurelia looked back at the castle and pulled at the ends of her hair, something he hadn't seen her do for a very long time. She looked fragile. She looked human. When they were younger, she had looked this way, when she worried about the trouble the brothers got themselves into, or the trouble waiting for them when they returned home. But this anxiety wasn't for them now. It was for a situation she could not control.

He rested a hand on her shoulder and tried to comfort her. She touched hers to his, and he felt her warmth. How different they were. "Perhaps you should leave."

She nodded, shrugged off his hand, and the majesty in her face returned. She required no more comfort, and they were once again Tomas and the Marquise, not brother and sister.

"I am needed elsewhere. I had hoped you could control him while I was away, but I see that's now beyond your capacity. However, if something happens and you need me, I'll return."

"You worry too much, Aurelia. The pain will be momentary. It will be contained."

She knew he lied but she accepted it. There was never any telling how far Olivier would go. "I'll leave tomorrow."

She headed back to the castle and left him to wonder what could be so important to drag her away. Either way, she was going and wouldn't have to witness Olivier at his worst. As she exited, Reiner passed her, and he bowed. She gave the curtest of nods without stopping. Reiner looked puzzled.

Aurelia might not have been pleased to see Reiner, but

Thierry's mood lifted once he appeared. He itched to hold him in his arms again, to feel skin against skin, to taste his tongue and flesh. When Reiner smiled, he almost pounced.

"Do you know the Marquise well?" Reiner asked.

"Not particularly. She reminds me of my sister."

"My aunt is very fond of her. She considers it a good omen when she appears."

Thierry smirked. "Does she visit often?"

"A few times a year. Without warning, though. If it was anyone else, my aunt would consider it rude, but as it's the Marquise, all sins are forgiven."

"If only they were."

"Pardon?"

"Oh, nothing." Thierry closed the small distance between them and hoped that would be the last they would speak of Aurelia. "What do you have planned for the day?"

---

AURELIA MADE A GREAT SHOW OF LEAVING BY carriage, but once it was out of sight, the whole thing would vanish. It was nothing but magic and air. Even so, it was as solid as if it really was a black travelling coach, drawn by four somber black stallions and a driver who said nothing while waiting for his mistress.

She said her farewells as if it were a funeral and wrapped the Baroness in a long embrace. They clung to each other, and when they separated their eyes were wet. Thierry realized too late that these people, particularly the Baroness, were Aurelia's family, one more caring and loving than her real kin had ever been. She held the Baroness's hand until the last moment.

"I will see you again soon," she said softly. With fingers pressed against her lips, she took a few deep breaths and turned away.

Olivier was next. He bowed and kissed her hand.

"May I offer some advice, Orlando?"

"Certainly, my lady."

"Be careful. One who offers his charms so readily usually has them taken away when he least expects it." She studied him like a mongoose baiting a cobra.

"Wise words, but I hardly feel they apply to me." He gave a reptilian smile. "I hope we meet again soon."

"I am sure we will."

She gave Thierry a pointed look and climbed into the coach. He remembered her pledge: she would return if needed. With a flick of the reins, the carriage pulled away from the castle and out the gates. The Baroness waved until it could be seen no more. Thierry had a moment of regret and wished he'd spent more time with his sister, without Olivier lurking in the background. He would have to wait until next time—if she could bring herself to look at him.

"Baron, has that attendant shown up?" Olivier asked.

"I'm afraid not, Orlando. He has either left our employ, in which case may the Devil catch him, or else he fell into some misfortune on the day of the hunt. My men conducted a search but failed to find anything." The Baron may as well have been talking about an old horse for all the concern his voice held for the disappeared man.

"That is a shame."

The Baroness cut across their chatter. "We must do something to cheer ourselves up." She dabbed at her eye. "The Marquise's departure always saddens my heart."

Olivier turned to speak to Thierry, but the Baroness

sidled up to him and laced her arm through his. "Would you mind keeping me company, Orlando? I feel a conversation with you would lift my spirits." Her red-rimmed eyes beseeched him. She was not the woman of power Thierry had first met, jockeying for the favor of bright, young things. The quaver in her voice and the soft, sad smile she gave his brother were anything but predatory.

"Of course, Baroness. I would be honored to chase your dark clouds away." He smiled at her as if she was the most beautiful woman in the world. She blushed and coyly hid her eyes. There was nothing she could have done about it. Olivier could make an executioner feel desired. With a nod to Thierry, the pair disappeared inside.

He seized Reiner's hand and held a finger to his lips. Tempting as it was to use his invisibility, Reiner might notice a change. Instead, he had to rely on regular artifice. He peered into the hallway and, once he was sure Olivier and the Baroness would not see them, dragged Reiner up the stairs to his room.

Once he closed the door and locked it, Reiner fell on him, kissing him, and trapping him in a tight hold. His eagerness made Thierry laugh, and Reiner gave him a bashful look. He was too delicious, and Thierry's body ached for him. He scooped Reiner off the ground and lay him down on the bed. Nuzzling against his neck and blowing hot air onto Reiner's skin, Thierry's lungs were suffused with his earthy scent, so unlike many of the powdered ninnies of the aristocracy. It grounded him, which only made him want Reiner more. He fumbled with belts and buckles, trying to break through the clothes to reveal Reiner's beautiful naked body.

A knock at the door.

They stopped, listened.

Another knock.

Reiner slid off the bed and ran into the antechamber to arrange his clothes. The handle turned but the lock held.

Thierry tucked in his shirt, checked Reiner was out of sight, then opened the door.

*Olivier.*

Nails of ice splintered Thierry's spine and his jaw hardened, keeping a snarl fastened in his throat. His fingers tightened on the door handle and the metal buckled in his grip. It was all he could do to not attack his brother in Reiner's defense.

Olivier seemed not to notice. He leaned against the doorframe, inspecting his nails, but only a fool would think he was truly so nonchalant. When he deigned to lift his head, he wore a smile never designed to put anyone at ease.

"I thought the Baroness wanted you." His voice was leaden.

"She is consoled. May I come in? There is a delicious smell of fresh meat emanating from your room." He leaned close to Thierry's body and inhaled, closing his eyes as he breathed Reiner's scent. "And from you." He pushed his way into the room.

Thierry reached out and grabbed his shoulder. "You need to leave." Olivier spun round, flinging Thierry's arm off him. He showed a flash of anger and then it was gone, replaced by that menacing grin. Henri had never looked so threatening.

"But I feel I have hardly seen you since we arrived. Me running off with young Wolf, and you running off with what's-his-name."

Thierry's hands clenched into fists. *How did he know? What did he know?* They'd been careful. Thierry had not spoken Etienne's name once in Olivier's presence. Though he had said it to Aurelia. Could she have said something? Could Olivier have overheard? There was nothing he could do about the scent. Olivier had always had a sensitivity for aromas, pontificating over them like a *parfumeur*. Likely, Olivier would believe Reiner was just a toy. Thierry would have to convince him that was the truth.

"Get out." The order rumbled low through his teeth. "You'll ruin everything."

A thud came from the antechamber.

"Hmmm." Olivier gave Thierry a jackal's grin and loped into the other room.

Thierry closed the door and ran to catch him. But it was too late.

Reiner hovered over a fallen chair. He straightened under Olivier's gaze; the chair forgotten.

"Hello, Orlando." He crossed his arms, his voice strong with a touch of displeasure.

Olivier inclined his head a bare inch. "Hello again, Reiner. I hope my brother is being a good companion."

"Certainly. It's refreshing to find a countryman so interesting. It's quite *unique*."

Thierry wished he was holding Reiner's hand and could squeeze it in warning. Then again, the veiled insult made him smile.

Olivier's empty laugh wiped it from his face. "I wonder what you two could have been doing."

Reiner's his lips closed with all the warmth of a dungeon. Olivier crossed the distance between them in a few quick strides. Thierry followed, ready to intercede.

Olivier was close enough to touch him. He looked Reiner up and down, a seductive curve to his mouth, a

whisper of desire in his voice. "Do not fear. You see, my
brother and I have no secrets. We share *everything*."

"Not this time," Thierry snapped.

Olivier grunted. "We shall see." He appeared relaxed,
almost playful, but Thierry had seen him kill while in this
mood, taking down men without baring his fangs. Thierry
coiled his muscles, ready to spring at the slightest indication
Olivier might harm Reiner.

A minute dragged as they stood in this little trio until
Thierry was forced to break the silence.

"Don't you have someone to see?"

"Why, yes, I do," Olivier said with mock delight like
some fop dispensing pleasantries at a ball. "I shall leave you
to it. Enjoy."

After a lingering glance over Reiner's body, Olivier
stepped lightly from the room, closing the door behind him.
Even though they were alone, they remained still, waiting
for the other to make a move.

Olivier had found Reiner. But did he know what that
meant? Thierry had tried to keep him a secret, and he'd
tried too hard. Even without revealing Etienne's return, he
would have to stay by Reiner's side. Olivier would not allow
him to keep Reiner to himself.

He slowly reached out with one hand to touch Reiner's
arm and pull him close.

"Will he keep his mouth shut?"

"Yes. He's got his own secrets to protect." Thierry
hugged him and kissed his cheek.

"What if someone suspects?"

"Don't worry about it. I won't let anything happen to
you." Reiner had no idea how close he'd been to a killer, so
his worries were, to Thierry, more mundane. Ignorance was

about as safe as he was going to get. But one day, he'd have to hear the truth.

"You can't know that. Maybe this wasn't such a good idea." Pushing away, Reiner stepped out of his arms and headed for the door. Thierry followed and took his hand, but Reiner slipped free.

The taste of sour milk coated the back of his tongue. Olivier was one thing, but if Reiner rejected him there would be nothing left for him. He'd always believed Etienne loved him and Reiner had already shown shades of the same, but would it ever be enough? Had Etienne suffered like this when trying to convince him it would be all right? The dangers shone now as they did then. Exposure. Condemnation. Death. Yet Etienne hadn't let go. And now, neither would Thierry.

Reiner's hand touched the handle. Thierry held the door shut.

"I swear to you there will be no trouble. No one will discover us."

Reiner avoided his eyes. "Let me go, Tomas."

He put his other hand on the door, fencing Reiner in. "Look at me."

Reiner refused, and Thierry was faced with the back of his head and he felt shut off from the light. He'd seen Etienne's dead body, but this was different. Then he'd known Etienne had gone not cursing his name. Now, Reiner might have every intention of never talking to him again. He might even deny what they'd shared. If that's what he meant to do—*God, please, don't let it be so*—then he needed to be certain and see it in his eyes.

He grabbed Reiner and spun him round. Offence swept away the glint of shock on his face. He hated using force, but everything depended on this.

He spoke fast and low. "Now that I've found you, I'm not going to lose you." Reiner fixed him with a stare that would make a rock wither. It was that strength he'd loved in Etienne—even if it did sometimes border on stubbornness. "I give you my word, Orlando will not tell anyone, and you will be safe."

He detected a crack in the stone wall, a slight softening of Reiner's cheek. Thierry's lips brightened, which only made Reiner harden again. Still, Thierry knew his words had had an effect. Like a tree's root upsetting a foundation.

He leaned closer, an inch separating them. The artery in Reiner's neck throbbed, faster than normal. "Please, Reiner. You know this is right."

"I said n—"

Thierry kissed him, stopping that hideous word from touching the world. Olivier had always chided him for never taking action; what would he think now? He pressed against Reiner, the coarse cloth rasping against his skin, creating a friction that made him all the more aware of how confined he was, of how his skin ached to feel Reiner's body. Reiner's lips resisted at first, but his grunts of protest changed to soft murmurs as he opened his mouth and allowed Thierry in.

Reaching behind him, Thierry turned the key in the door with an audible click. Lips still touching, they tore the clothes from their bodies and threw them to the ground. Reiner pushed him back towards the bed. Their skin connected and Thierry vibrated. A bolt of energy crackled along his muscles and burrowed into the bone, deep into the marrow. He gasped like a man showered with water after a trek through the desert. He held Reiner tighter and kissed him deeper. Thierry's knee parted his legs and ground against his groin. Reiner moaned loudly.

"You'll need to keep quiet if you don't want everyone to find out," Thierry said with a lightness that made his heart swell.

Reiner laughed and twined his legs around Thierry's hips, forcing him down harder. "I'll try, but I can't guarantee anything."

## XI

Olivier's smile crashed as soon as the door closed. His fangs itched to bury themselves in someone's flesh. Any neck would do, though ultimately it would have to be Reiner's.

Barely mindful of how fast he moved, he hurried down the stairs and out into the courtyard. He vanished into the forest but couldn't move fast enough to get away from the pain swelling inside him. Molten anger cloyed his throat. As it travelled to the very edge of his body and cooled, he sensed a deep-buried line of jealousy and snarled.

All it had taken was seeing that look in Thierry's eyes: love, protection, need. He'd never thought Thierry would find someone to love again. All for that human. There had been those they'd fucked, but none of them had ever touched his brother's stone heart. No amount of pleading, no protest of undying love could melt his ambivalence. And so, Olivier had believed their own love was safe and inviolate. They existed for each other alone, despite never succumbing to that which Olivier longed for most.

And now, everything was under threat because of this

mortal. He considered abandoning his plans for the Duke and killing Reiner instead. Then they'd leave and find somewhere new, somewhere without distraction, where it would just be the two of them once again. Perhaps the wastelands of Siberia or Persian deserts.

He heard laughter.

Then more in response. People played in the forest, not far, blessedly close, manna from heaven. His fangs unleashed. His senses sharpened. When the laughter came again, he heard the rub of cloth, a boot heel disturbing the soil, rapid, shallow breathing. The colors shone around him, the greens, the browns, the red on the berry bushes, and the smells of earth, decay, new life. Sweat.

Olivier disturbed nothing as he stalked towards where they lay on the ground. One male, one female, young, about seventeen years, disheveled, poorly dressed, oblivious to the danger around them as they kissed and fumbled. Olivier's every muscle tuned to the movements of his prey. If they ran, he would meet them. But they weren't going to run—well, one of them wasn't. But which one to choose first?

In the end, the choice was made for him.

They rested against a trunk, the girl in between the boy's legs. She sat back on her knees as the boy stood to take off his shirt. She glanced at him from under her eyelashes, a coquettish smile on her lips. The boy was too eager and got tangled in the cloth. The way he blundered betrayed his naïveté, and she rolled her eyes at his foolishness. Finally free, he smiled triumphantly, as if undressing was a task beyond anyone else.

Olivier sprang, knocked the boy to the ground, and squatted on his chest. The girl screamed, scrabbling in the dirt. She could scream all she liked. The sound made his body tingle.

The boy looked into Olivier's face, seeing the bright, burning eyes, the fangs, the face of a monster. He screamed and lurched, but Olivier dove forward, sinking his teeth into the boy's naked shoulder. His teeth gripped skin and muscle. He pulled back, and a chunk of meat hung from his mouth. The boy bellowed. Olivier spat the flesh on the ground and bit into his other shoulder. The boy convulsed underneath him as he went into shock. Olivier stayed buried and sucked out his blood. A rush spread through him like cold river rapids. He drew more as the boy shook. Olivier's hand snaked up his naked chest and gripped his throat. He forced it to the right and sought the jugular.

The girl ran. Only seconds remained to finish the boy. He bit his neck and crushed his windpipe. Olivier ingested as much as he could and left the boy to drown. Thrilled at the struggle, tantalized by the chase to come, he hunted the girl.

She'd stopped screaming, but sobs broke from her as she tried to get away. When she turned to look back, she tripped on a tree root and hit the ground hard. She looked up, and dirt smeared her cheek. Olivier stood at her head. She choked on her cries and cowered at his feet.

Olivier's groin pulsed at the beautiful sight beneath him. He crouched and combed his fingers through her matted hair. "Didn't your mother ever tell you to stay out of the woods?"

She put up her hands, begging, pleading, praying.

"Don't cry, little one. It'll be all over soon," he cooed. "They're coming to find you. They're going to see what you were doing with that boy." He let the gold of his eyes dissipate and replaced it with calm blue. She mewled but listened entranced to his words.

"They're going to think you hurt him. What you did

was a sin." Olivier loved that word. It rolled off the tongue so well, and it was a perfect companion to the blood of an innocent.

"Please," she begged. "Please let me go. I didn't mean to. I'm sorry. I'm sorry. I'm sorry."

She rambled as Olivier edged closer. All but paralyzed, she couldn't stop him from lifting her chin and kissing her. He pushed her back on the ground.

"Shhh." He reached in between her legs to rub against her core with his bloodied fingers. She didn't respond, but that didn't matter. His fingers felt the lightly furred mat, the warmth that emanated from her.

He lifted her skirt. She tried to cover herself.

He slapped her across the face.

"Don't," he said calmly but firmly.

She winced and covered her red cheek. Tears eked out from behind closed eyes, and her mouth screwed to a grimace.

He rubbed her thighs, massaging the supple, smooth skin, and sensing the pulse of her femoral artery. How he'd enjoy this. He restrained himself, built the anticipation, the excitement until he could bear it no longer and then plunged between her legs and bit through the skin. His teeth found the prize as if magnetized, and the blood came fast, coating his tongue with sweetness. She gasped, she sobbed, she tried to get out from under him, but he pinned her down and her struggles only made him hold on tighter. He gripped her wrists and held them together to stop her from beating his head.

"It hurts," she managed in between her rising screams. "Please, let me go."

He groaned like a wild animal feasting on fallen prey. In a few minutes she would be dead and at peace.

And that wasn't right.

He'd spent time dragging her to the point of breaking. This was no quick kill. This was effort and consideration. It had required a piece of him, and to kill it off so quickly was an insult to his very nature.

She could live: bruised, tormented, tortured, guilty. And what stories she would tell.

His fangs retracted, and he healed the wound with his own blood taken from his tongue. He wiped his mouth. He crept up her body and looked down on her. He grinned, leaned next to her ear, and whispered, "Remember my face. It will haunt your dreams."

And then he was gone.

# XII

THIERRY AND REINER JOINED THE RUSH OF GUESTS hurrying to discover the source of the shouting. They met the Baroness as she peered out the front door, preferring to stay in the shadow of the house.

"What happened?"

The Baroness started at Reiner's voice and touch. "There was screaming in the forest. A woman, a girl they think. It's stopped now, but even I heard it." Her fingers wound through the lace about her throat and began tapping a fast beat on her chest. Reiner put his arm around her and guided her into the parlor. She left, muttering for the Marquise.

Thierry closed his eyes and swam through his blood to fish for Olivier. It was harder now that he'd fed, but the bond was there. He concentrated, trying to find a sensation that would indicate where he was, how he was feeling.

He almost missed it, mistook it for his own contentment. Olivier was close. Having found his brother, he was ready to reopen his eyes, but something tugged at him, something he hadn't experienced for a very long time.

The tug became a pull.

He couldn't leave Reiner's side again.

The noise in the courtyard grew and compelled him to see what Olivier had wrought. He rushed to Reiner and took his hand. "Come with me." He dragged him away from his distraught aunt, leaving her to the ministrations of others.

Once outside, he saw the damage wasn't as bad as he'd expected. The girl was breathing. She sat in front of one of the men as they rode in on the horse. She faced his chest, clutched him, and sobbed. The other horse carried the man's drained body. The wounds were a glorious mess of broken, bloody tissue. Thierry growled and twitched. He forced himself to look away and focus again on the girl.

Her dirty brown hair clung to her face and neck, matted with sweat, grime, and blood. The Duke shouted at a servant to hasten to the village and tell them they'd found these two in the woods. Others helped the girl off the horse. She trembled and shrank from their touch, but slowly they brought her down. Olivier had drunk from her. She was pale and weak. Wiping away tears, she lifted her head, and looked at the assembly.

Her eyes landed on Thierry and she fainted.

The men didn't catch her in time, and she collapsed on the stony ground. Thierry swore aloud. She hadn't eyed him long, but who had seen her look at him?

They carried her inside as she hung like a slaughtered lamb. He and the other guests trailed them into the castle. She was taken to a bedroom upstairs. Any moment she might wake and search for the face of her attacker. How long did he have? The girl was going to live, and he wished her dead.

He wanted to take Reiner's hand and feel the soft

human comfort he offered so freely. He needed it desperately, because to not hold him would be to lose him—a possibility that crept closer to certainty, thanks to this girl whom Olivier had allowed to survive.

Christine, the one who had fawned over his twin, appeared and forced her stricken visage upon them. She clutched at her throat, and her eyes took on all the horror of one a little too excited with gruesome events.

"Isn't this simply awful? How do you think she got like that? And did you see what happened to the man?"

"Wolves? A bear? Who knows? Excuse me." Thierry was in no mood for her chatter. He nodded to Reiner that they should find somewhere else to stand.

Back in the courtyard, they watched as the men lifted the dead body off the horse and lay it on the ground. They covered it with a cloth and stood around muttering. One of the servants crossed himself.

"If only the Marquise were here," Reiner said to himself.

Thierry knew better. He was about to ask Reiner what he thought Aurelia could have done, but the Baron's shouting stayed his voice.

"Reiner!"

He was quick to answer and ran to his uncle. "What is it?"

The Baron took hold of his arm and pulled him aside, out of earshot of most of the guests. Thierry edged closer, intrigued but wary. His hearing was good enough to keep a certain distance, yet still be privy to their conversation.

"She doesn't look good. I think..."

For a moment, Thierry thought his hopes would be fulfilled. The girl was going to die without waking. There would be no need to kill, as Olivier had already done enough harm, taken enough blood, frightened her beyond sanity. He wouldn't have to leave Reiner behind as he went on his grim mission; there would be no mission to undertake.

But then the Baron fixed Reiner with a knowing look, and some secret meaning passed between them.

Reiner stammered. "Uncle, I can't. We don't know if it's real. What if it doesn't work? Then what? I'll look a fool, and she'll still die."

"You need to try. We've seen what you're capable of."

Reiner's shoulders fell. He looked up the stairs at the solid door to the girl's room. Thierry struggled to make meaning of their words. How could Reiner help the injured girl? What secret had Reiner kept from him? The girl needed a miracle, nothing else would—

The realization infected his mind, and he could barely hold himself back. He groaned, earning himself some worried looks from a couple of the men and women.

He'd missed it completely. Reiner's touch. He'd been so convinced the spark that passed between them was the reawakening of a connection so deep it transcended time that he'd missed the truth. The thrill of Reiner's hands on him, like fire that lit up his skin, his senses, his heart—the way Etienne had.

But it wasn't anything to do with Thierry.

It had always been there. It had all come from something Reiner possessed, a life force—a force that could heal. Reiner's hands had awakened more than his soul. They had tried to bring him back from the dead.

If Reiner laid his hands on that girl, it would be over. She'd awaken and point her revitalized finger squarely at Thierry.

He couldn't let Reiner go through with it. But before he

could act, the Baron turned Reiner towards the stairs. He ran to stop him, caring nothing for the scene he was going to make.

"What are you doing?"

"I...I'm going to try to help the girl." He saw Reiner didn't believe in his power, that he was going on a fool's errand. What had Reiner done in the past that had convinced the Baron, and most likely the Baroness, of his healing abilities? A dying bird? A sickly relative?

"But how?"

The Baron interceded at that point. "Never mind, Tomas. Reiner knows what to do." The Baron pulled his nephew up the stairs.

Thierry forced himself to follow, but each step towards the girl was another bell toll signaling the end. Could he stop him? Could he kill the girl before they got there? But the Baron was relentless in his march, and Thierry ran out of time.

"Let me help you." The words fell from his mouth without him knowing how. Reiner creased his brow, sadness darkening his beautiful face. He shook his head slowly, and they disappeared into the room and closed the door.

A moment later, the Duke, the Baron, and all the other men emerged, leaving Reiner behind. They milled around in the hall. Thierry watched them as they paced.

Minute dragged after minute. There was no movement behind the door. Reiner and the girl were quiet.

*What is he doing in there?*

After a long while, he heard the girl take a deep gasp of air. One or the other of them moved. Reiner's whispers tried to soothe her while she sobbed.

"Please. Don't let him get me. He killed Jakob. He drank his blood. He drank from me." She spoke in staccato.

Until then, Reiner had shushed her, but now he stopped and listened.

"What am I going to do? He's here. He's here. I saw him. Those eyes, those golden eyes that burned right through me. Help me, please. He's going to kill me."

Then silence.

When Reiner opened the door, she was unconscious on the bed, but apart from an occasional cry in her sleep, she breathed easy. Reiner had saved her. Thierry couldn't help the disappointment that stole through him.

"She is better now. She will live," Reiner said softly, avoiding the questioning looks of the men—and Thierry.

The Baron thanked his nephew and followed as the men rushed into the room to see the girl.

Thierry touched Reiner's arm, but he withdrew it slowly.

"What did you do?" he asked.

Reiner shrugged. Was he just modest or ashamed? He looked into Thierry's eyes, and he understood what troubled him. Reiner turned away, shaking his head.

"Reiner..." Thierry called out, but he'd already gone, pausing once to look back, about to say something, but thinking better of it. He joined the others in the courtyard.

Soon enough, Wolf and the men from the village arrived and told about the miracle inside. Four of them thundered into the castle. Thierry hung back, trying but failing to look concerned rather than guilty.

A bearded man emerged with the girl in his arms. Her chest rose and fell, despite Thierry praying for it to stop. He hoped she would stay asleep and silent until he had the chance to get to her.

Three of the villagers wrapped up the boy's body. The

blood turned the white sheet red. They lifted his corpse onto a horse.

But Thierry barely registered what they were doing. Instead he kept his focus on the girl, remembering her features and memorizing her scent.

Reiner watched him from a distance, his arms folded, a glint of iron entering his eyes. Was it worth it? If he killed the girl, the secret of what he and Olivier were would remain hidden, but how much would Reiner accept? Better Reiner should hear it from him than from a peasant girl.

"What have I missed?" Olivier appeared at Thierry's side.

"As if you don't already know." Thierry fought to stay calm when what he really wanted to do was knock Olivier through a wall.

"Is she still alive? I was wondering if I'd stopped in time."

"It's too bad you didn't blind her as well."

"Oh, you know I haven't done that in years."

"Pity. She recognized me—or should I say, you."

Olivier chuckled, and heads swiveled to glare at him. He ignored them. "Interesting. This could turn out to be a lot more fun than I'd anticipated."

"You don't anticipate anything."

"Are you worried the girl will give us away? Or are you worried it will interrupt *your* fun?"

Thierry held his tongue and kept his eyes on the scene in front of him—the body draped over the horse, the girl slunk in the bearded man's arms, and Reiner watching him and Olivier.

"The idea of villagers turning up here with pitchforks and flaming torches sounds like great sport," Olivier said. "This place is a little boring."

Thierry's skin prickled at the last word. Olivier never used it unless he was ready to move on. There wasn't much time left.

The men gave a few parting words to the Duke and the Baron and left for their village. Would the jolts and bumps of the journey home wake the girl? Would she scream? How long would it be before she marched back to the castle at the front of those torch-wielding peasants?

"If you'll excuse me, brother, I must have a word with Wolf." The dust hadn't settled before Olivier was after his quarry.

Wolf beamed at him, pleased to be spoken to, to be given attention.

Reiner avoided Olivier and walked back up to the castle, brushing past Thierry with barely a glance.

He had to go after him.

The girl could wait until nightfall.

# XIII

OLIVIER GAVE WOLF ORDERS TO JOIN HIM IN HIS ROOM later that night and left him to slide next to the Duke. The man watched after the now-departed villagers. Where the body had lain, a bloodstain remained. The Duke called for the men to bring water and wash it away. They jumped at his deep, strong voice, and Olivier appreciated the effect the Duke had on the lower classes. One minute he was revered for his bravery, the next despised for his power. They did his bidding regardless.

Standing beside him, Olivier couldn't help but feel a little small in stature. The Duke was about a head taller than him. Henri had been tall as well, and thickset. His shoulders and arms suited the heavy lifting the abattoir required. It also made him a force of nature in a fight. Olivier rubbed his jaw from still-smarting memories of when he'd been on the receiving end of his father's clenched fist. A quick look at the Duke's hands told him that both men were hacked from the same carcass.

The Duke ignored Olivier. It seemed he was lost in his own thoughts at what might have happened and what he

could do about it. Olivier suspected the Duke was purely a
man of action, one who preferred there to be no mysteries
and no crime left unpunished.

"These are terrible times," Olivier said.

The Duke grunted which only thrilled Olivier more.
He wanted to bait the giant.

"Oh, I didn't just mean what happened to those poor
people but...well, Duke, I think I have some bad news. It's
about your son."

The Duke's eyes fixed on him. "Wolf? What is it?"

Olivier stepped closer, lowering his voice, drawing the
Duke down towards him.

"It's rather delicate, I'm afraid. Do you think we could
find somewhere private to discuss it?"

The Duke grunted again and strode into the house.
Olivier trailed behind. The Duke climbed the stairs two at a
time, barging through the castle and ascending to his rooms
on the first floor. The Duke held the door open for Olivier.
He shrouded himself in a veil of abasement. He prepared
himself for a chastisement, though this time he presumed it
would be without the fists, and he wouldn't wake the next
morning with a black eye.

As the door closed and he was trapped in the room with
the Duke, old fears jammed his throat. Many times he'd
been marched home through the streets with Henri cursing
his name, aiming kicks at his legs and backside. Thrown
inside their small house, he'd tried to get away, but Henri
had filled the room.

The Duke's grim face pinned him to the spot. A need to
hug the wall and find the shadows pricked at his consciousness, but he fought it. It hadn't done him any good then, and
it certainly wouldn't help him now. His pleas had gone

unheard, his childish defenses brushed aside like grass beneath a hailstorm.

As the Duke neared him, Olivier flinched and remembered the nights he'd spent with his face pressed against the sawdust-covered floor. The grunting that came from behind him, over him, inside him. Worse was the night he showed Henri he had grown to accept it, even like it. His wicked smile brought broken lips and swollen eyes, but it delivered him from his father's favorite form of control.

By the time the Duke sat, Olivier had steeled himself with the memory of besting his father that night.

"Say what you have to say." He didn't gesture for Olivier to sit, so Olivier didn't.

He held onto the back of a chair. "Thank you, Duke. As I said it's about your son, but it is also about Anna, his betrothed."

"And what about her?"

"I'm sure you noticed how quickly she left after hearing she was to marry your son."

The Duke didn't reply.

"And I'm sure you don't fully believe her reasons of having to talk with her parents. Young women these days seems quite content to accept certain decisions, particularly when it is to do with something they want. I'm not alone when I say that Anna's affection for your son was evident the moment you arrived and has probably been a verifiable fact for some time."

"Do you have a point?"

"Sorry, my lord, it is rather delicate, but as is so often the case, delicacy can be rather long-winded."

"Orlando..."

"Duke, I'm afraid I think the reason Anna left in such a hurry was that she discovered something about Wolf that upset her. It appears your son prefers the affections of another."

"Impossible. He told me himself how much he wanted to marry Anna."

"Things change."

"Who is the woman?"

"It pains me to tell you, but it is not a woman."

The Duke glared at Olivier. His jaw took on all the suppleness of a mountain. "What are you saying?"

"I am saying he prefers the company of men, rather than the affections of women."

The Duke darted at him from across the room. Olivier forced himself to cringe when he preferred to kill. The Duke fell on him and pinned him against the wall. Olivier's face contorted into that of a sniveling fop, waiting for the blows to fall. He gazed into the Duke's fiery eyes, and there was all the burning anger and spite he'd seen in Henri. He felt his soul split at the dual warring forces. His body remembered the routine, his mind rebelled and raged.

*Stay down. Stay down, and it will be all right. You'll get vengeance one day.*

The Duke's face loomed. "How dare you malign my son's honor with talk of a sin against nature and God?" He rained spit on Olivier's skin. "I will have restitution for your evil little lies and expose you for the odious man you are. If I have my way, you will be shot on the day of Wolf and Anna's wedding."

"Please, Duke," he whined, "it is no lie, and I don't tell you this to embarrass you, but instead to warn you. Since coming here, I have noticed his attention drift from Anna to men in the castle. I say this as a fellow countryman, and to save you and your son from ridicule."

"The only thing that will save me is to see you dead."

"But what about Anna? She discovered something about Wolf that upset her, and now she has left, perhaps never to marry your son. And who knows what she is saying back in Dresden?"

"Even if she believed a lie like this, there is no way she would impugn the son of a Duke. I would destroy her."

"I believe there is still time to get them back together."

"All you speak is lies." The Duke released him and stood, but as Olivier attempted to straighten his clothes, the Duke punched him in the stomach with the strength of a pugilist. He faked the yelping, but for a moment he was back in Carcassonne, cowering in the abattoir as Henri rained another blow down on him.

The Duke strode towards the door and wrenched it open. Olivier rushed to bow before the Duke.

"Forgive me. I am only looking out for you and your son. I would hate to see something evil befall him."

"In my opinion, Orlando, you are the evil one, and I instruct you to keep your despicable thoughts to yourself, unless you wish to find yourself strung up by your entrails."

He whimpered as he left. The door slammed behind him. When the air settled, he straightened. With each step away from the Duke, each measured movement down the stairs and once again out to the courtyard, his stride lengthened, his chest inflated, he unfurled out of his subservience and emerged a wasp.

The closeness of the Duke's breath on his face, the fists holding him to the ground, and the sting of memory spurred him on.

He smiled with purpose as he searched for the next piece of his plan.

XIV

REINER TRIED TO STOP THIERRY FROM CHASING AFTER him, but it was no use. Cornered in his bedroom, he kept his distance and furniture between them.

"What's wrong?" Thierry attempted to get close to him, but Reiner was adamant. Fear and anger battled for prime emotion in his eyes. Lurking behind it all was the specter of suspicion, like a fog on a moor.

"Stay where you are."

Thierry stopped and held up his hands, showing Reiner his palms. "It's about the girl. What did you do to her?" He tried to speak calmly in the hope Reiner would relax.

"Me?" Reiner bared his teeth.

There would be no way to avoid what the girl had said, but Thierry had questions he wanted answered.

"She was going to die when she arrived, then you went in the room and she recovered. What did you do?"

"I don't know. I just... Why am I trying to explain this when it's you who is keeping secrets?" Reiner jabbed a finger at him.

His stomach twisted. If he knew the truth, Olivier wouldn't let him live, and whatever Thierry did wouldn't be enough to stop that awful fate. "I had nothing to do with the girl."

"I'm not an idiot. Of course you didn't. We were together when it happened."

Thierry almost sighed in relief.

"But the girl said...she mentioned something about..." He took a couple of steps to the left then paced back to the right, unsure of which way to go.

Reiner would understand it eventually. Maybe he already had but refused to believe it. He watched as the man he loved wrestled with the idea that, if not his lover, then his lover's brother had brutalized two innocent people. If only he could erase those painful thoughts. Instead, all he could do was twist them.

*To keep him safe.*

"Yes?"

Reiner looked at him, and all indecision fled. "She recognized you! But it wasn't you, I know it wasn't you, but then that can only mean it was..."

"Orlando."

Reiner's eyes widened. "You knew, didn't you?" He came out from behind the chair. "That's why you tried to stop me helping her. And you're protecting that...that monster! Why?"

"I'm not protecting anyone. Orlando's not a killer. What did she say exactly?"

"She said something about your eyes."

"What about them?"

"They were golden...like yours." Reiner frowned.

Thierry tried to keep his eyes neutral whenever around humans, but he must have slipped, once, around Reiner.

Now they were dull grey, but even so they were too bright for how he felt inside.

"They're not golden. Look. Neither are Orlando's. Do you think there is any way either he or I could have done this to her, to that boy?" He disgusted himself the way the lie so easily sailed off his tongue. But Reiner had to believe they weren't anything other than innocent. The moment Reiner had confirmation of their true nature he'd shout it from the top of the castle. They'd flee, but not before Olivier eviscerated Reiner.

"I don't know what you or Orlando are capable of."

The accusation struck him between his ribs. He sucked in air against the wound. "I give you my word. He had nothing to do with this."

"Then where was he?"

"Does that matter? After what state those two were in, do you think anything human could have done such a thing? Well?" He sighed. "I don't know where Orlando was, but I can assure you he wasn't out killing anyone."

"Are you lying to me?"

He'd called Olivier a liar so many times he'd never thought anyone else would be worthy of such a name. Yet here he was. Each lie hooked into his flesh and pulled him further away from his love. Reiner might discover the truth one day, but hopefully by then he would be an old man and have lived a full life. To know now meant death.

"No. I'd never do that to you," he said in a voice level and sure. Reiner still didn't look convinced. "Whatever that girl saw, it wasn't me, and it wasn't my brother. I can't believe I have to try to convince you we had nothing to do with it. I thought...I thought I meant more to you than that."

Everything he said took away the possibility of a smooth revelation. When Reiner discovered the lie, there would be nothing that could hold them together. In lying to protect him, he was ensuring they could not last. The best Thierry could do was see him survive. Then leave.

"I'm sorry. It's just, your eyes. I was sure...She was so afraid, so certain in her pleas. Of course, I know you had nothing to do with it, but your brother frightens me." Reiner softened, looking slightly guilty. He slid his arms around Thierry's waist, and their bodies pressed together. The closeness after such distance was like blood after a month of thirst.

Thierry hugged him tight and nuzzled against his hair. "I know, but he is not a killer."

"Of course. The girl will wake soon, and we'll learn what truly happened."

Thierry murmured an agreement, but his spine stiffened. He had to find the girl before she told anyone else what she'd seen. Not for his sake, but for Reiner's.

———

NIGHT FELL. MOST OF THE GUESTS BRUSHED AWAY THE memories of the day's events and enjoyed the generous feast. The Baroness retired early to her room. The Duke sat at the end of the table, speaking to no one, despite the Baron's best efforts to talk about what had happened in the forest and what they should do about it. Were they in danger? Should they leave? The Duke barked at him to hold his tongue. The Baron, chastised, chewed on his meat. It looked tough.

Olivier kept up the camaraderie at his end of the table, eagerly urging the gaggle around him to drink more, to laugh louder.

"The Devil hates nothing more than joy and merriment among friends," he shouted.

Wolf joined in. Thierry saw the adoring look he gave his brother. Thierry couldn't wait to get away from the table. Despite his assurances, Reiner studied Olivier. Thierry prayed his brother's eyes stayed dull.

However hard Olivier tried, once the meal finished, the guests fled to their chambers.

Thierry and Reiner hurried to Thierry's room, using the commotion and loudness caused by Olivier's group as cover. Once the door was closed and locked behind them, Thierry attacked Reiner with a passion that spoke of finality, of fear for the future. He tore Reiner's clothes as he tried to get them undone and ripped open his own, tossing aside the expensive and articulated fabric.

*I have to feel his skin against mine.*

Reiner didn't have time to protest as Thierry stripped him naked. He laughed, and his brooding vanished.

Thierry paused to look at Reiner's body and feast on the vision of his muscles, his chest and stomach, and his cock already twitching in anticipation. His hands buzzed to touch him. Scooping him up, he placed him on the bed and kissed him forcefully, their lips pressed against each other, tongues reaching and meeting. He kissed Reiner's cheeks, flicked his earlobe, and breathed hot air onto it before caressing his neck with his lips and sucking at the vein. Reiner groaned and wriggled underneath Thierry's weight. The blood, the force, called to him, and he was helpless.

They kissed and Thierry's hands explored. His fingers dragged across Reiner's tense skin, each moment of pressure releasing a spark that made Thierry shiver. He worked his way down Reiner's body and slipped his hand underneath his balls, gently cradling them. They radiated heat, and the healing force buzzed here with extra intensity. Thierry gripped them, and Reiner grunted.

He released him, walked his fingers between his legs, and pressed against his hole. Reiner's heart beat faster. He sweat as he allowed Thierry into him. Staring at him, with hungry, desperate eyes, was his long-lost Etienne. Sadness and lust swirled in his groin, knowing this was only temporary, and one day he'd have to again say goodbye. The memories would have to endure.

Thierry withdrew his finger and positioned himself between Reiner's legs. "Are you ready?"

Reiner struggled to catch his breath but grabbed Thierry around his waist. He guided him forward, lifted his legs and grasped his rod. With the head pressed against the opening, he bit his lip, and Thierry edged forward.

Reiner winced, but he held Thierry with a firm hand and forced him on. The pressure was enough to make Thierry want to lunge and bury himself inside his lover. The feel of him wrapped around his shaft, warmer and softer than his hands could ever be, closer than anything else except to drink at his neck, sent a swell of starvation up his body. He wanted to devour Reiner until they were as one. A moment of resistance, a chance for Reiner to relax, to lick his lips before he encouraged Thierry, slowly at first, pushing him in, then out, the gentle rhythm built in speed, strength and intensity. Thierry teetered on the edge, remaining gentle while wrestling with a need for brutal conquest.

Reiner's nails clawed at Thierry's buttocks and pushed him deeper. Each thrust brought an affirmation. His eyes were open now, finding and holding Thierry's gaze. Fast then slow, deep then shallow, he drew the sounds from Reiner's lips.

"Give me your hand," Reiner commanded.

They touched, and Reiner pulled him close, so their torsos met. Thierry pinned him down.

"I'll forever remember the way you look now," Thierry whispered.

Reiner shivered at the words.

Thierry drove him to the precipice until his face twisted in pleasure and pain, and then thrust harder until Reiner came. His eyelids flickered and Thierry was cast back to a time when he made love beneath oak trees. As Thierry came, he grunted. It was the sound of old wounds reopening. His need for the past left him hollow. Reiner's eyes closed and his head turned away. His breathing deepened. He slept with a smile on his lips.

And Thierry was lost.

Could that time be resurrected? Here was Etienne reborn, willing to give him love he had no right to take. But was there a future when all he longed for was the past, and Olivier had burned so much of the present? This was Reiner, a person in his own right, not just some shell to be ignored. Because if this was Etienne, who had Etienne been?

Thierry lay down next to Reiner, covered him with the sheet, and watched his chest rise and fall in steady rhythm. An hour passed in silent thought as he considered what needed to be done.

A jumble of soft, murmuring voices filtered through the door to his sensitive ears.

*Olivier.*

He sharpened to his whispers as his brother talked with Wolf.

"I will join you soon."

"Can we meet in your room instead?" Wolf asked.

"No."

The finality of that word stopped Wolf from saying anything else. He walked away, but Olivier stayed. Would he knock? Did he smell Reiner? Thierry watched the door handle as a minute went by, but it didn't turn. Olivier left. A door farther down the hall clicked shut.

It was time.

He slid from the bed and dressed in trousers and a shirt. The usual fineries were unnecessary, as were shoes. He checked the lock on the door and went to the window, opening it to the night.

Reiner turned in the bed, the sheets shifting as he moved.

Thierry didn't want to leave, but Olivier was busying himself with Wolf. Even so, he reconsidered leaving. Even if he stayed, Reiner would always be in danger, as long as Olivier roamed these halls.

With a last look at the sleeping Reiner, he dove out the window. His feet touched the stone ground for the barest of moments before he hastened into the forest as swift as death.

## XV

Olivier didn't have to try hard to bring Wolf to climax and unconsciousness; a few standard tricks were enough. Wolf collapsed, exhausted. Sweat slid down his body and soaked the sheets. His breathing labored, then slowed. In the dim light of the bedchamber, a satisfied smile rested on his lips.

Olivier's satisfaction would come later.

He dressed and returned quickly to his rooms where, curled in an armchair, rested a stable boy drugged with laudanum.

Olivier stripped him. Smears of dirt covered his skin, but otherwise he was a beautiful specimen of youth. He smoothed his hand down the boy's cheek, feeling the warmth of his blood, the supple smoothness as he trailed further down his body, touching his neck, chest, stomach, groin. Where his hand went, his nose followed. The boy smelled of sweat, hay, horses, and the earth. He licked his thigh and tasted salt. The artery pulsed. Olivier pierced his flesh and a soft, short cry slipped from the boy's lips. He tasted sweet blood mixed with the heady perfume of the boy's scent and an undertone of copper, the trail of the drug. Olivier couldn't suppress a murmur. He wanted more of these young things, their simple life force, but his plan niggled at him, cracking through the haze of his lust, to bring him back to reason.

*Later. There will be more later.*

He withdrew his fangs and licked the wound closed.

He carried the boy to Wolf's bed and lay him beside Wolf. Standing back, they looked perfectly suited, both innocents, both unwilling participants in a game they knew nothing about.

He left the room and gave the barest of taps on the Duke's door.

It opened with force, and the Duke's eyes narrowed. "What do you want?"

"Duke, I know you don't want to hear this, but I want to show you I'm right, if only so you can save Wolf from a life of depravity."

"Keep your voice down." The Duke grabbed his shoulder and hauled him into the room, shutting the door behind them. "What do you want to show me, you sniveling worm? I see the way you are with the other guests. You're not fooling me. If anyone should come under suspicion, it's you."

Olivier impressed himself. He'd infiltrated the Duke's life deeper than he'd thought. "Duke, please, I do not deserve this attack. I understand your anger, but I am only trying to help."

The Duke picked up a short sword from the table and held it up for Olivier to see.

Olivier retreated. "Please, Duke, just hear me." He backed up against the door. The point of the sword inched forward to rest between his ribs and over his heart. He couldn't die, but the Duke plunging a sword into him was not going to produce the right result. Begging might.

*It never worked with Henri.*

"You have a choice. You can leave and remain alive, for now, or stay and be run through. It's your choice."

Olivier stammered. His hand tremored as he reached for the door handle. "I'll go. But for your sake, go into Wolf's room now. You will see I am right."

The Duke raised the sword, giving Olivier enough time to flee. He hurried back into Wolf's room and hid in the antechamber where he couldn't be seen. In the darkness, he heard Wolf and the stable boy breathing as they slept.

A minute later footsteps stamped down the hall. Olivier's mouth curved in a satisfied arc. He knew the ways of fathers; they never trusted their sons.

# XVI

When Thierry had last visited the village, he'd kept to the edges, but now he was forced to venture further in search of the girl. The narrow streets led to the town square. In the center sat a fountain of the goddess Diana holding a drawn bow, with hunting dogs at her feet. Water dribbled out of the arrow into the pool below. Dim light glimmered from a few streetlamps, illuminating only the barest parts of the path over which they stood guard. The town slept; the houses were shut tight.

He paused outside each building, listening to what lived inside. The heady mix of other people and the lack of sanitation smothered the girl's scent.

With each house he passed, his impatience grew. Here he was again, in a village that reeked of fear and mourning. The taint stirred Wildenau's specter where death and cruelty had overwhelmed him as they committed one vile act after another.

In Wildenau, it had started so simply. First the tailor, then the butcher and his daughter—only a few deaths and disappearances. But then it—they—gained momentum, and the bodies had fallen like wheat beneath the farmer's scythe.

The six-year-old on the side of the road—the one that tried to get away—had been the hardest. But Thierry did it. He picked up the screaming boy after gorging on his mother's blood. He put him to his lips, and the poor thing froze. As Thierry bit into his neck, the boy cried. He drank until there was silence.

The blood, usually the perfect balm for all troubles, tasted of ash.

The next night, Thierry tried to shake the ghost of the dead child from his mind. He matched Olivier kill for kill in the vain hope that the blood of many would be an elixir for his torment. But as the bodies piled up, and the town grew more suspicious of them and mistrusting of each other, he knew he couldn't match Olivier's cruelty again.

He'd lost his appetite.

But now he hunted a girl who may or may not pose a threat to them. And what threat could that be? They were unstoppable, outside man's law, uncontrollable and unaccountable. Thierry cursed his false high morals. He didn't care about keeping him and Olivier safe. He just wanted to stay with Reiner until there came a moment when they could leave together. Without Olivier.

Now was not that time, and if the girl came looking for them—with an army of angry villagers behind her—then there would be nothing he could do.

Reiner would only feel revulsion for Thierry and the things he'd done. In his eyes he would see Olivier and Thierry as the same, as monsters who could rip the throat out of anyone they met, feeding on their blood and bringing nothing but pain and cruelty. Thierry wanted distance from that. Mistrust had already penetrated their relationship like mold. He wanted time so Reiner could see that he could be different—was different—from his twin.

He lied to himself. The best he could hope for was a life where Reiner lived. And Thierry wasn't part of it.

The scent of the girl scattered his thoughts. The sign on the door indicated he was outside the tailor's house. She was upstairs, a candle burning in the window. He tested the front door, but it was barred. He scaled the wall and peered into her open window. The light shone on her fevered and furrowed brow. Her clenched fists held the twisted sheet. Her teeth bore down on her bottom lip. A woman sat asleep on a chair in the corner. In her lap was a shirt she'd been stitching. He slipped into the room and leaned over the girl. Neither she nor her mother woke. His fangs neared her neck.

*Forgive me.*

The door burst open. A shot ripped through his back and threw him against the wall. He grunted from the surprise as much as the assault. Annoyance ran along his jaw and dug in harder when six men entered the room and beamed a spotlight on him. Their muskets trained on his chest. All had swords at their waist. A bell rang. People pour out into the street shouting as they came to kill the monster.

He looked down at the girl's wide-open eyes, her sleep a fabrication. Another shot fired and hit him in the chest. There was no sting, just a force that he could shake off, but as one shot followed another, and more people ascended the stairs to hand out loaded guns, his anger grew.

The bullets buzzed like bees. After brushing one off, another attacked. He pulsed with rage at being made to suffer this on his brother's behalf. Olivier should be the one here feeling the force of human justice. Once again, he was cleaning up his brother's mess, ensuring their secret remained, putting the tortured out of their suffering. But now they could all see what he was, they all learned about the monsters that inhabited this world. It was supposed to be simple, but that hope had been dashed like a child's head against a rock. His fury fed the one option now left open to him.

*They must die.*

They couldn't be allowed to live with the knowledge that vampires had been here. Word would travel to the castle quicker than an arrow. Reiner would know Thierry had lied. He could kill them in no time. He could slaughter the whole village if he had to. And the thought of that much blood provoked the beast within.

People gathered in the streets, shouting for his obliteration. He let their cries of "Monster!" and "Devil!" infect him and steel him for what he must do. His fangs dripped with saliva as he anticipated an endless flow of blood to cleanse, nourish and revitalize. He roared with the ferocity of a pride of lions. One of the men dropped his gun and ran, knocking people as he went.

Thierry crouched, ready to spring at the next one to shoot. It didn't take long. A balding man pulled the trigger. Then the others joined in. But Thierry dodged the pellets with ease, dancing as they hit the wall behind him. When their guns emptied, he lunged forward and took the first shooter by the throat and bit into his neck. The man jolted, first from fear then from death. Thierry drew the sword from his belt as he dropped the man and faced more frightened men.

Raising the sword, he made quick work of the four defenders left in the room. They fell with barely a sound, barely a resistance. Their guns were useless, their blades undrawn.

Another shot fired from the doorway as more men ascended the stairs, ready to exact revenge for fallen heroes. The bullet hit him in the left shoulder, and he spun with the force to stare into the tortured eyes of the girl on the bed.

She cried, the sheet pulled close to her body, her knuckles white with the strain. Another shot in the back, then another. His clothes shredded. But the girl on the bed held his focus. That pitiful creature. That ordinary girl who had done nothing except be the one Olivier had stumbled across. Madness crept into her eyes with each minute. So much damage had already been done, and here he stood, surrounded by corpses of his own making. He was no better than Olivier. In fact, he was worse.

He'd been foolish enough to think he could follow Olivier's example and expect everything would turn out right. His whole life he'd insisted they were different, and the moment he was tested he embraced his brother's evil. He couldn't go through with it. He knew the girl would not recover. She would never laugh easy. Olivier's torture would not fade. The damage had been wrought, and he couldn't unmake it. This was Olivier's responsibility, not his.

And if it wasn't his, then he was free.

Aurelia's old dictum to watch over Olivier crumbled like dried cow dung. He'd told her that he didn't owe anything to the people in the castle, and apart from Reiner, he'd meant it. But that didn't mean he had to watch Olivier tear them apart. He could convince Reiner to come with him. They could leave before the peasants tore down the castle walls.

Bullets and blades pierced his skin, but he brushed them aside as he stalked to the window. They stung like wasps now, but for the first time in centuries he felt truly invincible.

When they tried to block his way, he pushed them aside but didn't attack. With a last apologetic look at the ruined girl, he flew into the crowd below and ran back to Reiner.

# XVII

THE DOOR OPENED. THE DUKE HESITATED ON THE threshold. The dim lights revealed enough of his scowling face as he stomped to the lamp beside the bed and turned its flame to full force.

The two males in the bed became obvious.

"What is this?" The Duke grabbed Wolf.

Wolf's eyes opened. Startled by his father, Wolf scrambled to get away and bumped into the boy. His brow knit at finding Olivier's replacement.

"Answer me," the Duke growled, punching his son's arm.

Wolf spun around and raised his arm to protect himself from the threat of a second blow. "Father—"

But the Duke had crossed to the other side of the bed to wake the stable boy. No matter how much he shook him, the boy didn't stir. He shot his son a look heavy with disgust and headed for the door.

Wolf clambered over the bed, ran to his father, and grabbed his arm. "Please, listen to me. I don't know who that is."

Wolf tried to pull the Duke back into the room while he demanded to be let alone.

"I can explain."

"I don't want your *vile* explanations." His voice carried the full weight of a thunderstorm battering a fishing boat on an open sea. Even Olivier shivered.

"Father, please listen—"

"I want nothing to do with you. You are not my son." The Duke grabbed him and pulled him close. "Do you hear me? You are no longer my son." The Duke spat in his face and threw him away. Wolf lost his balance and collapsed on the floor.

The Duke sneered at his naked son and left without a backwards glance.

Wolf looked around, unsure of what had happened, who was in his bed, why his father had come in. Olivier watched these questions play across his features, watched the anguish and the heavy loss attack his mind and made his body shrink and slump. Wolf closed the door and hunched over the edge of the bed, his back to the still slumbering stranger.

Olivier stripped out of his clothes. He rubbed his head and attempted a groggy swagger as he staggered from the shadows. He groaned, surprising Wolf, who dropped ready to defend. When he saw it was Olivier, he rushed to him.

"What happened?" Wolf asked.

Olivier didn't answer at first. He continued to massage the phantom wound on his head as he lurched to the bed and steadied himself. He looked at the stable boy.

"Who is this?"

"I don't know." The words winged from his mouth like a frightened dove.

"Really?" Olivier liked to push his prey to the point of madness. Wolf was very close.

"Yes!" It was almost a screech. "Where were you?"

"The last thing I remember was lying in bed with you, and then I woke up on the floor feeling like I'd been in a fight. Did I hear someone else in here?"

"My father. Oh God, my father. He found me in bed with this boy. He won't wake up."

Olivier nudged him. "Something's not right here. I don't think he's pretending. Poison?"

"What? Why him? Why me?"

"I don't know. Looks like someone is trying to cause a rift between you and your father."

Wolf crumpled onto the bed and sobbed. Olivier grimaced. When men cried, they sounded like bellowing heifers.

Olivier embraced him. Wolf had lost his smile and the twinkle in his eyes. Here was a broken man at the mercy of others, and with so many unanswered questions. That is how they would remain.

As Olivier hugged him, he swayed him a little before raising his head, opening his mouth, and sinking his fangs into Wolf's neck.

Wolf sucked in a rapid breath and struggled, pushed desperately against Olivier, but that only made the fangs tear at his flesh. Olivier would not let go. Wolf's hands turned into fists and beat at him, but they made no difference.

*If only he'd shown that force in bed.*

Wolf's hands clawed at Olivier's skin, but he continued to drink. Olivier crushed him to his body, ribs breaking, his lungs unable to expand, suffocating.

For all its violence, it happened so slowly. Each moment

passed in exquisite pain as Olivier took out his vengeance on the Duke's son. Soon, the Duke would feel guilt at causing his own son's death. The Duke would crumble beneath the weight of the knowledge and beg for mercy. Then Olivier would kill him too. He drank, holding Wolf in the grip of death until his strength finally weakened. His heart beat. Just.

Wolf's body sagged. Olivier retracted his fangs and carried him in his arms to the window. Wolf stared at him with unblinking eyes. A few tears skipped down his cheek. Olivier smiled at him and bent down to kiss his forehead.

With one hand, he opened the window and pushed through the curtains. He held Wolf over the edge of the window and let go.

He listened.

The sound of cracking bones and wet flesh hitting stone thrilled him, and the sensation mixed with the fresh blood he'd swallowed.

Olivier turned back into the bedroom and unsheathed Wolf's sword from the scabbard hanging over the chair. He jumped on the bed and flipped the stable boy onto his stomach. Straddling him, he pulled his head back by his hair and slit his throat. The blood sprayed over the bed and the wall, and the body jounced beneath him. He bit his lip to stop a moan escaping and drove the sword between the boy's shoulder blades. Climbing off the emptied body, he licked a little of the splattered blood off his hands, but the rest he wiped with a sheet then went and dressed.

After a final survey of the bloodied room, he opened the door.

Reiner stood at his door opposite.

Olivier didn't have time to close the door. He could see

the blood and the body and Olivier's terrible hand in the whole thing.

Reiner opened his mouth, his chest filling, ready to shout, but Olivier was too fast. He sped across the few yards separating them, covered the human's mouth with his hand and muffled his cries. He forced him back into his room.

Reiner couldn't break free, and Olivier used his body to shut the door behind them. Olivier turned the key and waited. Reiner gave a horse kick to the wood but Olivier bore his full weight down so he couldn't move. He shouted into Olivier's suffocating hand. His fingers tried to injure his arm, but Olivier didn't relent.

His senses strained for signs of life on the other side of the door.

The longer he held Reiner, the greater the man's attempts at freedom. The persistence broke through Olivier's concentration, and he was forced to deal with his prisoner.

"Listen to me, Reiner," he whispered into his ear. "You need to keep very still, very quiet, or when I'm done there won't be anything left for them to bury."

Despite the warning, Reiner kept up the fight. There was still no movement in the hallway, but Reiner's muffled grunts and curses could still rouse suspicions. Olivier's hand moved the barest of inches and covered his nostrils and his mouth. Reiner railed harder but that used up his breath quicker, and soon he slumped into Olivier's arms.

He carried him to a chair and propped hm up. Grabbing the sheet from the bed, he tore it into strips. He wound the first through Reiner's mouth and around the back of his head. He bound his hands to the chair arms, and then one leg to the chair. He'd finished tying the knot when Reiner's free leg hit him in the chest, catching him by surprise. He looked up into wild, angry eyes. The boy had recovered quicker than expected. Olivier growled and grasped the leg, binding it tight and cutting into the flesh. Reiner winced, but when he opened his eyes they were filled with cold hatred.

For a second, he recognized that hate. He was sure he'd seen that scorn before. But the moment passed when the Duke's heavy gait marched down the hall.

It wouldn't be long now.

Half a minute later the Duke ran back the way he'd come, down the stairs, while calling for help. How Olivier wanted to be there when the Duke saw his dead son, to see the contempt in his eyes turn to grief. He wanted to see the broken and bested man, but Reiner demanded his attention as he tried to break free from the binding rags. He almost toppled himself, but the chair was made of sturdy stuff and would not break easily.

Olivier could just kill him now, be done with it. He could throw him from the window like he'd done to Wolf.

But those burning eyes gave him pause.

He remembered where he'd seen them before.

The commotion outside was a mere hum to the sound of blood filling his ears as he looked at his old foe. He glowered at Reiner, piercing him with his gaze, searching for some confirmation that who stared back at him now, who had been almost inseparable from his brother since they arrived, was the soul of Etienne de Balthas.

He roared in Reiner's face, the sound forcing him back in the chair, his eyes flaring at the terrible noise and the fangs that dripped with saliva.

At the moment of what was to be his triumph over the Duke, he was brought low in the face of this resurrection.

"How did you get here? How did you find him?"

Accusations poured forth as if this was truly Etienne, as if he was really here and not ashes and bones buried beneath an oak outside Carcassonne.

Remnants of his human life pursued him. His hypocrite sister, the shadow of his father, and now the revenant of his greatest rival.

Thierry had found him.

And kept it secret.

Olivier tipped back his head and howled. His body boiled with too many emotions, and he clutched his head to quiet the voices. But they shouted at him, scalding him with their words.

*Thierry lied to you! Thierry betrayed you! Thierry abandoned you! Thierry hates you! Thierry doesn't love you! Thierry! Thierry! Thierry!*

"Stop!" he screamed.

When he opened his eyes, the voices had silenced. Reiner said nothing, attempted nothing, and regarded Olivier like some plague-ridden dog. The fear had worn off, the strength and fangs no longer a stick with which to beat him. He had shown his anger and jealousy, and now his madness. Reiner thought he'd won. Old hatred died hard.

"You think he's yours? You have no idea."

He opened his mouth and bared his fangs, wound his fingers through Reiner's thick hair and roughly exposed a neck destined for biting.

## XVIII

THIERRY MADE HIMSELF INVISIBLE TO AVOID THE MEN as they crowded in the courtyard. Whatever the cause, Olivier would be to blame. The sooner he got back to Reiner, the better and safer he'd be. All he had to do now was convince him to leave. The villagers wouldn't be far behind.

He scaled the wall, slipped through the window, and stood behind the curtains. Reiner might be awake, wondering where he had gone. To suddenly appear two stories up and enter the room through his window would not help. But he paused and listened. Nothing stirred inside: no rustle of the sheets as Reiner turned in the bed, no murmurs as he drifted through dreams, no breath.

Panic rose like a plague of locusts in his chest, and he burst through the curtains to stare at a chair with its back to him. Reiner's head poked over the top. For a moment, Thierry made himself it was Reiner waiting for him to return. He prayed that was all it was. If he asked how he'd got into the room, he would tell him the truth and accept the punishment, even if it meant denial and banishment.

The lies had become exhausting. One slow step after another, he crept towards the chair, refusing the truth behind his earlier observations. He'd been mistaken. He could hear him breathe.

*Yes. There it is. He's breathing lightly. He's only asleep.*

He stood behind him, unwilling to go forward as sinister whispers overcame his thoughts.

He forced himself to walk around the chair, keeping his eyes fixed on the wall ahead until the last moment when he was compelled to look.

With a strangled groan, he collapsed, kneeling in front of his slain lover. Reiner's open eyes stared. His hands and feet bound. His neck was bloody and rent, and his shirt ripped open, his chest a gaping hole where a heart once beat.

Thierry bawled ugly tears and keened like an old crone over the bodies of her dead grandchildren, rocking back and forth in front of this empty shell. Etienne had been taken from him again. No goodbye. The smell of his blood was sulfur to his senses and burned into him, blaming him, cursing him.

His shaking hands caressed Reiner's once-beautiful face, his lips. He avoided the wounds, unable to bring himself to touch them for fear they would scald. There was no more power left in him, no life. He couldn't heal himself, not after such an attack.

Even Thierry's blood couldn't save him.

He rested his head in Reiner's cold lap, gripped his legs over and over as if trying to rouse him in one last vain attempt. Bloody tears fell.

"I had to."

Thierry was airborne the moment he heard Olivier's voice behind him. He struck his brother with the full weight of his body and strength and propelled him to the ground. Wild rage burned through him at what his twin had done.

Unlike before, when Etienne had died that horrible death in the woods, Olivier did not accept Thierry's beatings. Barely had they fallen to the ground before Olivier punched him in the face. The brunt of Olivier's own anger stormed behind the impact, and Thierry lost his hold. Olivier slithered out of his grip. He clamped his hand over Olivier's ankle and dragged him back, and this time landed a heavy blow on the side of his twin's head.

Thierry sought some purchase on Olivier's body, to hold an arm, to grip his hair, but Olivier was slick with Reiner's blood, and Thierry only became stained. Olivier took each attack and served it back with his own viciousness.

Thierry stung with the fire of betrayal and loss—not only his, but Olivier's as well. It found those vulnerable places and stuck a hot poker into the open wounds to make him gasp and quiver. Rather than break him, it drove him harder.

They broke apart, and Olivier crouched beside Reiner's corpse, his usual smirk replaced with an angry sneer, his fangs dripping, his fingers like claws.

"If you hadn't—"

Thierry couldn't let him finish the accusation. He flew at his brother, summoning strength from the hope that one day he would be free of this monster and that day could be now. They splintered the door and crashed into the hall.

The weeping of women and the cursing of men soared up to them from downstairs. They called Wolf's name and prayed to God.

The brothers rolled on the ground, desperate to make

sure the other didn't get away. They grappled and roared, the sound reverberating off the castle's walls.

The wailing in the hall stopped.

They fell down the stairs, their snarls like a pack of wolves. Screams preceded them and people fled.

Hitting the cold floor hard, they tore into each other again, unconfined in space, unbothered by the castle guests and servants hugging the walls. Only the Duke stayed where he was, slumped on the ground with his dead son resting in his lap. The man sat in a daze, unaware of the maelstrom around him.

Thierry leapt at Olivier, gripped him and sunk his teeth into his shoulder, the first real blow he'd had so far. Blood stung his tongue, soiled by the hate that coursed through him. He remembered their maker and how they'd defeated that sack of flesh. If he drained Olivier of enough blood, would he be as easy to kill?

Olivier kicked him and he soared into the air, landing on the stairs.

Through the castle doors, the night turned orange as flames filled the courtyard, and bobbing torches illuminated swords and guns held aloft by the people of the village. Their shouts entered the hall and forced Olivier to turn.

Seeing the ordinary folk armed and angry, the Baron regained his authority and called for arms. Thierry couldn't laugh at their attempts to rid themselves of these devils. He couldn't laugh at anything, but Olivier did.

The villagers swarmed into the hall, screaming out "Unclean!" and "Undead!" and "Kill the vampire!". They charged Olivier.

He roared with the force of Hades. The sound knocked people off their feet and compelled them back. Their bravery fled.

Thierry saw his chance. He attacked Olivier from behind, grabbed his hair with one hand, and held him up for all to see.

"This is your demon! He is the one who has terrorized your people and slain the Duke's son. Have your vengeance!"

"And what are you?" Olivier hissed at him. He flung his arm around to grab at Thierry and break his hold. His fingers were wound tight through Olivier's hair, but he'd underestimated the pain Olivier was willing to put himself through to be free. Olivier kicked at him and he skidded backwards, his fist holding locks of Olivier's black hair.

When Thierry regained his footing, he expected Olivier to be on him like a cat on a dove, but his brother's attention was diverted elsewhere.

The Duke had left Wolf's body and taken up one of the swords that littered the room. An awful calm clouded him as his eyes fixed on Olivier. Those armed shouted and bayed to attack, but he held up his hand, and they fell back.

"It was you all along, wasn't it?"

Olivier tried to grin, but it was only a half-smile. One corner of his mouth twitched up and exposed a canine.

"Of course. How does it feel to lose everything?"

The Duke howled a battle-cry, raised the sword above his head and charged. Olivier sprang at him.

"Enough!"

The Duke and Olivier shot apart. Bergamot hung heavy in the air, and Aurelia advanced out of nowhere into the middle of the fighting circle. Her green dress glittered. Her feet were bare, her raven hair unbraided and cascading down her back. She looked like a simple farm girl—except for the hard glint in her eye and the aura of powerful magic that clung to her.

The Duke lay dazed on the ground, Aurelia's power having knocked him against a marble column. A few of the men dragged him to safety.

Olivier crouched and circled around his sister. "Had to come here and fight Thierry's battle for him, did you? Again."

Thierry snarled at him, but Olivier didn't take his eyes off Aurelia.

She held up her hands as if laying a benediction. It encompassed both brothers. "Enough of this fighting" She spoke softly but clearly, the sound cutting across the people's murmurs.

"Kill him, Aurelia. He murdered Reiner!" Thierry's voice echoed in the hall, the castle all but silent as everyone watched and waited, terrified at what they witnessed. Only a gasp was heard from the Baroness as she learned the news of her nephew's death.

Betrayal beat a weak pulse in Thierry's veins. It belonged to Olivier, wounded by his brother's words. Thierry hardened himself and drowned it in hatred.

"Go ahead, Aurelia. Finish me off, the way you always wanted," Olivier scoffed.

"No."

He circled around her as if he baited a bear. "Because you can't. You don't have the power, you weak bitch." He spat blood at her.

Calmly, Aurelia raised her hand, and Olivier floated off the ground. He looked uncertain at first, but then laughed to cover his unease. "Cheap tricks."

She closed her hand in a tight grip, and Olivier screamed in pain.

"Never underestimate me, brother."

Her face never registered the tormented howls that

rallied forth, not even as Thierry collapsed to the ground, the agony seeping into his body.

"Finish him," he gasped at her, half fearful that if Olivier died, he would too. He prepared himself for the terrible affliction. Others joined in the call for Olivier's death, but their voices barely rose above his howling.

Thierry saw the fight in Aurelia's eyes, the tensing of her jaw, the flaring of her nostrils as she considered ending Olivier's unnatural life. Her hands trembled as they wielded an invisible power. She took a deep and long breath.

"No, it's not time." It was barely more than a whisper, but Thierry heard it and moaned.

She released her fist. Olivier fell to the ground, unable to rise. Aurelia disregarded him and knelt in front of Thierry.

"Kill the monsters," the villagers shouted and ran forward.

With the slightest of gestures, she opened her hand and blue light enveloped her, Olivier, and Thierry. The shield kept the crowd at bay.

"Thierry, I know you're in pain, but I can't kill him," she said, her voice gentle and laden with sorrow. "He is needed." She touched his face, trying to soothe him.

He recoiled from her touch and glared at her pitying eyes. "But he killed Reiner," he begged. "He's again taken from me the only thing I love. He doesn't deserve to live." Thierry sobbed. Bloody tears flowed down his cheeks to drip onto the floor and stained the marble.

"I know, but he still has a purpose to serve."

Hate welled at hearing her give that excuse. Ever since they'd rediscovered Aurelia and found her to be filled with this power and a blood-free immortality that

Thierry envied, she had expected him to trust what she said.

But not this time.

She was wrong. Olivier was not needed. He was not important. He was nothing. Thierry burned to fight again and rip his twin apart, not caring how long it would take. No battle could be too long to be rid of this fiend.

Olivier struggled into a crouch, waiting, glowering. Thierry dashed for him, about to fire into him like a cannonball.

But his brother vanished, and Thierry rebounded against the shield. He spun, hunting for Olivier, thinking he might simply have fled to the opposite side of the room. As he searched and found it futile, his roar grew. "Why?" he screamed at Aurelia.

She was unmoved and replied with the coldness of stone. "I told you why."

A final bellow ripped from his throat, and he shook as the sound soared to the heights of the castle, and his rage fled with it.

Thierry turned away and wept. The hate had demolished him and turned his sorrow into vengeance. Now, with Olivier gone, he was left with the hollowness of being alone. Surrounded by loathing eyes, he craved the chance to touch Reiner again, to say goodbye, even if he never received an answer. Looking around, all he saw were people who detested him for what he had brought into their lives.

Aurelia faced the audience, their swords held warily in front of them, the torches still burning. "Go back to your homes. We are leaving. Your village and this castle will be safe. You will not be troubled again."

"Witch! How can we trust you?" The Duke stood at the front of the crowd, his courage and strength returned, his

sword ready to strike against these forces if only the magic
hadn't repelled him.

She glided over to face the Duke. The closer she came,
the more people backed away—except him. "You will just
have to take my word for it. I am truly sorry for your loss."

Thierry heard the sadness in her voice, its softness
meant to soothe, something he remembered her doing to
Henri. But even under that there was a genuine note of
regret. He realized that while he had lost Reiner, Aurelia
had lost a deep friendship with the Baroness.

The Duke would have none of her conciliations, and his
voice carried with it the weight of his authority. "We
demand justice for the havoc these demons have brought
into our lives." The crowd cheered.

"There is nothing I can do. I am sorry."

"You lying witch!"

"Do not try my patience, Duke!" She raised her voice,
the gentleness gone. "Mourn for your son and your lost
friends. You are not the only one to grieve tonight."

"We will have vengeance," he whispered, the threat
laced with menace.

Aurelia didn't respond. She turned to Thierry. "It's time
to leave."

He looked at her with blood-stained eyes. "Why did he
have to do it? Why couldn't he..." A sob broke from his
mouth and halted his words. He closed his eyes against the
tears.

She touched his shoulder and they vanished.

## ❦ III ❧
# A BORED VAMPIRE IS A DANGEROUS THING

**Present Day**

Perth, Australia

I

As they entered the club, Olivier drank in familiar and favored sights: half-naked, sweaty men; drunk, drugged and delirious boys in bright clothes gyrating on the dance floor. The bars overflowed as servers rushed to ease insatiable thirst. In the dark places, men executed dark deeds; hands and mouths groped and rubbed while bouncers looked the other way and sniffed. The dirty music drowned moans. Queues for the toilets. Bodies everywhere. The place was fertile.

The brothers swam through the sea of men and few women to the center of the dance floor. They moved in time to the *thump-thump-thump* of the music, a replacement for their long-lost heartbeat. Eyes followed them, unable to resist.

They danced in perfect rhythm, hypnotizing the men with the thrust of their hips, the glide of their hands and arms. Olivier knew the moment when the first few realized what they were; the word "twins" uttered in reverence.

The brothers removed their shirts with seductive slow-ness, revealing their hardened bodies, the play of light and shadow on the hills and valleys of their muscles. They dropped them on the floor, lost amongst the broken glass, gum, and plastic packets devoid of their illicit contents. They smiled wickedly at each other.

One guy broke the circle surrounding the brothers to go behind Thierry and wind an arm around his waist. He was taller by a couple of inches. His bare torso free of fat, his muscles big, a testament to a life in the gym. Thierry ground his ass into the guy's crotch. His eyes closed. He bit his bottom lip and ran his free hand down the man's body and against the bulge in his pants. This wasn't just for Muscle Man's pleasure, but for everyone else who couldn't look away.

While their gaze roamed over Thierry, Olivier left the circle to explore the deeper darkness. It was a spectacle Olivier had seen his brother perform before. There was never anything more to it. Nothing lasted. He always returned.

As Olivier slithered around the bodies, he saw the questions on the faces of many. For all the drugs and the dancing, apprehension vibrated in the air. Will I? Won't I? Will he? Won't they?

*This is going to be fun.*

After his round, he returned to the dance floor. Thierry and Muscle Man had disappeared. He thought of finding him and watching, but there would be another opportunity later, and he had the urge to be the one on show.

He gathered around him a collection of men of various ages, races, shapes, sizes. He used his body as a conduit to connect one lust-riddled male with another. The shaven-headed Germanic body builder with the slight, effeminate Italian; a smooth and toned, ageless Asian with the preppy, college kid with his perfect, cheeky smile and green eyes.

Olivier let each one possess him. Their hands explored his body, in his jeans, tongues and lips around his neck, his nipples. Heated bodies masked his deathly coldness. Knowing he was watched drove him on, charged him, fueled his lust. The men pressed harder. He heard the pumping of their blood.

They spoke to him, told him what they wanted to do to him. How they'd tie him up and ride him until dawn. They wanted to be used. Abused. Tormented. They wanted him to come on them. They'd swallow for him. They'd let him fuck them raw. They'd do anything he wanted.

The music rolled on. Hours passed as Olivier moved from one to another, indulging them, kissing them, allowing them to bite his nipples, to grip and rub his dick. He lost count of the hands that touched and the mouths that sucked. Eventually, all that drove him was a thirst that needed to be quenched with their blood.

He had denied himself long enough. Being this close to so many bare bodies fashioned his craving to a needlepoint. The heat drew sweat from their pores and opened their veins like blooming flowers. A garden of delights waited to be decimated. The moment his teeth sliced through yielding flesh would be like the first time, the blood would taste sweeter than just an ordinary kill.

Olivier's discerning eye settled on the college kid, and he pulled him close. He looked at Olivier the same way Thierry looked at him when they were young, and Olivier meant everything. The kid rubbed against him, touched his face, kissed his lips, thumbed his nipples. For all the alcohol he'd seen him drink, for all the hours they'd been dancing, the boy kissed him with fierce, sharp desire.

Olivier returned the fire, caressed the flesh with his tongue and tasted salty sweat. His fangs extended and he homed in on the boy's jugular. He'd have to be gentle but that was all part of the fun, trying to restrain himself. Trying. That first drop was what he chased. The boy wound his fingers through his hair and pushed him towards his neck.

He smelled it before he saw him. The stench raped his nostrils. The kid's ripe scent evaporated, replaced with the trace of a witch. Olivier looked around. His fangs were so close to their mark, but a witch studied him, and that thought drenched his libido with ice water.

Against a wall near the exit, Olivier spied him. Dark-haired, slight build, young, early twenties. Power swirled around him as if he stood in moonlight. He held a glass of something in his hand, a neat shot. He met Olivier's eyes without fear. The look verged on boredom.

*A witch with a superiority complex. How rare.*

Olivier straightened, the blood in front of him forgotten. The kid tried to relight his interest, but he was nothing, a shadow in a room without light. He was aware of the other men around him, how they watched him, waiting for his attention to return. But he ignored them too as he stalked through the crowd to his new quarry.

The witch didn't attempt to flee. He sipped from his glass and waited. As he lifted the drink to his lips, Olivier caught sight of the tattoo on his left forearm: *aut inveniam viam aut faciam.*

*I'll either find a way or make one.*

Olivier stopped a foot away. Now he was this close, the air was thick with the smell of rotten oranges. He sniffed in contempt.

"Hello, witch."

"Good evening, vampire," the boy replied, his voice level.

"What's your name?"

"Oberon."

Olivier laughed. "King of the Fairies. I might have known. Did you enjoy the show?"

"Immensely. I came to watch you. And your brother."

"I love being watched." Olivier took a step closer. The air crackled around them. "Especially as I bite into the flesh of young things such as yourself."

"I could see that." Oberon remained still though the disturbance of the air as he readied his power was enough to tell Olivier he had the young witch worried.

He took the glass out of Oberon's hand and drained the last of the alcohol. Whiskey. Straight. He put it down on the high table next to them.

"Do you like watching?"

There was no space between them now as he pressed himself against Oberon.

"Did you get off on seeing me about to pierce that kid's skin and lap at his blood?"

He traced a finger up the witch's arm, parted his legs with his knee, and ground against him, using the wall as an accomplice.

"Did you wish it was you?" His lips descended to the witch's neck. The witch bared his throat and inhaled sharply.

Olivier's fangs were ready. The impulse to taste blood gripped his guts and squeezed, threatening to overwhelm his control. He knew he couldn't be gentle, couldn't hide this. The electricity in the air made his teeth buzz. He would feed and it would be messy. The sharp points slowly pressed against the witch's skin. Oberon was his.

The witch's hand touched his chest, and fire burned through his body. Olivier flung his head back; his teeth denied their rightful home. He cried to the dark roof, but music cloaked him. The pain raked up and down his spine like a tiger with steel claws, along his arms and legs, coursed through his veins, shattering any attempt at resistance. White heat consumed his mind.

He collapsed to his knees, eyes wide and unblinking. The witch's hand remained on his bare chest. He looked at it, no tell-tale flames, no blue light, just a plain, human hand —that burned like a brand. He forced his head to look up at this child who had him on his knees and starred into weariness matched with a pitying, sad smile.

People looked at them, but no one stopped to help. Olivier and Oberon were in a world of their own. The pain burned on, but he fought to keep from hunching over. Too many times Aurelia had bested him. This witch would not do the same.

Oberon leaned down and stared into his eyes.

"I know about you, Olivier. I know what you're like." Oberon removed his hand and the pain lessened. Slowly. "Watch yourself while you're here, because I will happily bring you to heel."

The witch turned, descended the stairs and exited the club. A moment later, Thierry's cold hand touched his shoulder.

"What the fuck was that? Was that Aurelia? I thought I was being burned alive. I nearly ripped a guy's head off."

Olivier stared after the witch. Thierry's bleating was as nothing to him. The embers of the pain sparked his own angry fire. He snarled like a slavering dog fighting to be let off its leash.

"Come on." Olivier grabbed Thierry's hand and pursued the witch.

Oberon—*that fuck*—was no doubt laughing at him but

wouldn't be for much longer. The witch was going to die, slowly and in immense agony.

They burst out into the piss-and-vomit laden air. Overtones of that stench of magic were the only sign the witch had been there. Olivier looked left, right. Oberon was hurrying down the road. Olivier growled and pulled Thierry behind him.

With two of them, and the resilience the anger gave him, the witch would be in pieces before the night was out. Though it hadn't been easy, he'd killed enough of them to know they bled like everybody else.

And they could scream, too.

## 11

ONE MOMENT OLIVIER WAS IN FRONT OF HIM AND gaining on the witch, the next he was pulled into the darkness beside the footpath. Thierry made a sharp right and came upon Olivier wrestling with someone with a death wish. He kept his distance. Olivier was unlikely to require his help. But when they broke apart, he saw his brother's opponent in the weak light.

The Duke had returned.

Thierry charged him, knocking him off his feet and sending them farther down the dark passageway towards a parking lot. The Duke landed on his back but kicked Thierry off him with strength not usual for a man of two hundred years. Thierry sailed past the blur of his brother as he raced to meet the Duke.

A car broke his flight. The sides of it crumpled beneath the impact. The Duke had gained even more strength, or so it seemed, from the last time they'd met, some hundred years ago. He'd been strong then. Perhaps his frustration at failing had given him something extra.

Olivier and the Duke rolled, trapped in each other's

steel hold. The Duke head-butted his brother, Olivier tried to tear at him with his fangs. The Duke always had a grim look, but now his face seemed forged from granite, determination sharpening his features. And that determination was focused solely on Olivier, the only one he ever really wanted.

Even when the Duke had come after Thierry.

The Duke released one of Olivier's arms, quick enough to pull a blade from behind his back and shove it into Olivier's descending forearm. Olivier and Thierry howled in unison as the pain seared through flesh and sinew. Panic cauterized the wound. This was something new.

Gasping, Olivier looked at the weapon. "New toys, Duke? You must be desperate. Immortality not enough? The witches had to give you the tools to finish the job? That must really crush your balls."

The Duke withdrew the blade and spun it around in his hand as he raised his arm, ready to bring it down into Olivier's chest. Though it burned, Thierry cast aside the mirrored pain in his arm to assist his brother. Olivier blocked the blade as it came down, pulled his other arm free from the Duke's grip and punched him in the guts. Thierry launched at the Duke, and they tumbled together.

*Watch the blade.*

They skidded against another car and shook free from the collision. Thierry flipped backwards and landed on his feet.

The Duke was quick, and his knife pierced Thierry's stomach.

He fell to his knees, the hilt, still held, sticking out. The Duke twisted it, and it became a hot screw churning through his insides, scalding his intestines, muscle and innards with its poisonous touch. He looked up at the

Duke's face, a sneer across his lips, cold eyes bearing down on him. With his free hand, the Duke pulled another blade from a hidden holster and readied for the next blow.

Olivier flew at the Duke and toppled him. The blade slid from Thierry's stomach, leaving a trail of sulfur in its wake. They tumbled and turned, the blades flashing but never finding their mark. Olivier ducked, punched, and kicked at the Duke just as he sought to fell his foe. They chased each other around and over cars, but now their blows met less often. Soon, the Duke broke from the fight and sped away. Olivier pursued.

Thierry lay on the loose gravel, one hand covering the gradually healing wound. The other he brought to his mouth to lick his own blood from his fingers. After the incident in the club and the fight with the Duke, his reserves of strength ran low. He'd need to feed soon to drown the pain. It hummed through his body, a stinging tickle that raced beneath his skin. He had to go back to feeling nothing.

He supposed he had something to thank the Duke for. Giving them a warning. And now he'd done it once, he wouldn't be able to surprise them so easily again. Would they have to leave? Weariness swamped him.

*No. Olivier would stay and fight.*

He probably shouldn't have run off alone, but the Duke wouldn't allow Olivier to catch him now, not tonight, not until he was ready. Even then, Thierry wondered if he should be at Olivier's side.

Though Thierry had met the Duke a few times since the castle, the last time was the most telling of the Duke's plans. All he sought was Olivier and when he'd found Thierry it was as a last resort. His brother had disappeared, and the Duke thought Thierry might know where he was. He never knew how the Duke had found him, but when he'd told Aurelia she insisted he relocate and forced him to feed farther afield to throw whoever might be watching off his trail. The Duke didn't appear again.

Until now.

The last time they'd met, Thierry had fought the Duke well enough. He had never been much of a fighter, and the Duke's prowess put him to shame. But a few well-placed blows and he rendered the Duke helpless. Thierry had carried him away, left him somewhere to be found and tended to. Why hadn't he killed him?

Because he had a small hope that he would find Olivier and kill him.

But knowing now the weapons the Duke possessed, could he withstand the pain?

He cursed as he sat up, out of tiredness more than any aches that troubled him. The wound had healed, the sting now washed away. And he sat alone.

And hungry.

Crumpled shells of cars with broken windows surrounded him. The fight had lasted seconds but the damage had been great. A crowd was gathering, and he'd be better far away.

He stood and took a step in Olivier's direction when he saw a head disappear behind one of the cars. Of course, they hadn't been alone. How much had this person seen? How much would they reveal? His veins constricted and pulled at him, eager to have fresh blood.

*Two birds, one stone.*

He crouched low and raced around the cars, a shadow amidst the hulking masses, his feet barely touching the gravel. A young man lay on the ground, peering for feet coming to get him. His breathing was loud and rapid, and his head jerked from side to side trying to make out any movement. Thierry appeared next to him. He stopped searching and stared at Thierry's boots. His fingers scrabbling through the gravel, shaking, searching for something with which to defend himself. He looked up as Thierry descended. He spun him around, sank to the ground and cradled him in his lap. He plunged his fangs into his neck.

The young man struggled. He was strong. He beat at Thierry, thick fists striking Thierry's chest, trying to break free, but that only made Thierry's teeth tear. The blood tasted of fresh, sweet peaches and quenched his deep thirst. It pulsed through him, filling his old organs with electricity. His prey stopped struggling, though he lived still, and Thierry removed his fangs to savor the honey on his tongue.

A crowbar smashed him in the center of his face. It didn't hurt but it startled him. He tried to open his eyes to see his attacker, but the crowbar beat him again. And again. He caught it as it swung and wrenched it from the wielder. Thierry flung the almost-corpse off his lap and rose.

He faced his attacker, a middle-aged man, slight belly but broad shoulders and thick arms. Fading tattoos wound their way around his neck. He was bald, missing a tooth. He drew a knife, and it seemed to rekindle some courage in his eyes. Though Thierry's lack of injuries or pain had unsettled him plenty.

"Wh...what were you doing to him? Anyone hurts him, they answer to me."

"He's yours?" Thierry advanced on this piece of filth. He'd seen the type before. Criminal. Thinking Thierry was someone who would just lie down and take whatever abuse he had to give. The body behind him was necessary; the one in front of him would be fun.

"I paid for him." He leaned forward and spat the words.

Thierry understood. The john looked prepared to stand his ground.

"I've already had him. Looks like you're due a refund."

"I'll take it from you. In blood."

"Blood? Now you're talking a language I understand." Thierry's voice was like a hiss that cut the guy. He backed into a car and lowered into a fighter's stance with the knife held in front of him.

"I'm going to gut you."

"We'll see about that."

Thierry moved fast, sweeping the crowbar across the john's legs and shattering his shin bones. The man screamed and fell to the ground. He dropped as he reached for his legs. Thierry swung again, battering his left arm, rendering it useless, and the man bellowed, eyes widening at the pain that he couldn't escape. Thierry swung again, and it tore his skull apart, blood and bone and brain splattering across the cars. The screaming stopped. Thierry dropped the crowbar next to the headless corpse and turned back to his earlier meal.

He had to leave quickly. Those screams would bring people running no matter what, even just to see someone die. But he'd been denied his full hunger and wanted those last few drops, especially from one so delicious.

When he crouched down beside the unconscious figure, he saw he'd chosen well. The young man had short blond hair and an open face, soft without being fat, smooth without seeming fake. Thierry caressed his cheek, trailing his hand down to his neck to finger the puncture marks.

But they were gone.

*Healed?*

He turned his victim's head to look on the other side of the neck, in case he'd been mistaken, but there was nothing there either. He was whole. Thierry listened to his breathing, a little shallow but not struggling. He put his hand over his heart and felt a heart beating as strong as any other, blood pumping normally, blood that had been replenished.

The young man's open eyes caught his attention. He stayed still, not moving, not trying to get up or away. He stared at Thierry with fearful eyes.

Sounds of people running, sirens getting nearer. He tried to block them out to listen to the body in front of him, desperate to feel the shimmering power he suspected coursed through this body. He longed for it, but he was also afraid, frightened he'd done everlasting damage, frightened he'd wasted his chance.

Then he felt it.

The spark.

He looked into the man's eyes and saw what he'd been searching for.

"I've found you." He whispered it like a devotion, a prayer of salvation to the Almighty.

The man's brow creased, but he didn't speak. Maybe he was still shaken from his attack. Why should he know who Thierry was? And now what had he done? He'd nearly killed the one person he never wanted to hurt.

The sirens were outside the parking lot now. Many feet crunched the gravel. Torchlight shot through car windows, hunting for the source or cause of the screams. They were getting closer to the dead body.

Thierry swore under his breath. "I'll come back for you."

The man's eyes widened.

"I won't hurt you again. I promise."

Thierry scurried into the darkness, avoiding policemen and onlookers, and ran in the direction Olivier had gone.

His brother waited for him on the other side of the street. He leaned against the link fence, his lips pursed in an appreciative smile, an eyebrow raised. "Impressive." His hand waved over the collection of police and the chaos Thierry had caused. "What did you do?"

"Getting rid of witnesses." Brushing aside his brother's amusement, he took him by the hand and pulled him away.

# III

THE BROTHERS SPENT THE MORNING INSIDE, SLEEPING like the dead they were. They stayed in a recently unoccupied house set back from the street and surrounded by high walls and thick gardens. No alarms, no dogs, no people. With the curtains drawn and the TV volume low, there was no reason to expect anyone was home.

Thierry rose before Olivier, woken by an itching anxiety that wouldn't shift. Without disturbing his sleeping brother, he left and returned to where he'd last seen Etienne.

The city looked different in the light of day. It was a Sunday, with people walking as if the sun forced them to take it easy. The energy of the night before had been swept away with the coming of dawn like litter caught beneath a street sweeper, the fights replaced with pleasant chat, short skirts with summer dresses. Thierry wore jeans and a white T-shirt. Sunglasses covered his bright eyes. People noticed him and looked back as he passed. They didn't know what he was, just admired. Slowly, he faded from view and walked unseen.

When he reached the parking lot, people gathered on the path to gawk over the police tape and ogle the officers searching for clues to the violence. The parking lot remained as Thierry had left it the night before. He spied the crumpled car Etienne had cowered behind.

*God, he'd bitten him.*

But he'd healed; the marks had faded as if they never were. Then he'd looked at him with those memorable eyes. The joy at finding him again and the panic of Olivier being so close had withered with the hours. Now he was left with an ache in the pit of his stomach because this time he had been the one to draw Etienne's blood.

*It tasted so good.*

He snarled at the voice inside his head. He'd never taste Etienne's blood again. But how would he know? Sure, he knew who Etienne was now—after such a long wait—but what about the future? He would have to stop killing.

He laughed without mirth. He may as well ask the same of Olivier, for all the good it would do him. Death found them these days. They barely had to try.

This search for Etienne had already proved disastrous. Without knowing, he'd nearly killed the one person he needed above all others. And that was because he'd become embroiled in Olivier's spat with the Duke.

Wherever Etienne was—and he prayed to whatever god listened that he was safe—he was better off without Thierry in his life. He slumped against the fence. That thought had always been more than he could stand. But it was right. He knew it the first time Etienne had died.

Turning his attention back to the police, he wished he knew what had happened to Etienne. It would be easier to say goodbye if he knew he was all right. Had he stayed for the police to take him? Did they think he was the one who'd killed that lump of flesh? Would he talk about Thierry? If only...

But there he was.

Thierry picked him out of the crowd. A hood covered most of his face but as he tried to push out of the crowd and away Thierry spotted him.

*So he had made it out safely.*

But not unscathed. His eyes were deeply shadowed, his mouth downturned. He hunched himself under his jacket, melting into the hood's shade. Thierry had done that. Now he was going, and Thierry doubted he'd get another chance to find him again. He had to talk to him. Just to make sure he was okay.

Before he could reason himself out of following, he'd crossed the street. He threw off the invisibility as soon as he hit the pavement and matched Etienne's stride, keeping at a safe distance until they were out of sight of the police. Etienne turned a corner. Thierry followed and was brought up short as a knife flashed at his throat.

"Stop following me." Even with Etienne's face screwed up with anger, Thierry's body vibrated.

*So close to him again.*

Thierry raised his arms, palms open, and smiled.

Etienne gasped.

"You're the guy from yesterday. You..." His hand tightened on the knife, his mouth moved, trying to form the words that wouldn't come. His eyes shifted around, behind Thierry, searching for signs of anyone to help.

"Please, I don't—" Thierry began, but Etienne stabbed the knife at him.

"Don't talk. I'm going to walk away from here, and you're going to stay where you are and never come near me again. If you do, I'll bury this in your throat."

He had eyes of steel, hardness fighting with the panic that threatened to swamp them. If only he could calm him, then he could apologize. Again.

"I'm not going to hurt you."

"I said, don't talk." He jabbed the knife at him.

Thierry deflected it easily, grasped the weapon and wrenched it from Etienne's hand. He pulled Etienne against his body. He sensed the buzz of the healer through his clothes, sparking against his skin. He closed his eyes and breathed it in.

"I promise I'm not going to hurt you," he whispered in as soothing a tone as he could manage. "Last night was a mistake. If I'd known..." He couldn't finish what he'd wanted to say.

"Let me go or I'll call for help."

He sighed. "I'm going to let you go, but not because I think you'll bring the police running. You wouldn't want them around you anyway. Too many questions, right?"

His head rang with accusations. *Manipulator. Liar. Tainted.* He was sounding like Olivier, trying to swing all this to his favor when it had faltered from the start. Reiner had been so willing, so ready for him. Etienne had protected him. This incarnation stared at him with daggers.

He released Etienne and stepped back. "I'm sorry." He bowed his head as if he were a supplicant to a lord. He slipped the knife into his back pocket. "I didn't mean to hurt you last night, but you seem to be all right."

"What are you?" Etienne inched back.

"I think you know. And I know what you are as well. You're a healer."

"I don't know what you're talking about."

"Yes, you do. And I want to know you. Better."

Etienne's eyes widened at that. "I said I wouldn't hurt you. Can we go somewhere to talk?"

"Leave. Me. Alone." Etienne walked backwards, bigger steps now, then turned and jogged away.

Thierry let him go. He pulled out the wallet he'd swiped from Etienne's pocket when they'd been entangled. He flicked through to his license.

Alex Roche. Twenty-three-years-old. He memorized the address and slipped the wallet into his pocket. He'd return it later.

IV

Olivier visited the museum then the art gallery. He didn't much care for what he looked at. He had seen plenty of art over the years and seen relics when they were first made. As with other cities, there wasn't much for him to do except hunt, terrorize, and fuck.

Luckily, that was all he'd ever wanted. Without Thierry around—where he'd gone, he didn't know—he had to make his own fun. Today, he'd decided to hunt.

While looking at a painting by McCubbin, he noticed a tall, Scandinavian male: short blond hair, impressive muscles. He wore sandals, shorts and a tight blue T-shirt. Olivier followed him as he took photos of Aboriginal dot paintings, of sculptures and their placards. He savored the slow journey through the galleries, up and down stairs, keeping far enough behind, not looking over too often. Twice, Olivier deliberately caught his smile. Once, he waved. He got a positive response in return, but the tourist probably thought Olivier was just being friendly. There was no come-hither look, only innocence.

Olivier licked his lips.

With the artwork experienced, the Nordic Wonder left the art gallery and headed away from the cultural center to walk down soulless city streets populated with lunch bars and offices, a metropolitan church, places surrounded by concrete and brick, uneven, mismatched, unattractive. Olivier kept out of sight and let him gain some lead before he raced across the tops of buildings to get ahead of him and wait.

Before the Nordic Wonder reached a busy intersection and the openness of the park at the end of the street, Olivier dropped behind him without a sound. He shadowed him, falling in with his stride, his left foot landing at the same time as the Scandinavian's, his right with the Scandinavian's right. Ahead, Olivier saw an opening between two buildings, a driveway to an out-of-the-way parking lot. Olivier coughed and tapped the man's shoulder.

The Scandinavian jumped and turned. Olivier smiled, but then his welcoming grin opened to reveal protruding fangs. His prey's eyes widened, and he turned to run, but Olivier grabbed his thick neck and hauled him into the driveway. He struggled and beat at Olivier, but Olivier withstood it all, waited for the man to tire, to realize it was futile. The Scandinavian shouted out. Someone might come, but they usually didn't. He threw the man to the ground. He landed on his camera, smashing it under his weight. He scrambled in the gravel, tried to get up, holding one arm in front of him while shooting glances around in the vain hope someone would help.

"My God, you're beautiful." Olivier pounced and sank his teeth into the Scandinavian's strong, sweaty neck. His lips formed a seal over the holes, and he caught the blood in his eager mouth. The blood was a cool drink under a scorching sun, and he sucked harder.

The Nordic Wonder fought less as the seconds passed and his body emptied. Olivier hugged him close, wanting to feel a human form against his ancient body, feel muscles tense and relax. A moment before the Scandinavian died, Olivier withdrew his teeth and kissed his lips. They were already going cold.

He closed his eyes to the bright day and hummed as life flowed through him. He floated.

A blaze tore through his gut and forced a roar from his throat as a blade protruded from his stomach. He flung the corpse away. The metal burned his skin, muscles and organs. He'd been spit like a pig on a feast day. He scrambled away and the blade slipped out. He grunted as it withdrew. Though it was now free, the metal's fire still travelled throughout his body, singeing his nerves. With a quick turn of his head, he saw the Duke standing there.

He spun his body around, fighting against the agony that threatened to cripple him. Olivier sneered at the Duke's lack of a smile. No triumph at the surprise point he'd won against his foe. Before the Duke died, Olivier would carve a grin onto that stony mask.

The wound healed, but not as quickly as it should have. The skin bubbled around the edges as it reformed.

The gravel crunched under the Duke's booted footfalls as he came at Olivier. He swung the sword, readying it to find its home in Olivier's chest. It came down. He rolled out of its way, and the blade hit the road with a sharp twang. The Duke readied for another strike. Olivier rose, gaining a little space to give him some distance to defend, moving left then right, trying to force the Duke into a sloppy attack. There wasn't much hope of that. The Duke watched him with the precision eye of a well-trained hunter. He kicked the dead body out of his way and sent it skidding across the concrete with no more effort than a child kicking a teddy bear.

"You should show some respect for the dead, Duke." Olivier laughed in between his gasps, and the corner of the Duke's mouth twitched. They weren't laughing at the same joke.

The Duke swung his sword, close enough to force Olivier back further, and the blade sang as it cut through the air. He made another pass and clipped Olivier on the shoulder. He swore and clutched at his arm. Another swipe cut his leg, and an unholy shriek fled his mouth. He buckled and fell to the ground.

"Aren't you worried about witnesses? I can hear them coming now." Olivier ground his teeth through the pain. He was healing, but the magic of the sword made the sting linger.

"I wish the whole world could see you die." The Duke raised the sword above his head for another thrust.

Slime oozed along Olivier's bones and infused his muscles. He would not die like this. Not after all this time. He braced himself for the attack, readying his body to defend until the end. Even if he did die, he was going to take the Duke with him. The sword came down, and his fist came up to meet it.

Barely a whisker before impact, Thierry scudded into the Duke with a thud. They rolled and wrestled each other like two mountain lions, and the sword flew from the Duke's hand and skittered across the gravel. Thierry smashed the Duke's head into the ground. Nimbly, he jumped off him and grabbed Olivier.

"Come on." Thierry dragged him away a moment before two police cars arrived at the driveway.

From the top of a nearby building he felt safe enough to

look back, but the Duke was gone. Only the Scandinavian's body remained.

Thierry tugged his arm. Olivier spun around and snarled like a Dobermann. Thierry's eyes narrowed to slits and he shoved him hard. "You want to get skewered again? Be my guest, you fucking lunatic."

Thierry sprinted away. Within a few steps, he'd vanished, and Olivier looked at empty air. He hoped Thierry was still there, just invisible, but he felt no other presence except a hot wind. He cursed the nothingness and, with a final look at the police swarming through the parking lot, ran in Thierry's direction.

V

THIERRY REFUSED TO TALK TO OLIVIER WHEN HE returned home, but he couldn't hold back his rage for long. It wasn't Olivier's stupidity or the fact he'd been caught, it was the pain Thierry had felt, so many miles from where his brother and the Duke fought. Coming out of nowhere, it nearly rendered him unconscious. He had stuffed his fist into his mouth after the first cry broke free, then wrestled with the agony to find a moment of stillness where he could feel for Olivier.

He'd gone to his aid without a second thought. It wasn't until later he admitted it was simple self-preservation. God, he was becoming more like Olivier with every passing day. He couldn't be sure killing Olivier with the Duke's new weaponry wouldn't also annihilate him. He didn't want to take that risk. Not after finding Etienne—Alex.

Eventually he calmed down, and Olivier looked contrite enough to make a kitten look guilty. All part of the show. Thierry had long since given up his need to find anything sincere about his brother. In a moment of truce, they decided the Duke must die. Obvious, really, but Thierry had been the one to say it. Olivier flinched. Perhaps he thought it meant solidarity.

Whatever. Thierry knew his course of action.

Eradicate the Duke.

Neutralize Olivier.

Regain Etienne.

Olivier voiced some worry over who might be behind the Duke's crusade, his immortality and weapons, but that was a problem for when maggots infested the Duke's corpse.

And so Monday brought with it purpose, and they fanned out through the city. Thierry suggested they separate, saying they would do better searching alone for the Duke, rather than waiting for him to come to them. If they could find where the Duke was camped, then they might have a better chance of killing him quickly.

Once Olivier was out of sight, Thierry changed course. He had faith Olivier would find the Duke first, and right now he had someone else he wanted to see.

He made a quick detour through some of the suburbs to the east of where they stayed. It didn't take long to form a picture in his mind and recall the names of streets, or the locations of parks and houses. The mental map finished, he headed to Alex's apartment.

Thierry stopped in front of an ugly, three-story building made of white-painted bricks with steel railings around the balconies. They were small apartments, one-bedroom places from the look of the outside. Aluminum foil covered many of the windows. Bore-water had stained the walls. A baby cried in an apartment on the upper floor, a television blared in another, shouting came from the first floor. All doors were shut tight. The stench of rotten food and unwashed bodies laced the air, but it was petunias compared to what Carcassonne had smelled like. He wrinkled his nose from the memory of his first whiff of that putrid city after being made vampire.

He climbed the steps to the second floor and rapped on the door of number twenty-four. Feet scuffed across the apartment floor. The door moved as hands pressed on the timber either side of the peephole. Rapid, shallow breathing followed. Rattled cutlery chimed through the flimsy wood.

"Alex, please open up."

All motion and sound stopped.

"I promise I'm not here to hurt you. I know it's difficult for you to trust me after what happened, but I'm telling the truth." He felt a fool for speaking such lies. He'd never deliberately tried to make Etienne suffer, but it had happened anyway, like a plague didn't intend to decimate populations.

The door remained barred. It was such a frail thing, easy enough to splinter. Three breaths and it would fall down.

"What do I have to do to convince you?" Would all this noise on the landing raise anyone's suspicions? He couldn't imagine someone poking their heads out of the safety of their private caves. Maybe if they heard gunshots. Nothing else.

"I've got your wallet. If you want it back, you'll have to open the door."

He waited.

Nothing.

"Would it help if I told you my name?"

Silence.

"I'll tell you anyway." He leaned against the frame, half-turned so he could talk to the door. Loud enough to be heard on the other side, soft enough to make it intimate. "My name is Thierry d'Arjou. I was born in Carcassonne. You might have guessed I have a brother. He was there that night we...met."

"You're a killer," Alex whispered. He said it with resignation as if he talked about the rain or a dog with black fur.

Thierry couldn't lie anymore. Not that he wanted to. Lies had chained him when Reiner lived and left him with the taste of rancid blood. "I am. It's who I've become. I could tell you a whole lot of shit about not meaning to hurt you or that guy, but the truth is, it was instinct. If I'd known it was you, I never would have..."

Speaking with Etienne had always been so easy, and now he couldn't keep the words from falling out of his mouth. His bones squeezed with the need to tell him everything, but at the same time "everything" would be too much.

"I would rather kill myself than hurt you." The pause had only been short. Perhaps Alex hadn't noticed it. "And if that man meant something to you, I am truly sorry, from the depths of my being, for causing you more pain. I just needed to know that you're okay. You healed. I saw it. And I almost cried that you could get rid of those scars, that your blood was replenished so fast."

Desperation made him speak so freely. Olivier would have laughed at his clumsiness. He'd seen men in bars trying too hard to get the girl or the guy and watched as they were laughed at. There was no need for pick-up lines when you were a vampire; a weighted look, a caress was enough to bring anyone under your thrall. He could have tried it here, but that only meant more falsities. What he was doing might not work, but at least it was honest.

Alex didn't seem impressed.

Thierry sighed. He'd ruined his chance yet again. Perhaps if Olivier didn't exist. Perhaps if he stopped feeding on humans. Fancies and improbabilities all. The only thing he knew now, while he stood, pleading for another chance, was that if he didn't leave Alex behind, the whole dreadful cycle would happen again. He screwed his eyes shut against the sting of tears and bit his lip until he drew blood.

"I'll go now." *Oh God, please, there must be another way.* "You won't see me again." He didn't want to speak those words. They dug deep furrows in his throat as he forced them out.

He placed the wallet on the welcome mat. With a final touch of the door as if it were Alex's face, he walked away. His feet dragged like a tired horse pulling a funeral coach. He wiped his eyes, and his hand came away stained red.

The door opened, but he didn't look around. He couldn't bear to see, even through rose-colored vision, the hint of a spark of hope on Alex's face. It would only sputter and die.

"What did you mean when you said if you'd known it was me?" Alex asked with the wary curiosity of a mouse sniffing around a trap.

He had to stay firm. He'd made his decision. It was for Alex's own good. The less he knew about their shared past the better. "It's best you don't know."

"If you want me to trust you, you'll tell me." There was a touch of hardness in his voice. That he came outside was a sign he was made of strong stuff, but even that wouldn't be enough to withstand what Thierry brought in his wake.

The path was set. It was time to go and forget this life. "We've met before. Though you won't remember it."

"When?"

Thierry let out a long breath. His mind raised long cherished memories of Reiner and when they lay in each other's arms. A sharp ache drilled through his body. "A long time ago."

*Best to leave now, while I still can.*

He fled down the stairs, pledging never to return.

# VI

"ANY LUCK?" OLIVIER LOUNGED ON THE COUCH, channel surfing, staring at the fast-changing images on the screen.

"What do you think?" Thierry snapped. "Why aren't you out there looking for him? If he's going to appear, it'll be to gut you. Not me."

Olivier turned his attention from the television to his brother. He raised an eyebrow.

"Fuck off," Thierry fired.

After leaving Alex, he'd spent hours sifting through the city for signs of the Duke, but that had brought nothing but frustration. He'd fed off a woman in the hope that might draw him out but to no avail. And the blood had done little to drown his pain. He'd made the right choice with Alex, but that didn't mean he had to like it. And to come back to find Olivier here, wasting time while the Duke plotted? The sooner the Duke died, the sooner they could leave this town, and he could avoid the temptation of going back to Alex.

Olivier slid off the couch and over to him. Thierry

looked away, not wanting to give his brother any more attention than he deserved. He was sulking, and he knew it.

Olivier tried to catch his eye. "Want to have some fun?"

"Killing the Duke would be fun. But what are we
doing? Sitting here, waiting to be attacked, *watching
television.*"

"His time will come. We'll find him." Olivier rubbed
Thierry's arm in what was meant to be a soothing way. His
touch felt like sandpaper.

"It can't come soon enough."

"Let's go out again. We'll find some guys and fuck 'em."
Olivier's greedy smile told him his brother's mind was
already made up. If blood hadn't made a difference, he
doubted sex would be the salve he needed. In fact, the
thought of being with anyone other than Alex made him
cringe. But Olivier had an insistent look in his eye, and to
say no might rouse his suspicions.

And so, nights and days passed. They searched
without reward, and they fucked and drained when they
could, hoping it might stir the Duke from his nest. No
matter how much time passed, Thierry couldn't forget
Alex. The longer he stayed, the greater his need to see
him. He did his best to avoid any places he might go,
especially that parking lot, and for the most part it
worked.

The end of the week rolled around, and the town
ripened again. Late on Friday they descended on a night-
club and mixed with a crowd winding down from their
week of work. The crowd craved some debauchery.

Olivier led them through the throng, looking up and
down the boys and men who parted before him. They
regarded him back, an appreciative smile on their glossed
lips. His upright posture, his fine build, chin slightly up in

the air, his superior smirk and the expensive clothes they'd bought with stolen cash all contributed to his desirability.

Thierry, trailing behind, was almost invisible. Just how he liked it. While not totally see-through, he'd allowed his ability take over and faded into the background, no need to hold a smile he didn't mean. It allowed him to cast his attention further afield and see what was really going on.

A fight between two girls, a young guy crying on a couch in the semi-darkness, three mates throwing back pills —and Alex on the arm of an older man. He paused, taking in the scene and making sure he'd seen it right. The man must have been in his fifties, well dressed, and not unattractive with his grey styled hair and perfect-fit shirt. Money, power. Alex laughed at something he said, touched his leg. The man's arm was around Alex's waist. He sat with his knee pressed into Alex's groin. A low growl rumbled in Thierry's throat as he continued behind Olivier. There was a moment when he thought Alex looked right at him, but his face didn't change.

Olivier's head turned back a little, a question in his eye. Thierry sneered at him, and Olivier looked away. Stupid. How could he be so stupid? They were stuck here until the place closed, or Olivier selected someone to take home. How could he ensure he avoided Alex, but also Alex avoided him, particularly when there were two of him around? He could have spent the whole night in the shadows, but Olivier shone. Alex wouldn't be able to resist. No one could resist.

Three areas made up the club: a main bar, a dance floor and a beer garden. They swam through the dance floor, around flexing and contorting bodies writhing to the latest hits spun by the DJ. Olivier's busy hands touched one man then another, slid up and around torsos and asses.

Thierry waited for him to finish and move into the open air.

More people filled the outside, glasses in one hand, many with cigarettes in the other. Music blared, and voices raised to match. A few of the guys they had screwed before were in attendance. Thierry saw their hungry eyes as Olivier talked to some of them and met their friends. He did his best to join the conversation, but it was easier to stand back and let Olivier do it all. He had better things to worry about.

What if Alex came outside? What if he saw Olivier and went up to him? What if he spoke to him thinking he was Thierry? What if he warned security, or called the police, or made a scene? The memory of Reiner's death replayed in his mind, and he knew Olivier wouldn't care about witnesses. Alex wouldn't get out of here alive.

He couldn't win. He'd tried to do the right thing by staying away, but this town was too small for the three of them.

Someone bumped into him, and he snarled without thinking. Olivier glared at him without missing a beat in the conservation. That reproachful look was enough to make him want to beat Olivier as near to death as he could.

Olivier wound his arms around two men, both wearing tight shirts and jeans. Their hair was arranged in small mohawks. Their muscles were large. With a few encouraging words whispered in their ears, Olivier led them to the raised dance floor and pulled them up to join him. Olivier hadn't fucked either of them before; they were as-yet-unconquered territory. He left previous conquests holding their half-finished glasses and casting lascivious looks. Thierry rolled his eyes and moved away.

His brother danced while this small part of the world

watched. His two admirers, neither of whom could keep a beat, molded themselves to his body and became his props. Other dancers stopped and stared, their body temperature rising at the display. This was nothing, though. Olivier held a lot back. He was building up their tolerance to his exhibitionism so eventually everyone would be as free as he was. He'd done it before.

Thierry was one of the few people not affected. It was just another of Olivier's games, and he'd grown weary of it long ago. The crowd swelled until it became harder to move and any space was filled and pulsed with sexual energy. Faces buried in necks. Bodies clung to one another in the storm. The couple beside him ground their pelvises together. When one of their hands gripped his shirt and sought to touch his skin, he knew he had to get out. He pushed through the crowd, shoving aside those who refused to move. He was in full color now. He climbed the steps to head back inside, and when he looked up, he was face-to-face with Alex.

Alex didn't notice him because the spectacle of Olivier filled his focus. There was no longing, admiration, or desire in his expression, just shock and horror. He barely moved.

If Olivier looked over and saw him talking to someone, he'd be suspicious. Thierry never spoke to anyone. Thierry took hold of Alex's wrist, and the invisibility flowed down his arm and cloaked Alex. A heavy-set bloke rushing from inside to outside bumped into them without a backward glance. The illusion would hold while he touched Alex.

But that would prove difficult.

Alex blinked out of his daze, his eyes twitching from Olivier to him. Though the invisibility stopped others from seeing them, they could see each other clearly.

Alex tried wrenching his arm free. Thierry attempted to calm him but didn't release his hold. He couldn't.

"Alex, it's me, Thierry. That's my brother, Olivier."

Alex tensed. "Let me go." His voice was low but hard.

"Listen to me. You have to leave." Alex had to get out soon. However slim, the chance of Olivier meeting him was too great. Thierry had promised to stay away to keep Alex safe, and that meant Olivier could never know he existed. Alex struggled like an eel caught on a hook; difficult to control, all too easily able to slip away.

"So you can slaughter everyone?"

Thierry flinched as if he'd been struck. "No. No, because if you don't go, you might die." He hadn't really expected Alex to care what happened to other people. Altruism was not a trait Thierry had seen a lot of through the centuries. It was even rarer in this time.

"I can't leave." He continued to wrestle with Thierry's iron grip. "I'm working."

"So that's who the old man is." He even surprised himself with the barbed wire in his voice. Biting his tongue, he let his fangs descend a little and pierce the skin. Blood seeped out and equally soothed and incited him.

"I have to pay the bills somehow," Alex said. "And I've got a vacancy since you bludgeoned Paul to death."

"Am I meant to feel bad about killing him?" Thierry knew it wasn't the right thing to say, but truly, he would have torn this *Paul* apart over and over again if given the chance.

"I doubt you'd feel bad about killing anyone. Let. Go."

"No, you have to leave."

"And I said no."

Thierry ignored his protests and dragged him inside. He'd be happy with anywhere not in Olivier's sightline.

Then maybe he could properly explain. He took Alex to a dark part of the club and sat him on a couch. They were more or less alone except for a gaggle of drunk women out on a hen's night.

He still held Alex's arm. That in itself was enough to make him pause. His hand on naked skin, a strong pulse beating beneath the surface, and that electricity buzzing through the connection... It rang loud in the emptiness inside his undead heart, but it couldn't bring him back to life, no matter how powerful.

"Why do you want me to leave? Is it so you can get me alone and drain my blood?"

Thierry sighed. *Fool. As if a touch would be enough to break through Alex's barriers.* He suddenly felt all six hundred plus years pressing in on his bones. He didn't want to fight any more, but to give up meant abandoning Etienne again. And who knew if he'd get another chance? Like a pilgrim on a march across mountains, he set his mind to the track ahead.

"I've already told you I'd never do that to you again. It was a mistake."

"Too fucking right, it was. So why the need for me to go? I'm working. I can't just disappear."

"You're not safe here."

"Nowhere is safe with you two running free. Why should here be any different?"

"Because if my brother sees you, he'll kill you."

Alex's mouth opened, but no sound came out. He blinked a couple of times and tilted his head like he was unsure he'd heard correctly above the din.

"Why me?" Alex asked.

"Just trust me on this."

"Stop saying that!" He pumped his fists. "Just because

you say something doesn't mean I have to believe you. You've given me nothing to make me think you're speaking the truth, or why I should believe your words about protecting me."

He was right. Of course. Thierry brought nothing but more trouble. But whether Alex accepted it or not, Thierry had to do the right thing and get him out of there. "This isn't how it's supposed to be at all," he muttered under his breath.

Alex was expecting an answer. He wouldn't give up; he was too strong for that.

"If I tell you what's going on, you won't believe me."

"Try me." Alex did a good job of looking like someone holding the power, even with Thierry gripping his wrist. He sat rod straight and glared down on Thierry. It was only then he noticed his own shoulders had slumped.

*The weight of years...*

He rolled them back, adjusted his spine and lifted his head so he now looked directly into Alex's eyes. He allowed the glow to shine and injected glittering blue into his irises. Not to lull Alex—that was too close a coercion—just to impress on him the seriousness and the need for action.

Even if that need meant running away.

"You saw my brother out there with all those men and all that attention. He feeds off it as surely as he feeds off blood. But the one thing he craves more than anything is me."

Speaking it aloud brought the danger into sharp focus. Thierry had very rarely told anyone how Olivier hungered for him like an addict for his next fix. Now to hear it said raised the hairs on the back of his neck. Etienne and Reiner had suffered because of Olivier's obsession. Thierry had always tried to brush it off, but he should have put a stop to

it years ago. When they were still human. Another lot of
blame to heap at his own feet.

"If he sees me talking to you, if he sees I have *any*
interest in you, you're as good as dead."

"So why do I have to leave? Why don't you go?"

"I can't leave without raising his suspicions. And if you
stay, I can't guarantee he won't stumble across you."

"Your brother sounds delightful."

"Look, we don't have much time. He'll notice I've gone
soon, and you need to leave before then."

Thierry pulled him to his feet and made for the exit.
They passed Alex's trick at the bar; Alex waved but the
man looked right through him. "Why didn't..."

Thierry didn't stop, just tightened his grip on Alex's
wrist.

Once outside, Thierry released him, and the world
could see them once more. The bouncer flinched at their
sudden appearance. Thierry smiled at him sweetly; the
bouncer grimaced. With Thierry's hand resting in the small
of Alex's back, they walked down the street to the end of the
building, away from any possibility of seeing Alex's paying
customer or Olivier. Police cars and taxis crawled the street
and groups of shouting men and shrieking women staggered
around. Thierry stopped on the corner and lightly pushed
Alex away. His hand buzzed with the aftershock of Alex's
energy.

"Go straight home," he choked. This could be the last
time he'd see him. At least he'd live. "Don't stop. Please."

Alex rounded on him, his chest forward, his fists like
hammers. "I told you I'm not going."

Thierry bared his fangs. He hated doing it. But he was
desperate.

*Just go. Before it's too late.*

Alex's eyes widened, but he quickly recovered and fired back a metallic glare. He turned and marched away. He looked like a young lion that had tried to best an old bull elephant and failed, yet still managed to leave with some dignity, a swagger in his hips, his head held high. The kid was tough.

But Thierry still wanted to protect him. He should walk with him. To see him safely home. To stay with him and guard him.

At least Alex had spoken to him. True, the hard edge of mistrust never left his voice and he looked at him with little affection, but that might change, with time. He laughed. For all his immortality, he didn't have any time for this. The Duke skirted the edge of their world, threatening to overcome them. He meant to finish the job. There would be no respite for them until it was done.

Olivier pulled him like a vortex. Thierry started to turn back to the club, but a fast-moving shadow caught his attention.

A shadow making its way to Alex.

He forgot his brother and sprinted down the street. The Duke had a head start and was faster than Thierry expected. He roared as the Duke collided with Alex, punching him in the face and throwing him over his shoulder. Alex's head lolled. Thierry closed in on the Duke, his attention fixed on Alex's limp frame. Five yards separated them, then four, three, two...

The Duke halted and spun around, a knife in his hand headed straight for Thierry's chest. Almost too late, Thierry slid down, sailing underneath the blade that barely missed his head. His legs crashed into the Duke's and he fell. The blade struck the concrete with a spark.

Thierry slipped out from under him, hefted the still

unconscious Alex onto his shoulder and ran. A quick glance behind. The Duke followed. Thierry increased his speed even as Alex's weight bore down on him. He turned right down one street before going left down another. When he'd gained enough distance, he scaled walls and sprinted across rooftops, then dropped down an alley and let invisibility and shadows cover them. He didn't see the Duke again and, after a few minutes had passed, he felt safe enough to take Alex off his shoulder and sit him down. He propped against the wall. Alex woke. When he saw Thierry, his eyes opened wide and his mouth readied a scream.

Thierry muffled the sound with his hand and spoke as fast and as loud as he dared. "Stop screaming, or else he'll find you."

Realizing how that must sound, and what this all must look like—he doubted Alex had even seen the Duke—he cursed himself. He spoke even faster, trying to keep his voice to a whisper lest the Duke be lurking nearby.

"It's not Olivier. An enemy of ours attacked you. I fought him, but he chased us. I think I've lost him now, but you need to be very quiet in case he's still out there." His senses pulled taut, ready for any shift in the light, any quiver of sound to warn him to run. "I'm not here to hurt you. I'm going to remove my hand, but please, please don't scream. Both of our lives depend on it."

Hot air beat against his hand. Thierry removed his palm and peered up at the sky. Nothing yet. He scaled the wall like a gecko hunting mosquitoes. Poking his head up, he looked around. All he saw were rooftops scarred with shadows and humming streetlights. The Duke was gone.

But not all his problems.

VII

OLIVIER PRESIDED OVER A FEAST OF THE FLESH Bacchus would have envied. The men he danced with had stripped off their shirts. Their jeans hung low on their hips; perfect V-lines visible. Elsewhere on the dance floor, the masses followed in kind, all in various stages of undress. All fixed their attention on the hunk of meat in front of them, many slid their hands into secret places to rub and stroke and make wet.

The DJ's songs took on a dirty beat, a heavy bass like the drumming on a slave ship, forward, more, harder, faster. A woman in the crowd screamed out, an orgasm racking her body, convulsing as her partner's hand worked quicker and deeper.

Behind him, Olivier heard heavy breathing as Muscles Two rubbed against his ass, his hard cock pressing through the fabric. The friction brought him to climax, and his sweaty head collapsed forward and rested on Olivier's back. He reached around to touch the wet patch, his thumb slipping beneath the waistband to touch the sticky mess and rub the spent head. He put his thumb in his mouth and sucked. The saltiness made him think of the sweat that slid down their necks and bodies, between their legs, raising veins and arteries that begged to be pierced.

He hungered.

Muscles One bared his neck in front of him, begging for it to be kissed, licked, bitten. Not as hard as Olivier had in mind, no doubt. *Later*. He caged that beast and sought to sate the other.

With Muscles Two spent, he searched for a replacement, someone to be favored and join him on the dais. He cast his gaze around the crowd, skipping from one body to another, from nameless face to nameless face, refining his choices: that one too fat, that one too thin. That one's eyes too small, too close together, not the right allure. That one too short, that one too tall. His choices diminished in one glance to a bare handful. Other nights he wouldn't be so choosy, but tonight his lust fueled those around him, and if he wanted to keep it up, his tastes had to be obeyed.

He fixed his stare on one with chestnut hair, longer than he would have thought fashionable for today, but it reminded him of the bandits of two centuries before, those rough men who slept in the woods and gave a damn for no one. The modern bandit hugged some skinny thing in black PVC pants and a too-tight tank-top. Bleached blond hair, too. The men behind and in front of Olivier continued to worship his body and dance, a spectacle for everyone around, as his eyes burned to be noticed by one. Bandit realized soon enough he was being watched. His lips separated from Skinny's, and his attention rose to Olivier.

He smiled and that should have been it.

But Oberon slid in between them and blocked his view. Olivier hissed before he knew he did it. His fingers arched into claws.

Oberon's smirk and raised eyebrow almost ruined everything. As it was, the distance between people grew, and the music skipped a beat and clashed. People looked at their sudden hip-partners as if they'd never met before. Olivier had to decide if the night was worth ruining all because Oberon had shown himself.

It wasn't.

With the music back on track, he pulled up a few more of those at the base of the stage to join him and he lost himself amongst them. He wiped the snarl from his face and forced his fingers to straighten. His hands jerked as they explored the new bodies he'd collected. He was determined to wipe Oberon from his mind. Now was for fun, and that fucking witch couldn't stop him doing what he wanted.

But when there was a break in the crowd he quickly looked to see if Oberon still watched. He wasn't where he had been before, but that didn't mean he had gone completely. Knowing Olivier hunted here, he probably felt some duty to protect his fellow humans. Had Thierry seen him?

He laughed. Thierry probably sulked in the shadows somewhere. With all this eager flesh around, Thierry should have been happy. But something had upset him when they'd walked in, and he'd looked like a feral cat ever since.

Another thing to darken Olivier's mood.

He kissed a man with bright teeth, a shaved head and thick arms. Their tongues wrestled. The man held him, his hands descended to grip his butt cheek and pull him close, press against him. Muscles One moved to sandwich him from behind, his mouth over Olivier's neck. He lengthened so there was more to kiss. He bit him, nibbled at the skin, and Olivier growled. He felt them both, their hardness coming at him from both sides, their deep breathing and carnal bleating echoed loud in his ears. They smelled of sex, of animal need. He wanted to take them both now, on the stage. He'd put on a show that would make Oberon pant.

He sought the zipper of the one in front and slid it down. His hand slipped through the opening and over underwear wet with anticipation. He flicked the waistband down and the cock was free and in his hand. He gripped it hard, pumped it. He looked into surprised yet hungry eyes, and then they kissed with newfound ferocity. Olivier pumped harder while he freed the one that battered him from behind. He wanted it in him. Moans rose around him again. Olivier craved more.

But as he considered how best to get himself fucked, lights started coming on around the darker edges. The music wound down, the vocals fading, a beat lingering that soon would be over. Most people didn't notice but he did, and he growled. Two am and they were told to go home. Two cocks in his hand, and neither ready to blow. He'd have to finish this elsewhere. Not his preference, but there might be the chance for blood play.

"Come," he barked at them, squeezing their dripping dicks for good measure. They bitched but buttoned themselves and followed him as he stepped off the dais and set a course through a sea of half-naked men and women. Some still hadn't noticed it was time to go. Olivier smiled at what he'd created. Next time he'd go bigger.

He glanced around for Thierry, but he didn't appear. That stung. With two suitable specimens in tow, he'd hoped Thierry would join in. Watching his brother ride anonymous bodies always been a turn on. And sometimes, Thierry allowed Olivier to touch him, even rarer to kiss him. That was as close as he got. But it was enough—for now—to outshine the rest of the action. Maybe he'd be waiting at the house.

He strutted between the big exit gates of the club onto the street.

"Olivier."

He stopped and composed himself. Oberon wouldn't rile him so easily this time. He adopted the slyest smile he had and turned his head to look back at the witch leaning against the wall. He was dressed in black—*surprise!*—from the tight, low-cut, short-sleeved shirt to the cargo pants, his eyes heavily underlined and his hair spiked. Olivier saw the other tattoos that graced his skin. An O with a circumflex on his right bicep and the edges of a large, ornate tattoo etched on his smooth chest. It was thick and black, hours' worth of pain. Olivier was pleased.

"Did you enjoy the show, Oberon?" He stood close, hoping to intimidate. His entourage flanked him. "You should join in next time. It's much more fun."

"Are you joining us?" asked one in a sultry voice.

Olivier cocked his head a little, curious if Oberon would say yes.

"No. I don't think so. You boys play safe." Oberon walked away.

"Is that it? That all you're going to say? I expected more."

"How about this: come with me, and I'll give you something you've wanted for a very long time." His brow flicked up quickly, beckoning, testing, goading.

"Unless your dick is bigger than the ones these guys have, I doubt you've got much to offer."

He shrugged. "I can find him for you," Oberon said and walked away.

"Who?" Olivier called out.

Oberon didn't stop, but he swiveled and walked backwards. "The one who's after you." Then he laughed.

*The Duke.*

But how did Oberon know? The Duke was stronger, faster, deadlier than before, and Olivier assumed a witch had done it. Why not this witch? Was it a trap? Would he lead him into the Duke's thick fingers? But what if it wasn't a snare? He never trusted witches if he could help it. But Olivier hadn't seen the Duke in a week, and if he could come at him unaware, this whole thing would be over, and then there'd be no reason to keep looking over his shoulder for the next attack. But if it were a trap...

"Are we going, or what?" Muscles One said. The other guy leaned against him, his fingertips circling a hard, pierced nipple. The stud reflected the streetlight. Maybe he could do both—*or was that all three?*—by fucking these guys in a park, and then chasing after the witch. He looked after Oberon and saw him turn right and out of sight.

He made his decision. Disappointing as it was.

"I have to do something first. Tell me where you live, and I'll join you there in half an hour."

"If you've changed your mind, just say so."

"Oh, no. We're going to have a wild time." His eyes blazed crimson. They licked their lips in near unison. "Address," he commanded.

With the location committed to memory, he didn't wait to say goodbye. He sprinted around the corner after Oberon and almost ran past him leaning against a wall. Waiting.

"You're trying my patience." Olivier's voice rumbled.

Oberon just smiled, a big smile with lots of teeth.

*Smug bastard. Those lips will be the first to go.*

"How do you know who I'm looking for?" Olivier asked.

"I was told you were here and in spite of my own

opinion on the matter I was told to make sure you stayed safe. I learned there was someone else new in town, and after getting a look at him I relayed my information and was told this person would wish you harm. A great deal of harm," Oberon said as they walked.

Olivier sensed a familiar stain running across this conversation and was almost too afraid to ask who was going to the effort to protect him. But ask he did.

"I can't tell you. That would spoil the fun."

Olivier grabbed his throat and slammed him into the wall. "Tell me!" he growled, his fangs free. Oberon's hands instantly reached up to protect his neck but finding it gripped by such force he tried a different tack and put his hands on Olivier.

Fire burned through his skin, but Olivier had been prepared for this and steeled himself. The blaze coursed through him, his hands then his arms and into his chest. His eyes bore into Oberon's. He saw the strain around the edges. Just as the heat threatened to rise into his head, he released his grip and withdrew. The fire cooled. It had taken more than he thought to resist that pain. He wondered how Thierry would be feeling. But he was proud of standing his ground as long as he had, of not crying out.

And he'd learned something.

"Never mind. I can guess who's behind this."

"You're smarter than I would have expected." Oberon walked again. He rubbed his neck with one hand and shot dark glances at Olivier. He was no doubt sore that his magic hadn't been as effective as he had planned. Next time, the witch would probably try something else.

"How do you propose to help me with my problem?"

Oberon chuckled. "You're having trouble finding him, right? I mean, if you'd found him, there would probably be buildings lying in rubble, bodies littered far and wide, the sky filled with flames and smoke."

"He isn't worth such a fuss." All he wanted was to put his hand through the Duke's chest, pull out his desiccated black heart and devour it. His blood would run like oil down his throat.

"I can find him for you," Oberon said. "I just need something of his. Get it. Bring it to me. I'll work the magic, and you can trace him wherever he flees."

"But if I'm able to get something of his, then surely I've found him." Was it a trap after all? Olivier scanned the darkness for any sign of that familiar shape.

"Yes, but it seems you have no idea where to look, so he'll come at you when you least expect it. And then you'll die. Not that I'd lose any sleep over that, but someone else would be very upset."

Olivier doubted Aurelia cared if he died. Thierry, perhaps. That's probably why she was involved. "Very well. If I get something from him and don't kill him, I'll come to you. How do I find you?"

"I live here." They hadn't walked far from the club before they stopped outside a block of flats: new ones, modern architectural design in a soulless grey. He'd expected something more "of the earth" for the witch. "Number eleven."

Oberon unlocked the door to the lobby and started to go through. "And vampire, don't even think about trying to attack me while I sleep. You won't like the consequences." Oberon flashed him a sour smile and entered.

Olivier couldn't blame him for thinking it. He bowed lavishly to Oberon's back. "Sweet dreams, king of the fairies."

# VIII

THIERRY STUCK TO SHADOWS WHEREVER HE COULD ON the way to Alex's apartment. Beneath a cloudless sky, the city streets lay open. Even cloaked in invisibility, he felt exposed crossing roads and dashing through parks.

Alex struggled to free himself from Thierry's grip for the first few hundred yards, despite being told what was happening. Eventually he accepted Thierry's grip wasn't going to lighten and allowed himself to be dragged. Perhaps he understood Thierry wasn't the worst thing stalking the night.

The Duke didn't reappear, and they made it inside, after some arguing. The flat was smaller than Thierry would have liked, and for a moment he wished he'd stayed outside as Alex demanded. But he'd fought hard enough to be allowed in, and he wasn't ready to turn around and leave. It wasn't just the walls that made him uncomfortable.

Alex watched every movement, calculating, analyzing. There were viruses in labs that didn't undergo such scrutiny. Thierry tried his best to walk casually around the apartment, but Alex's glares turned his legs into gnarled tree-trunks. He lowered onto the couch and watched the front door. Now all he needed was for Alex's unfriendly eyes to soften. His skin crawled with the attention.

And the need to feed.

"Look," Thierry said, attempting to carve through the growing silence, "I didn't mean to get you involved, but if you could stop looking at me like I'm a slathering Rottweiler, it would make me feel a whole lot easier."

Alex folded his arms. "You think I should go easy on you?"

He considered telling him he was desperate for blood, but that would have made matters worse. Even thinking about it strained his jaw. "I'm not here to hurt you. I'm here to protect you."

"I've heard that before. From a lot of people. Turns out they liked to hurt me more."

"I can kill them, if you like." His voice was ice. "Just say the word."

Alex's eyes flared, but just as quickly returned to normal and he looked off to the side. Considering.

"Your clients?"

"Most of them. My bones heal fast. It makes me popular."

Thierry let out a snarl that filled the small room. Alex backed away and Thierry cut the noise. "You *let* people hurt you?" Thierry had been around plenty of sadomasochists— Olivier was a prime example—but they got their kicks from it. Alex didn't look the bondage type.

"I have to make a living somehow, and Mother always said use what God gave you."

"I don't think she had that in mind."

He shrugged and sat next to Thierry, carefully choosing his place so their bodies didn't touch. At least he was closer.

"It's not as if I really get hurt. I have to pretend sometimes, otherwise they beat harder and I pass out. Then who knows what happens."

He regarded Alex under hooded lids, looking for some falseness, trying to see if this was a joke. But Alex's face was open and relaxed. Believing it was true made Thierry hunger even more. He wondered if the guy Alex had been with at the club had chosen him for his ability to withstand pain. His face was committed to his memory. Whether he was guilty or not, being near Alex was enough to sentence him.

"And the money is worth it?"

Alex smirked. The walls were bare except for two framed large print photographs, both black-and-white male nudes. The couch had tears in its fabric, the coffee table legs were scuffed, and the books on top had mug stains. A cabinet with a TV, and a few DVD cases scattered around the floor finished off the decoration. A Spartan existence, but Thierry had lived with less in Carcassonne.

"It might not look like it, but I make plenty," Alex said. "I save most of it. One day I'll be old, and they won't want me."

Money didn't mean much to Thierry, but he could see Alex used it wisely. What his home lacked, he made up for with his clothes. The blue shirt was torn now, but Thierry recognized its fine cut and remembered the price. His cargo pants were designer, too. At least Alex had earned his money; Thierry and Olivier stole theirs. The clothes he wore had been paid for with money taken from a dying father's wallet.

Alex frowned at him as if trying to figure out the answer to a crossword clue.

"I'm a bit over six-hundred-years-old," Thierry said.

"Oh." His eyebrows rose.

"Both of us, of course. My brother and I."

"You look good for someone so old."

Thierry averted his eyes and smiled sadly. Little did he know how the years weighed on him, especially as the time lengthened since he'd last kissed Etienne. And Reiner.

"It's no wonder you've got enemies."

"There's a lot to atone for."

Alex huffed, half a nervous laugh, half an understanding grunt. "And the guy who punched me?"

Thierry hesitated. Alex had inched closer, seemingly eager to hear his history. Perhaps being on the end of a vampire's fangs had opened his eyes to another world, one he already straddled without knowing it. Healers were rare. From what he remembered, Etienne hadn't been one. At least not that Thierry knew of—and he was sure they shared everything.

Alex waited for an answer.

How much could he reveal? Razors sliced his flesh. No more secrets and lies. But it was a habit tattooed on his bones; hard to remove. "I can't remember his name, if I ever knew it, but we call him the Duke."

He recounted the whole sorry tale of the Duke, Wolf, and Anna, from the moment they arrived until Olivier dealt the final blow. Listening to his own story, his guilt rose at how he had refused to intervene. Sewer water would have been easier to swallow.

He didn't mention Reiner. He wanted to see if Alex had any flash of recognition, and then perhaps it would be easier to talk about souls. It didn't stop the memories from threatening to cleave him in two. While he spoke of Olivier and Wolf, he remembered how he'd met Reiner, about the connection, that blissful day at the lake and the nightmare of finding his corpse. It was all he could do to stop his voice quaking. When he finished, he had to force his fists open. His knuckles popped.

He watched carefully as Alex processed the tale. There was a glimmer of something like comprehension behind his eyes, quickly replaced with a query as if not everything was right.

"How can he be an ordinary man, yet be over two hundred years old and powerful enough to frighten you?" Alex asked.

He confessed he didn't understand it, either. "And I'm not frightened of him. Just wary."

Alex arched an eyebrow.

"What? I'm not." Thierry replied.

"Then why are you still here?"

"I'm frightened for you."

"But why? Why does this Duke want me? Surely you and your brother are his targets."

Thierry wet his lips. Alex had begun to warm; there was even a hint of a smile. They were closer than before, still not touching, but the distance was so small and buzzed with possibilities. He expected sparks to pass between them. Closing the gap, touching again, without having to hold him to rescue him, seemed almost impossible with what he had to say next. Olivier would laugh at his clumsiness.

"It's because of what you mean to me." The strength in his voice surprised him. No tremor, no softly spoken words. His back straightened, and he looked Alex directly in the eye. Pride swelled like an evening tide. At his core he cared for Etienne—and who Etienne had become. It was right and pure. And no matter how this ended, he had that knowledge.

The lines on Alex's forehead deepened. "And what's that?"

The moment was close, and he longed to reveal all. Talking about his history had felt like having a friend, someone who listened. It was akin to talking to Reiner, almost, but more like talking to Etienne when they were alone in the forest, holding each other, talking of their simple life. How would it feel to have no secrets? He ached to be free.

"Do you remember when I said we'd met before? That was both true and not true."

"Why am I not surprised?" He sounded like Etienne, then. What would he have thought of Thierry's lies? If he could, he would have blushed. He had to make this right. For Etienne's memory, if nothing else.

"When I was made, there was a man I loved more than anyone else. More than my sister, even more than my twin. We had known each other since we were children, and my brother was jealous of the bond we developed, but that didn't stop us from falling in love."

Alex shifted his shoulders. "I don't see what that has to do with me."

"We had to be careful. Anyone found doing what we did was tortured and burned at the stake." Those had been grim days. They were mostly women, and the screams before they burned pierced through flesh. The men babbled and wailed, too. Thierry had gone to watch, as nearly everyone did for fear that staying away might draw an accuser's finger. Grim days. "We managed, and despite the fear, they truly were the happiest days of my life.

"Then came the vampire. He took Olivier first, and my brother, being the selfish monster he is, lured my lover away and killed him. I found his body and was turned that night."

For the first time since sitting down, Alex leaned back in the couch. Thierry almost thought he'd relaxed completely, but then Alex put a finger to his mouth, bit a nail and frowned. "What was his name?"

"Etienne." Shivers raced up his arms and burst into the back of his head. The name was holy.

A smile like the breaking dawn broke on Alex's face: slow, gentle, warm. "Nice name."

But it was a smile of sympathy, not of recognition. Thierry couldn't smother the disappointment mewing in his chest. Not that he had really expected Alex's memories to shoot awake.

"There was nothing I could do for him, and at the time I didn't know Olivier had killed him. I thought it had all been a mistake, and the work of our maker. I made him pay with his life, and for a time I felt vengeance had been done and could continue.

"But I was wrong. Olivier and I roamed the earth. I trailed him like his shadow. He reveled in his new dark nature while I seemed to be a voyeur, never feeling the blood of my victims, never hearing their screams, never seeing the destruction I brought into the world. In some ways, I was a better killing machine that Olivier because I didn't care. I was bored, and a bored vampire is a dangerous thing.

"And then I found Etienne again. When I told you about Wolf and Anna and the Duke, there was someone else on the edges of our little drama. Reiner."

Once again, no recognition darkened his eyes at hearing Thierry had kept something from him. The build-up could only mean it wasn't going to be good.

*Be resilient!*

"I saw in him Etienne's soul, and the more time I spent

with him the more I believed it. By then, I had been four hundred years without his love. It was Etienne. I knew that with every fiber of my being. His soul had returned to me."

Alex leaned closer, his face a mix of thrill and uncertainty.

"But Olivier found out, and not content with destroying Wolf and the Duke, he took Reiner from me. Again."

"I don't see..."

For a second he almost believed him, but then Thierry looked at Alex with fine precision. A crack formed that allowed something to seep through. It was like watching two people meet for the first time and discover a lost kinship. But just as the crack grew, Alex tried to patch it.

"You do," Thierry whispered. "I know you do. You hear this story, and I can see in your eyes you try to grasp hold of things buried deep within you." It had worked. The memories, the tales, their connection were all trying to break down the dam, a drip here and there, and before long there would be a deluge. Thierry's mouth widened in awe. His body tingled.

Alex shook his head forcefully. "I don't remember anything. You are wrong. There is nothing there." His face was a mask of malice, his lips turned up in a sneer.

Thierry could see the danger in this chance slipping away as Alex's anger started sandbagging. They were almost there. He was closer than ever before. Full understanding was just on the other side, waiting to stream through. "Whatever remains, there is a trickle of memory and I am in it."

"No!" Alex shot off the couch.

Thierry rushed to him and placed his hands on either side of Alex's face. "Look in my eyes and tell me you don't know me." The joy had dried up. Now he wielded desperation like a sledgehammer. His voice cracked. "I see you."

"There is nothing," he said through gritted teeth.

"You are Etienne," Thierry pleaded. His throat was dry, but his eyes pricked with the heralding of tears.

"I am Alex Roche! No one else."

"I know you feel it. Please, just tell me."

"All I know is that you bring pain. Immense pain. I felt it before, and I know in every part of me that that is all you will *ever* bring. Now let go of me and fuck off."

Thierry's hands slid from Alex and he wrapped his arms around himself. He had been so sure Alex would remember. There was no doubt this was Etienne, but what did that matter now?

Alex strode to the door and opened it, but Thierry couldn't lift his head. He was made of shards of glass only barely holding shape. Eventually he found his voice. "But what if the Duke comes?"

Alex glared at him. "I don't care if Satan himself comes knocking, I don't want your protection."

"Alex, please." He took his hands, however much Alex resisted. "I—"

Heat flared in his fingers and hands, and he hissed. He let go of Alex. The fire leapt up his wrists and arms and reached into his chest. He grimaced against the pain. Alex was about to offer a hand but snatched it back when he realized who was in front of him. The fire burned brighter.

*Fight it. Don't scream.*

Was this Alex's doing? No, there had been that moment of surprise before his mistrust drowned it. Olivier? The Duke? It faded. He turned his palms over, looking at them, and the pain drained away like water down a pipe. Would it come back? He slowly opened and closed his fists, worried the skin would crack.

Alex held the door again. Waiting. Thierry wanted to explain but stopped himself. The flint in Alex's eyes said it all.

"Reiner was a healer too," he said, then stepped through the door.

It slammed behind him.

He spent the night watching Alex's window from the tree in the garden, shrouded in invisibility and his own self-pity. The lights went out at three-thirty, and all was still.

## IX

THE THOUGHT OF TRUSTING A WITCH LEFT A SOUR taste in his mouth, but Olivier didn't want to waste what might turn out to be help. He would have preferred to find the Duke himself, track him to his lair and set upon him when he least expected it, but that had proved fruitless. They had all the time in the world, or so it seemed, but he wanted to finish this. The longer they spent in the city, the easier they might be to find. The Duke could set traps, get others to work with him. Oberon's loyalties weren't exactly clear, despite Aurelia's intervention.

He fucked the night away with the two men he'd left the club with. He let them live. He had been in a giving mood. On the walk home, he tracked a couple of drunks staggering away from the pub and dispatched them down an alley. They barely registered the ambush and were too addled to put up a fight. They smelled of beer and cigarettes and, when he got home, he showered to wash away the feeling of their grubby fingers on his skin. Their blood warmed him, just as the sex had, and he was content.

For a time.

Thierry didn't return until well past dawn.

"Where have you been?" Olivier asked.

Olivier ignored his brother's leaden looks and told him about the witch, and the need to get something of the Duke's. Thierry said little in response to the news and grunted when Olivier said they were to search in earnest. He fixed Olivier with a meaningful stare and deliberately closed the bathroom door behind him.

Olivier had fed too recently to sense what bugged his brother. Yes, he'd learned the little secret that Thierry had obviously kept so well hidden for the better part of half a millennium. That had been hard poison to expunge.

While he'd always known there remained a connection between them through pain, as Aurelia had demonstrated the night after they were turned, he hadn't imagined he could regain the old intimacy by abstaining from blood. It had taken years of desperate searching after Thierry left to uncover it, when a few weeks went by without feeding as his desire to keep living faded. Like a tiny flame in the darkness, Thierry's emotions flickered.

At first, he thought he was going mad. Contentment crept into his being, a residual anger at himself. There was a longing, too. At first, he thought it was his own, but with more groping in the darkness he detected a difference, like a note played a semitone higher. His was the sharp pain of sudden loss, but there was another yearning that echoed beneath the surface of every emotion. The sensations grew over days. He believed it an effect of the hunger, as insanity took root, but then he knew it was real. Thierry was alive, and roamed the earth, and he could feel him on a level that no one else ever had. Not Aurelia. Not Etienne. No one.

He concentrated on the link to refine it, but the same limitations he had when he was mortal remained. He was only ever good at picking up the general feeling, except in close quarters where it sharpened. He couldn't pick out words or pictures. It was like seeing the world through cataracts, or so he understood. Location had never been a problem, but now it was muddled. It flitted everywhere, never fixing on one place. If he followed it too long, it made him sick. Probably something to do with Aurelia's influence.

He didn't understand why the connection had come back until, after two weeks of starvation, he celebrated Thierry's return with slaughtering a family of four sitting down to a meal. He'd never felt happier as he sliced into the father's chest and drank from the mother's breast. The young children hid under the table and whimpered. He felt he shared flesh with his brother once more, the way they used to. Then Thierry drowned in the blood, and Olivier discovered the secret. He howled and shredded the children in his rage.

Years passed. He sought a balance between the blood and the bond. He slipped all too often. Thierry blinked in and out of his inner life for nearly two centuries, the frustration and pain at not feeling him close spurred him on to kill more and more people, the joy at feeling him inside made him waste away.

And the Duke appeared every now and then, and he couldn't take the risk at being caught weakened.

That was what he told himself. Knowing Thierry was at least living with relative ease without him had hurt more.

When Thierry came out of the bathroom, his face had regained its normal passivity. He wore new clothes: a tight-fitting black tank-top that was barely more than a rag and dark blue jeans.

"Are you ready to hunt?" Olivier asked.

Thierry's lips turned up in a mirthless grin, exposing his ready-to-bite fangs.

They left the house, returning to the parking lot where they had first seen the Duke in Perth. If they started at the beginning, Olivier thought they might be able to tease him out. When they reached the spot, he suggested they split up, covering half the city each. Thierry grunted and disappeared west. His speed and his invisibility took him out of Olivier's sight; there was no point trying to follow.

Thierry had always fought against him. There were a few blissful years when they were human and had shared a bond unlike any other. But as they grew, Thierry didn't want to be his twin. He wanted to be Thierry alone. Bitterness scoured him as he thought of how that was exactly what he'd gotten the past couple of centuries, whiling away the years with Aurelia.

*If it wasn't for Aurelia...*

She had twisted Thierry against him. She was always there to whisper something in his ear, to drive a wedge between them, to act the caring mother that they lacked but only to Thierry. Olivier was always to blame in her eyes. Thinking about her did nothing to brighten his mood.

Then Thierry had returned, and the past twenty years had been spent adapting to one another again as Thierry struggled to become his brother once more. Of course, he wondered why Thierry had returned. The hate in his eyes was evident when he found Olivier again, slumbering in a drug den in Amsterdam. He'd looked down on him then, as he always did. He asked him why he'd come back, and Thierry had lied. He said he'd forgiven him and missed him. Lies about the bond, about needing to be close.

Olivier had swallowed them whole as an antidote to his pain.

He wandered with half an eye on the faces around him, down alleys and in places where the darkness might hide, but thoughts swirled inside his head about Thierry's fidelity. All Olivier wanted to do was hold him close. The more he searched, the further he felt from Thierry. Not the bond, of course, that was well and truly silent. But his need to be close to the one he loved.

Over time he'd suspected Thierry had other motives, but he could be patient, especially when it came to his brother, and encourage the return of once-felt desires, of companionship and need. His twin sulked like a five-year-old girl, but there were fun times. And Thierry had warmed. Of that he was certain.

He stopped and looked around, hoping Thierry might appear.

Instead he found the Duke.

## X

THE ATTACK ON HIS BROTHER HURLED THIERRY FROM the tree he'd been perched in outside Alex's apartment. A rush of phantom pain tore through his shoulder. He barked as it ripped into him. He hit the grass, his spine jarring from the impact. He rose to his hands and knees and crawled to the base of the tree, rested against it, his gaze flicking from left to right waiting for another blow to fall. But there was no way he could see where it came from, and he wasn't the prime target. He gasped as another bolt shot through his chest, like an arrow pinned him to the tree.

Slowly, the pain faded to a dull throb, and his senses returned to normal. Someone else was on the lawn with him. He sniffed the air, and a smile fluttered across his lips.

"Thierry?"

He peered from behind the trunk at Alex, standing there like a child worried about an injured dog. Would he get bitten? Could he help without getting rabies?

"Hi," Thierry croaked, his throat dry.

Alex's eyebrows knitted together, and he crossed his

arms in front of his chest. "What are you doing outside my house?" The worry was gone.

Thierry got to his feet, taking a moment to trust nothing else would floor him. *Not that I'd know.* When he was sure, he spoke. "I was checking to make sure you were okay."

"Me? You might not have noticed, but you were screaming your lungs out. Everyone's turned their TVs up. And why were you lying on the ground?"

"It's complicated."

"Whatever. I told you this yesterday. Keep away from me." Alex turned to walk off.

He couldn't let it end like that. Alex came out for a reason, and Thierry had seen real concern on his face. Thierry grabbed for his hand. Alex struggled but Thierry didn't let go. "Will you just listen to me, please? I know this is hard. I know this is difficult to hear, but what I said was the truth."

"So what?" Alex's mouth twisted in an angry snarl. "Just because we fucked in a previous life, I'm supposed to fall for a murderer like you just for old time's sake? What kind of idiot do you take me for?"

"There's something between us. You know it. I'm making a mess of this, but time is running out for us."

"There is no us!" Alex snatched his hand free and stormed back to his apartment.

Thierry followed, trying to get him to listen. He said all the wrong things, but he couldn't help himself. He'd wasted so much time with Reiner, and that had ultimately led to his death. He wouldn't allow Alex to end up the same way.

All through his life he'd taken the easy approach and allowed everything to happen to him. It was easy to get swept up in Olivier's momentum and say what will be, will be. But here he had a chance to take control of his life.

"Listen to me," Thierry tried again. "Look deep inside yourself and think about what I mean to you. What I *really* mean to you."

"You're a killer. That's all you are. I saw you splatter Paul's brains across a parking lot. How many other people have you killed? How many of the people I care about will you hack to pieces in your fantasy to own me? You'd kill every person I've ever slept with or taken money from." Thierry tried to respond, but Alex cut across him. "Don't deny it. I saw it in your eyes yesterday."

When they reached Alex's door, he opened it and stepped through. "I don't ever want to see you again."

The door was closing.

*No! This is not how it ends.*

Thierry slipped in behind Alex and shut them in together. Alex receded into the room, his brave mask slipping. Thierry didn't move. He'd frightened him enough, and it wasn't fear he wanted. Which was a pity. He could inspire fear very well. And anger. Even lust. It was the other emotions he wasn't so good at.

He felt the door, the plastic feel of the paint, the fragile wood beneath that. He could break it apart without thinking and his fist would splinter it into kindling. Yet it had almost stood between them. Now there was a gulf of emptiness, of mistrust and fear and harsh words.

"Alex, this is not—"

The pain returned, fierce little attacks, one after another. He hissed like a snared leopard, his body twisting to the strikes of ghostly weapons, the anticipation of the next making the pain sharper, fear for where the next one would fall, how deep it would go. He roared as one sliced across his chest, his hand shooting up to cover a wound that wasn't there. Another across the side of his neck, more on his arms. He hugged himself and crouched to the ground. He screwed his eyes shut. What had Olivier done? How could he be so beaten? The attack paused, but his body buzzed with the pain's eruption. He bowed over himself.

"Thierry?"

He peered up at Alex, thankful that he'd taken a step closer, but he couldn't dwell on it. His stomach burned, and he screamed. The sound filled the small place, reverberated on him, crowded back on him. Was Olivier dying? What about him? What would happen to him? Would this pain end? Would he survive? After a while the agony decreased to a steady pulse. His body quivered as the torrent departed.

There would be no denying the screams from Alex's apartment. Everyone in the block would have heard them, even if their TVs were at full volume. He rolled on to his front and got on all fours. Alex had crouched down into a ball, his hands covering his ears, his eyes squeezed shut. Thierry crawled to him and soothed him. "Alex, it's okay. I'm fine now. It's gone. Look at me, Alex."

He touched Alex's arm and his head shot up, his eyes stark with fear, his skin pallid. "What happened?"

"My brother. He got in a fight."

"And you felt it? I thought you were dying."

Warmth spread throughout Thierry's chest at the concern in Alex's voice. His hand came closer to touch Thierry's face, whether to comfort or heal he didn't know. "Yes, sometimes I feel what he—" He reared up and Alex's hand drew back.

*No, please no.*

"What is it?" Alex asked.

Thierry's mouth opened, his eyes not seeing Alex but instead looking inwards. His brother's torment pounded, but that wasn't the worst. The curtain of blood that kept them separated had been drawn, and he could see Olivier clearly.

"I have to go." Thierry fled the apartment, using whatever strength he had left to cross a great distance and get far from Alex. If Thierry could see through Olivier's eyes, his brother could do the same to him and feel Thierry's concern for Alex. He needed to find his brother and force him to feed.

XI

OLIVIER COLLAPSED BEHIND A DUMPSTER, AND Thierry found him not long after. Even though he sensed Thierry's weakness, his brother half-carried him back to the house and got them both to safety. He felt the emptiness inside Thierry, the strain on him. It was bittersweet, knowing he could once again feel Thierry so deeply and so close, his arm around him, body against body, his soul exposed.

But the demon within clawed for blood.

The thirst threatened to drag him down. Thierry insisted they wait until nightfall before they searched for replenishment. Olivier agreed, basking for a moment in his brother's torment, his worry and fear. He tried to examine it closely, closing his eyes and homing in on him.

He met a private strength that refused to let this beat them nor let worry overtake their endeavors. They would prevail. Thierry was wound tight, and he thirsted too. It flowed underneath his thoughts, a strong current that pulled him along.

When night unfolded, they hunted. They terrorized

people in their homes. The streets had been fine, but they could go door-to-door without raising too much suspicion. They found houses with one or two people, the humans' size and strength no problem.

With the first drink, Olivier's strength returned.

And Thierry faded.

After the first woman died, Olivier sat back on his knees and hugged himself tight. Shivers racked his body at the return of life to his old bones. The connection with his twin splintered. The sad inevitability of losing Thierry again shredded his heart. This must be what the guilty feel before facing the hangman. Thierry put an arm around his shoulder and helped him stand.

Then led him to the next victim.

By the sixth, Thierry was gone completely, and Olivier was strong again. They continued to feed to put something in reserve. By the time the sun rose, they'd fed on fifteen bodies and they returned home like engorged leeches to sleep off their bloated stupor. Thierry looked ill when they got back. His eyes were stained red and he could barely move. Olivier tried to talk to him, but Thierry headed into his room and shut himself in. Olivier sighed and went into the other room, stripped off his blood-stained clothes and climbed naked under the sheets. He slept.

## XII

AFTER RUNNING OUT ON ALEX THE DAY BEFORE, Thierry thought that was the end of it. But having led Olivier to drink from all those people—Thierry cringed at the memory of the systematic slaughter—he was confident that any glimmer Olivier caught of his inner workings was truly extinguished. He knew if Olivier was attacked again, the first thing Thierry had to do was get far away from Alex. Even with the exit plan decided, his hand stalled from knocking on Alex's front door. Then he gave one solid rap and waited.

There was a delay while Alex looked through the peephole. Then a sigh. Eventually he opened the door wide.

Thierry had hoped for some sign of relief on his face that he was safe and alive, and no longer in pain. There was no such welcome. Alex glared at him.

"Can I come in?" Thierry asked.

"Not until you explain what happened yesterday." Alex stood with his hand holding the door, and his arm barring entry. His stance accentuated the curves of his muscles, his white T-shirt taut across his hard chest. *No wonder men paid.* "Cops swarmed the place wondering what the fuck had happened."

"Because of the screaming." It wasn't a question. His voice had gotten him into trouble before, raising all sorts of alarms the louder he got. And now he'd brought unwanted attention on Alex. He'd spent enough time with hustlers to know they didn't mix well with the law.

"Even these neighbors can't ignore something that loud."

"Pity." Even though the doors were closed, and no faces peered from behind kitchen windows, Thierry wondered who listened. They needed to get inside, if only to quieten his paranoia. "We shouldn't talk about this out here. Let me in."

Alex opened his mouth to object but stepped back and Thierry entered. The door closed and Alex leaned against it. Thierry felt the distance stretch but remained cautious. Like trying to catch a finch. One wrong move and it bolted into the scrub.

"How did you get rid of them?"

"They didn't know exactly where the sound came from, though most of the trash around here pointed at my door. But no body, no blood, no sign of a struggle. The cops left. Eventually."

"Convincing."

"Lying comes with the profession. I thought they'd connected me with Paul, but I was lucky. Explanation, please."

Thierry allowed himself a small smile. Dealing with police left Alex unfazed. Part of the routine. What life had he lived to come to this point? What pain had forged him so strong? For all the softness and openness in his face, his eyes cut through the glitz and the bullshit and pinned Thierry like steel bolts.

"I said yesterday my brother and I are connected on a very deep level. In certain cases, what one feels, the other does too. The Duke's found a way to exploit that and cause a lot more pain than we thought possible."

"I'm guessing you're not used to feeling vulnerable."

Thierry went into the kitchen and drew a carving knife from the drawer. He held his hand out and drove it through his palm, cleanly, smoothly, without flinching. Alex's face paled and worsened when Thierry withdrew the knife and held up his palm. The skin knitted itself together.

No blood. No scar. No pain.

"You're fucking crazy," Alex said. "Warn me next time you're going to do something like that."

"Sorry." He wiped the knife on his jeans and threw it in the sink. He leaned against the kitchen counter, Alex nearer than before. His body radiated heat, just out of reach. Tantalizing. Like a bone placed too far for a chained dog. "Whatever weapons this guy has, they're able to cause us a lot of harm. My brother fought him yesterday and was nearly killed." His skin pricked at the memory. The wounds might have healed, but it would take a while before thinking of the attack didn't make his skin creep. "Every cut uses up our energy, whether it's to resist the pain or heal the wound. If he gets in enough hits, he'll weaken us to the point where he can dispatch us."

Alex took a step back and folded his arms. "But you're all right now? You look better than yesterday."

"I fed."

Alex cursed.

"If it's any consolation, it was quick. They didn't suffer."

"They?" His voice jumped. "How many?"

Thierry's mind calculated the numbers and bile swirled in his stomach. Too many. One was too many. He started to think about who they had been. Perth was a small place. Did Alex know any of them? "You don't want to know."

"You're probably right."

They stood in silence. Thierry thought of many things he'd like to say, but none that would be helpful. And none he really had a right to speak.

*I had to leave because I didn't want my psychopathic brother to find you.*

*I want you to come with me.*

*I want to hold you and never let you go.*

*You have Etienne's eyes.*

Alex broke the impasse. "Well, I'm glad you're all right, but you have to leave. I've got to go to work."

Thierry bristled at the thought of Alex beneath someone else. Images of whips and chains, of gags and blindfolds, clamps and hot wax flashed in his mind and stoked his own desire while also igniting his jealousy. Alex had said the men had broken his bones. A growl escaped his lips.

"Whatever you need, I can get for you. You don't need to do that anymore."

Alex smiled benevolently. "Depending on you would have to be the dumbest thing I could do. You're in a deadly battle with a guy with magic knives. You're a vampire who *needs* blood."

The Duke's blades were dull compared to this. "Can't you—"

"No, not now. I just need...look, please go." Alex opened the door. Sadness darkened his face. At least that was something.

Thierry ghosted towards it, not knowing how one foot

went in front of the other, not understanding why he was leaving. He felt like a slave, ground down to the point where there was no resistance. He'd seen them, their shuffling feet, the heavy way their heads and shoulders slumped. They didn't beg for anything, not even mercy.

Neither did he. He'd already lost enough.

But unlike those slaves' masters, Alex didn't look through him. Concern tinged the corners of his eyes, and his lips pressed together in a line of regret. No hate, just preservation. Thierry had done the same, turned away from his brother's excesses and forced himself to carry on. If only for the hope Etienne would return.

"Goodbye, Thierry," Alex said with an unhappy smile and closed the door.

It shut with barely a sound, but it may as well have been a pair of cathedral doors slamming for the effect it had. Denied. Again. And this time, by his own hand.

Etienne and Reiner had been snatched from him, but Alex had turned away rather than be involved with a monster. He could admire Alex's determination—rejecting a vampire was difficult on many levels—yet anger slithered through his body at being refused. And without so much as a fight on his part. This could not be the end.

He was certain Alex had begun to accept him. They'd spoken almost as equals. They'd *shared*.

This was not the end. It never ended.

Invisibility slid across his body, and he waited for Alex to leave. He watched him walk down the street and be picked up by a Mercedes. Inside rode a mustachioed man in his mid-fifties. They drove out to the suburbs to a large modern house with plenty of rooms. The streets were desolate at this time of day, and the house lay dormant. They went inside and closed the curtains. Thierry passed the tortured hour sitting outside the window, hearing Alex's moans, fake or otherwise, the rattling of handcuffs against the headboard, the heavy pressing on the mattress, and finally the protracted groan when the client came.

Thierry fought to remain still. Someone else was touching Alex, bringing forth those sounds. Thierry's nails cut his palm and broke the skin. His hands became slick. What he heard vibrated through his veins and his balls tightened at thinking of Alex beneath *him*, pleasing *him*. He nearly tore his lip off trying to stop himself from making a noise.

There was a bit of talk afterwards, not a lot. Another appointment was made for the following week at the same time. They got dressed, back in the car, and he drove Alex back to the city and let him out on the street.

Two more men in the afternoon. In the evening Alex went to the gym and talked with people, some of them who looked like friends. They chatted about things they'd done, guys they'd slept with. Later, Alex went home alone, ate some dinner and watched TV. At eight, Thierry left and returned to Olivier. They hunted and fed. They found a couple of guys to fuck. The seconds ticked by until morning.

# XIII

THEY SEARCHED FOR THE NEXT FOUR DAYS. OLIVIER returned to the alley where he'd last fought the Duke and went from there. He kept to deserted places: industrial buildings, parking lots and side streets where fewer people went, chosen with the belief that the Duke wasn't big on spectacle or witnesses. Every fight until then had been somewhere dark or hidden, and he saw no reason to ignore that pattern.

The number of people they killed did not interest the Duke. He wasn't a vigilante. Other humans were not important to him, so the body count was not an enticement.

Around noon on Friday, Olivier wandered around the park, just north of the city center. There were lakes and old trees, not as ancient as some he'd seen but old for this place. Their verdant and heavy limbs made their shade a place of cool respite from the summer sun. He'd been through here before, picked off a homeless man sleeping between the large exposed roots of a Moreton Bay Fig.

He walked along the paths, spying on the workers who sought the outdoors during their lunch break, the mothers with their strollers at the playground, the laughter and shouts of their children jumping in the sand. A dog on a leash snarled at him as its elderly owners walked past. They pulled the dog away and apologized.

As Olivier strolled, he saw a jogger on one of the park benches, stretching his legs, bending over, his shorts tight across his ass. He wore a T-shirt that left well-defined and well-tanned arms bare. He had headphones in his ear, the phone on his arm, the band across a bicep. He displayed himself in front of the male toilets. He watched those around him while he worked one leg, then the other. Spotting Olivier, his eyes roamed over his body. Then he looked away. Olivier smiled knowingly and headed for the toilet. He made eye contact as he passed.

The putrid stench of stale urine assaulted his nose before he blocked it out and concentrated on what he needed to do. There were two cubicles and a urinal. Both cubicles had lost their locks, an open hole in both doors where they used to be. There was a hole in the wall between them. Graffiti covered all surfaces. Olivier leaned against the one sink and waited.

The jogger entered, an expectant, cocky grin on his mouth. "Hey," he said, and walked over to Olivier then rubbed the bulge in his crotch.

*To hell with foreplay.*

Olivier pushed him backwards into a cubicle and closed the door. Their hands went immediately to the others' waist; Olivier pulled down his shorts, pleased to find him wearing a jockstrap, the jogger unzipped Olivier's fly and pulled his cock through the opening. Both were hard.

They fucked for ten minutes, the jogger biting his lip to stop from swearing too loudly. He still sounded like a bad porno. Olivier could have gone forever, but the jogger shouted as he came, shooting onto the toilet seat. His body rippled from the orgasm.

Olivier sped up and fucked harder, the jogger's body limp and pliable on him. He felt like he was screwing an untethered puppet. He came hard, raising his head to shout at the concrete roof as he spurted into the man. When the orgasm dissipated, he leaned back against the door, his head resting. The jogger still breathed heavily but had regained control of his limbs. He straightened, Olivier's dick still in him.

"Wow," the jogger breathed. "That was hot."

The acid burn of metal ignited between his shoulders as one of the Duke's blades drove through the door and into Olivier's back. He bucked at the pain, a thrust of his hips that sent the jogger off his cock and crashing into the wall. The other man slumped to the ground unconscious.

Olivier howled as a second dagger entered between his hips. The pain silenced his screams. He struggled to remain conscious, the first impact connecting with the second and obliterating all thought.

He heard the tell-tale sound of knife being drawn, and this one would likely be through his head. Olivier had to be quick. He pushed against the door and slid off the blades. He collapsed on to the jogger as another knife protruded through the wood, right where his head had been.

The Duke kicked open the door, armed with another two blades. He dove forward, ready to pierce Olivier where he crouched. With his head down, Olivier rushed to meet him, and rammed into his guts, forcing the Duke back.

The impact crumpled the metal sink, breaking the taps. Water gushed. They wrestled, switching places so Olivier's back was against the wall. He saw the door with its three blades. He punched the Duke in the face, his chest, his stomach, then kicked a leg out from under him. The Duke reached for Olivier as he fell, but Olivier jumped over him and up on top of the wall dividing the cubicles. He ripped a blade free.

The Duke dove for Olivier, his lip curled and his breathing heavy. But Olivier couldn't hang around to fight. He'd learned that lesson. With the knife in his hand, he flew from the grimy toilet block and away from the Duke as fast as he could.

# XIV

THIERRY HAD BEEN FOLLOWING ALEX EVER SINCE THE curtain between him and Olivier had fallen. Alex was popular and busy and there were plenty of men willing to pay for his services. On Wednesday afternoon, following another attack on Olivier that scalded the flesh between Thierry's shoulder blades, he tracked Alex to a client's house. The place was a regular-looking bungalow on a large block of land, near the river. The guy was fit, muscled, and in his late forties. When he opened the door, he sized Alex up like he'd planned exactly what he was going to do to him, exactly what cries he'd wring out. Alex entered the house without much outward care, his backpack hanging from one shoulder. The door closed and locked behind them.

Thierry went around the house, peering into windows to get a glimpse at them. From what he could see, the guy had a family. There were photos on the wall of him with a blonde wife and two young kids. Toys in one room confirmed the offspring. Thierry snuck around to the back-yard and watched through the open glass door.

They had already peeled off their shirts. Seeing Alex

half-naked made him hard, but the way Daddy loomed over him tensed Thierry's muscles for another reason. Alex played his part well, his fingers trailing around Daddy's nipples. He gripped Alex's jaw. He looked ready to kiss him, but quickly spun him around and bent him over the bench. He placed his hands on the counter.

"Don't move your hands."

Daddy reached around the front of Alex's jeans, unzipped and unbuttoned them. He pulled them down slowly, leaving his underwear in place. He lifted one foot, pulling one leg off along with Alex's shoes and socks before doing the other. He stood and pressed himself against Alex's back. Alex ground his ass against his crotch and placed a hand on Daddy's thigh.

"I said don't move your hands!" His fist smashed into the back of Alex's head.

Alex collapsed on top of the bench, and Daddy grabbed his hair, ready to smash his face into the hard surface.

Thierry burst through the screen door, slashing the mesh and ripping the frame into pieces of twisted metal. Daddy spun around, still gripping Alex. Thierry seized his arm around the bicep and crushed it, the bone breaking beneath his force. He released Alex with a loud cry. Thierry punched him in the chest. Ribs cracked. Daddy collapsed to his knees, and Thierry struck his face. His nose broke, and as he fell teeth skittered onto the floor.

He didn't stay down for long. He attempted to crawl away, but Thierry grabbed his ankle and pulled him back, lifted him up and flung him across the room like he was a doll. He crashed into a coffee table, glass shattering, wood splintering, and lay in a crumpled heap, unconscious.

Alex had fallen to the ground, but when Thierry knelt over him his eyes fluttered open. Even knowing Alex's power, he heaved a sigh. Thierry slipped an arm under him and cradled him. With one hand, he caressed his face, looking for broken bones. There was a small graze on his cheek but that healed as he watched. Shivers streamed up his arm and straight into his heart. The touch of a healer, the feel of his beloved.

"Are you all right?" he whispered. Like he held a miracle.

"Bit of a headache." A faint but warm smile spread across his face and entered his eyes. The defiance was gone, along with the hate. Alex tried to turn away, but Thierry had seen what he'd always hoped for. He wasn't going to let it get away.

"Alex, look at me."

Without a doubt, there was Etienne, but Thierry realized it wasn't really him. It was a soul he was tied to. It could have worn untold names and faces, but it would always call to him. Now, this was Alex, and he was what mattered.

Thierry kissed him, their lips meeting, Alex's warm ones to his cold. A chaste kiss, one of slow-burning passion, of compassion. Their eyes closed, and the world was shut away. He was whole again.

The sound of glass crunching and the man's heavy breathing stirred him, and Thierry's hand came up to stop a leg from the coffee table colliding with his head. He broke the kiss, pulled the weapon out of Daddy's hand and threw it away. Easing Alex out of his arms was like stopping feeding in mid-flow. But this brute had interrupted their reunion, and this time Thierry wouldn't hold back. He pounced on the man, forced him to his knees and loomed over him. He blubbered, begged, but Thierry was ice. He turned to Alex.

"I can't let him live for what he did to you, and what he would have done to you. But if you say the word, I'll let him go free."

Alex looked from him to Daddy, a troubled gaze that brushed over both of them. Thierry was worried Alex would want to release him, even after what he'd been through today and before this. Thinking about all the times he had been forced to bear pain made Thierry tighten his grip harder. But there was beauty in Alex's resilience.

For a long time they stayed in their strange tableau, the only sounds the pleas of a dead man. Alex rubbed his jaw, and his eyes lingered on the broken glass before returning to Daddy's bleeding face. He let out a soft but long breath.

"He's hurt me too often. He's yours now."

Thierry smiled and dove for the man's neck. He bit savagely but precisely into his jugular, cutting a scream short. He drank quickly, and blood exited the body in minutes. When the death throes stopped, Thierry withdrew. He stood and wiped the few errant drops from his mouth and chin.

He held out his hand, and Alex didn't hesitate to take what was offered.

"What does it feel like? To take a life?" Alex's eyes lowered to the body and then back to Thierry's face.

Dangerous questions to ask. Humans were always funny about death. Accepting yet unbelieving the effect, too abstract. Like understanding where the wind came from or how the moon affected the tides. Alex had watched him kill, and maybe that was too much for him to bear. Now Thierry regretted slaughtering the bastard.

"You shouldn't have had to see that. I'm sorry."

Alex's forehead creased. He walked over to Daddy's

body, his hand still holding Thierry's, and crouched down next to it. He placed his open palm on the corpse's face.

"You can't bring him back. Death is death."

Alex snorted like it was some droll joke. "I know that. I've seen dead bodies before, just not watched them die. Especially not by a vampire." His hand smoothed across Daddy's face. "There really is nothing left. I thought it might be different dying by your fangs but it's all the same."

Thierry tugged at his arm. "We should go. Someone might have heard."

Alex nodded, but remained kneeling a moment longer. What had this man been to him? How long had they known each other? How many injuries had Alex borne? Thinking about it made him want to leave even quicker. That, or shred the body to nothing. He looked up and saw photographs of the man's children. Beautiful, smiling children. For his own conscience, he hoped their father had been abusive so when they heard of his death there would be happiness instead of sadness. He didn't like his chances. He pulled at Alex again and this time he rose.

Thierry turned to leave, but Alex resisted. When he swung back, Alex watched him with a question waiting to be asked.

"What is it?"

"You didn't answer my question."

Thierry grunted. *No lies.* "Most of the time, I hate it." He held Alex's hand lightly, expecting him to withdraw and prepared to let him. But he stayed. He didn't flinch. Thierry closed the space between them until he could wrap his arms around Alex's waist. Still no resistance.

"Most of the time?"

Thierry's mouth went as dry as a year-old corpse. *No lies.*

"People like him," he jerked his chin towards the body on the floor, "I'd kill many times over if I could. I like finding them. The guilty. And then there are times when it doesn't matter who they are. The blood is all that matters and to stop mid-drink is torture."

"But you can stop."

"If I must." The last time he'd done that was with Alex. Before then? There hadn't been a good enough reason. Death had always been kinder. He'd left humans alive before and, when he saw them again, madness had overtaken them. Many found death in other ways, but he'd always been responsible. *Kinder to kill,* Olivier had once said. He'd meant it as a joke—as if he could ever be kind—but Thierry had chiseled the words on his heart.

Alex put his hands on Thierry's forearms, touching the skin. "When I feel you, it's like nothing I've ever encountered. You're not dead, and you're not really alive. It's like you're *more*. Have you seen those mosaics made up of lots of tiny photos and they create one big picture? It's like you're the big picture, and inside you there are other people but it's smoother than that, more subtle. Bits and pieces knitted together so you can't tell where one stops and another begins. I can feel myself going into you like there's supposed to be something to fix but it can't. It's not allowed." Alex ground his teeth. "I'm not explaining this right. It's beyond words."

Thierry felt the exploration. It penetrated deep, searching for something. Electricity sparked and, like Alex said, he felt *more*. From his skin, through muscle and veins and arteries, down, down to bone and marrow. He closed his eyes against the rush welling up, all from Alex's touch. He might not be alive like Alex, but he was as good as a newborn when Alex held him.

With eyes closed he sought Alex's lips. They pressed together and another jolt shot into him. He held Alex tighter, embraced him so close he almost crushed him. Alex exhaled loudly but not in pain. Lips separated, tongues met, and Alex slipped deeper into him, his power infiltrating another layer.

Thierry's eyes sprang open from the force of the connection. He craved more. His hands lifted Alex's shirt and Alex did the same for him, and in a flurry of thrown clothes they were naked, a strong current dancing from skin to skin. Thierry felt more exposed than ever before. No secrets covered him, nothing stopped Alex from taking all of him and burrowing into everything that was Thierry d'Arjou.

Hands caressed, skin shivered, and bodies hardened. Thierry lifted Alex and carried him to the couch. He lay him down and Thierry knelt on the carpet, glass pressing into his knees. Thierry was so hard, like he'd not done this for a millennium, and his cock so wet. He inched forward.

"Let me." Alex took hold of him, guiding him to that spot. Alex's eyes held his, his brow creasing a little in concentration until his throbbing head rested against the opening. "I'm ready." He smiled, one of joy and promise.

Thierry couldn't help but let out a little laugh. He pushed forward, slowly, Alex tensing and then relaxing. His muscles gripping Thierry's cock then allowing it in. He let out a long, loud sigh as he slipped in further. Alex's breath caught in his throat. Thierry's head snapped back, and white light obliterated his vision.

Alex's power flared bright. His touch paled compared to this, a dam bursting beneath a storm. Thierry fought to hold on to who he was, desperately scrambling for a branch, a rope, anything that would stop him from being swept away, but the water was warm and fast. He sank beneath the surface and suddenly there was no difference between him and the flood. He was the flood.

And it was beautiful.

Alex's consciousness swam through him and they merged, travelling together to where the river meets the ocean. At that moment they cried out together, waves crashing through them. Their bodies shuddered, and Thierry's head nodded forward to rest on Alex's chest. He breathed from impulse; Alex's need transferred to him. He blinked and the haze dissipated. He looked down on Alex's perfect chest, lines of come over his skin. Thierry licked some off one of his nipples and he swallowed, the milky saltiness coating his tongue.

When he raised his head, Alex's eyes held his. "I've never..."

"Me either," Thierry replied.

Thierry didn't want to pull out. Even thinking that he was still inside Alex made his cock twitch for more. But distant sirens made him cautious.

"I don't want to, but we should leave."

Alex shot a glance at the corpse behind Thierry. He showed annoyance more than anything. "You're right. We should be alone." Alex smiled, something more mischievous than even Olivier could manage. "And this time, I don't care if you scream the whole building down."

## XV

A<small>FTER HIS FIGHT WITH THE</small> D<small>UKE, AND REPLENISHED</small> on the blood of three, Olivier strolled through the warm night air, along emptying weekday roads to Oberon's apartment. Streetlights cast an unnatural glow on concrete and brick, splashing everything with an orange filter and making the city seem hotter than it really was. Crickets chirped their endless chorus. Olivier twirled the blade in his hand and used the tip to press the numbers on the intercom. It rang four times before Oberon answered. Too long.

"Yes?" the disembodied voice said through the speaker.

"I have it. Let me in."

"Who is this?" The goading made heat flush up his neck.

"Your friendly neighborhood vampire. Now open the fucking door, Oberon."

The intercom cut off with a click and the door unlocked. He went in, climbed the stairs, and struck the door with the metal hilt. It opened shortly after to reveal Oberon, dressed in a black tank-top and baggy shorts. More of the tattoo on his chest showed from around the edges of his shirt, sharp thick tendrils. He wondered how else the boy was marked. If he liked needles that much, Olivier would be happy to oblige.

Oberon wore calm like a cloak, but that would be easy to pull off. He greeted Olivier with a tight smile.

Olivier offered the knife, blade first. "Will this do?"

Oberon gripped it gently but firmly, no wince of pain, no drop of blood. Olivier thought of suddenly pulling it out to slice his hand but stopped himself. He could do that later. Perhaps.

Oberon took it from him, turning it to look at one side then the other as if judging a glass of merlot. It looked like he was going to sniff it. "Yes. This will do."

"Good," Olivier sneered. "It was hard enough to get. The next best thing would be his head."

"He's tougher than you gave him credit for?"

"He's supposed to be dead," he barked, and regretted it when he saw Oberon's smirk at the irony. "Can we get on with this?"

Oberon stepped back and waved Olivier in with the knife. The door closed behind him.

The apartment was open plan: a sitting room ran into the dining room which connected to the kitchen. It was a big place for one person. He saw a large bedroom with a king-size bed through a doorway. It was neat, despite the things littering the surfaces. Lights illuminated paintings and prints hanging on the walls. A ceramic statue of a nude goddess Aphrodite stood opposite a rougher model of a man constructed with sharp edges and hard angles. A marbled egg, candelabras with burned candles and other objects of an older style, no doubt some connection to the world Oberon lived in. Though they might have, they didn't clash with the modern, everyday things: a big, flat-screen television, and a sound system with many speakers dotted around the room.

"Witchcraft pays well."

"The gods are good to me."

Oberon stood with his hands clasped behind his back, his shoulders relaxed but square. A cocky smile on his lips.

"How does this work?"

"I'll need a drop of your blood."

Olivier suppressed a growl. "No."

"I see you're a taker, not a giver."

"I could say the same about you." He had to calm down or he'd lose all control, a dangerous thing around a witch. But it wasn't easy. He actually *breathed*. Definitely a bad sign.

"Your warm blood. Just a drop. It's to create a connection. I put the blood on the blade, and you'll be able to sense wherever he goes."

It sounded too easy, but he was short on choices. "One drop."

"That's all I need." He had the nerve to grin like he was trying to make a child take its medicine. After he took his lips, he'd take his tongue.

"And what do you do?"

"Work the magic, of course." The lights extinguished, and the candles dotted around the room flared into being. Oberon walked into the middle of the space and sat cross-legged on the carpet. He gestured for Olivier to follow.

Sniffing, Olivier's stomach turned at the scent clinging to the air like sewage in a humid climate. He surveyed the shadows in case they hid trouble. It could still be a ruse to make him lower his guard while the Duke snuck up and slit his throat.

*Never trust witches. Never.*

But with no other option, he sank to the floor and positioned himself opposite Oberon. The witch closed his eyes and laid the knife on the floor with the blade pointing at Olivier. He breathed deeply, slowly, and the sounds of the outside world faded. His hands rested on his knees palms up. Time slowed. He breathed three times.

*Theatrics.* Aurelia had just done whatever it was she wanted. No pomp, no ceremony.

Oberon's eyes shot open and the air around him wavered. Olivier sensed a wall going up, trapping him inside a cage.

"Your blood." Oberon's voice boomed.

Olivier bit into his wrist, and blood wet his lips. Holding his hand over the knife, three drops hit the metal. Two more than he'd wanted to give, but maybe that would increase the effectiveness. He needed to hunt the Duke wherever he went, however far he travelled.

*If this worked...*

He withdrew his arm and licked the wound clean.

Oberon's hands hovered over the blade. He closed his eyes and whispered, but the words were loud enough for Olivier to hear.

*Blood for binding,*
*Bound to blood,*
*Find the culprit,*
*In mist or flood.*

He repeated it three times, and the air electrified. Sparks fired from Oberon's hands and shot towards the blade. Energy surrounded it and power hummed over the metal.

But it remained the same, not taking anything in.

Abruptly, Oberon flexed his hands and the flow stopped. He frowned at it.

"What is it?" Olivier asked.

"Quiet." Oberon shut his eyes again and repeated the ritual. The air sizzled with more energy than before, and power beat at the blade.

Olivier stared, hoping it would work. It had to work. The witch promised.

*After his lips and tongue, his balls.*

Nothing changed.

"What's wrong?" He tried to keep the shrill tone out of his voice, tried to keep it low and menacing, but the doubts came thick and fast like tiny strikes with barbed wire. His nostrils filled with the stench of magic and the dome that covered them felt like it was shrinking. Relying on witches had always been a bad idea, and here he was, stuck with one. Was it a plot to hand him over to the Duke? Was Oberon really doing what he said he was doing?

Oberon's face hardened and sweat beaded across his forehead, the tendons in his hands strained, as did the muscles in his arms. He repeated the phrase constantly, more than Olivier assumed necessary. Any fear of Oberon double-crossing him at that moment vanished as Olivier watched the concentration etch itself into his face. He pumped more power into the working, his voice raising to a shout and filling the room. Blue light turned the air around the knife as thick as fog and Olivier shut his nose to the stink of oranges, burned oranges.

But no matter how much Oberon summoned, it wasn't working. Eventually he could sustain the magic no longer, and his hands closed. The energy dissipated in a rolling wave that rushed through Olivier's body and made him tremor. The lights stayed off and the candles still burned, but the rest of Oberon's power had fled like an exorcised ghost. He slumped forward, his hands resting on the carpet, breathing heavily, glaring at the unchanged knife.

Olivier almost felt disappointment, but it was swallowed by his contempt. "It didn't work," he said in flint.

Oberon's head snapped up and his eyes blazed hate at Olivier. "I can do it. It'll just take time."

"No. It won't. Something's wrong."

"There's an added enchantment on it that's difficult to get through."

"You said you could find him."

"And I will. You just have to be patient."

The witch wasn't going to put him off this time. He'd tried and failed. And worse, Olivier had almost believed him. "It's beyond you."

"It's not," Oberon shouted.

"Which means you're worthless."

Olivier launched himself at Oberon, but the witch flung his hands up to protect himself. Olivier hit a solid force and was thrown back into the wall and cracking the plaster. Oberon's power pinned him there. Olivier struggled to lever himself, scrabbling to raise his legs and push away. The witch jumped to his feet and advanced, his hands in front, the magic flowing from them, driving more into him. Olivier fought and groaned. New sweat burst forth on Oberon's skin.

*A chance!*

"I'd start running if I were you, witch."

Lightning fired through his body. He had to withstand. He could never submit to this witch. He ground his teeth against the burning. His mind returned and remembered, and a plan crystallized. He pushed himself on like he trudged through lava. How it burned. But then, he felt a chink in the flow and groped towards it.

Drops ran down Oberon's forehead. The gap in the flow widened. The pain faded until it was only a minor ache.

Then the force sputtered and failed.

Oberon dropped to the ground to grab the Duke's knife. Olivier heaved himself off the wall, his limbs exhilarated at being free. He attacked.

The witch didn't have time to react. They rolled over each other as Olivier tried to get a good grip on his arms. A shot of pain ripped through his stomach as the knife slipped into him. He released Oberon and jumped back. The weapon didn't hurt like it once had; his senses numbed by Oberon's earlier attack. He ripped the blade from his abdomen and flung it away. It buried in a wall, spraying plaster and cement.

Oberon rocketed to his feet and sped to the door. He pulled it open, but Olivier grabbed his neck from behind before he could run. He threw him back into the apartment, and Oberon skidded across the floor. Olivier locked them in.

He advanced towards the witch. Other prey cowered at this point or begged for mercy. Oberon was made of tougher stuff, but even stone shattered with enough force. Cold, determination glared up at him as he attempted to rekindle the magic. Sparks sputtered between his hands, but he couldn't summon anything more than the light of a dying candle.

*Pathetic.*

Oberon attempted to get to his feet, but Olivier jumped on top of him, holding him down. He brought his face within an inch of Oberon's. Still, the witch hid his fear. Eyes black like coal stared back at him. Whether it was the rush of the challenge or frustration searing his gullet, Olivier's fangs broke free and dripped with saliva.

"I can help you," Oberon said.

"That's right. Beg! I like it when they beg."

"I'm not one of your victims." The defiance was stronger than ever. And his stupidity.

"Hard to get. I like it that way."

He reached down and ripped the clothes from Oberon's body, revealing that brazen tattoo across his chest, two stars circled by reaching, thorned tentacles, beautiful and black and thick. Then another on his abdomen, 30 *April*, with twenty-two crosses beneath. Olivier took a moment to admire this canvas and imagine the hours spent in the tattooist's chair, lying back and maybe enjoying the pain. Apart from the ink, his body was smooth, even down to his crotch. Olivier licked his lips. Slowly. And smiled.

Oberon bucked, but Olivier took hold of him and flipped him, forcing his face into the rug. One hand was enough to hold him down. He slid a knee between his legs.

Harsh guttural sounds burst out of Oberon's throat. They were the cries of a doomed man, and they only added to Olivier's desire. The naked form beneath him, squirming to get away, that pliable, corruptible body. It made him hard.

Olivier unzipped himself, ready to conquer. He bit into his hand, and blood pooled in his palm. He slopped it between Oberon's smooth cheeks, marking him with his true essence. Oberon tensed, but Olivier's hand was stronger, and he worked his way in, coating the skin, wetting his hole, forcing a finger in. Oberon gasped, choking on the breath that caught in his throat. Olivier probed deeper and Oberon panted. Withdrawing his hand, he sank his teeth into it again, and this time coated himself with the red liquid.

He whispered into Oberon's ear. "This is going to hurt. But don't worry. I'll enjoy it."

Ignoring the squeals and the yelps, Olivier pried apart his firm, round ass, and speared him. He groaned as he sliced through Oberon's seal and penetrated his unwilling channel. The pressure made him harder, and Oberon's efforts to free himself only made Olivier impale him more, deeper, further. The carpet underneath Oberon's hands burned and blackened as he tried to master his faltering power. Olivier didn't care. It didn't touch him.

He could have fucked forever, but eventually Oberon lay still and compliant. No fight remained. There was nothing left to conquer. Olivier brought himself closer to climax and held it, the tension building to an exquisite peak that swirled in his balls. As he came, he bit into Oberon's shoulder. The witch cried out. Olivier pumped his hips harder and his cock spasmed, spewing forth into this reluctant lover. He drank, not to kill, but to weaken further. Olivier replenished his spent stores; the pain and his resistance had taken so much. But his heart warmed to know he could withstand—and had mastered—this witch sent by his sister to control him.

He withdrew his fangs and his dick at the same time. Oberon didn't move, but he breathed. Just. Olivier put himself back in his jeans and zipped up. He walked over to the wall and withdrew the blade.

He turned Oberon with his foot and crouched over him. Oberon didn't even attempt to defend himself. Not that Olivier wanted to kill him. Not now. Leaning close, his fangs sheathed, a wide smile slid across his face.

"You failed. And I could kill you. But I want you to live a life in fear of shadows and shy from the touch of another." He licked Oberon's face from his chin and up his cheek. He tasted salt, either from tears or sweat. Or both. Either way, it tasted of victory.

He walked to the door. The witch wouldn't rise, not until after he was gone. No chance of a bolt of fire hitting him in the back. The room was just an ordinary room now, perhaps a place where two lovers had shared a candlelit evening. Even the stench had been replaced with the aroma of animalistic sex.

*Not a totally wasted night.*

But he'd been a fool to trust a witch. He'd have to find the Duke himself—even if that meant tearing the whole city apart.

*Aut inveniam viam aut faciam.*

# XVI

"I COULD HAVE HEALED THAT SCAR SO NOTHING remained." Alex traced his fingers down the faded line across Thierry's back.

They lay on the bed with nothing covering them, the warmth of the night enough of a blanket to make sheets unnecessary and uncomfortable. For Alex, anyway. Such things didn't bother Thierry.

"In the end, I was glad to have it."

"Really?" Alex's fingers pressed harder, as if he tried to find a message engraved into his flesh. Thierry couldn't feel where the skin had knitted together. It may as well have been drawn on with chalk.

"It made me different from Olivier."

Alex lay down beside him and inched closer, his hand resting now, his arm embracing him. "There is more difference than just a scar."

He wasn't quite sure about that so murmured something non-committal. The last few years had shown him he shared more of his brother's nature than he'd previously admitted. Blood-stained walls and carpets were enough to convince him of that. And he'd been possessed by a singular purpose for longer than some cities existed. It was well inside the borders of fanaticism. He closed his eyes. Alex hugged him tighter and he calmed. In the back of his mind, doubts amassed like an army ready to storm the walls. Alex was his now, but Olivier still loomed large in their lives, threatening to bring everything down. How was this going to work?

Alex's fingers twined through Thierry's hair and brushed along his scalp. It was such a soothing gesture, laced with the purr of Alex's power. Thierry sighed. When they'd returned from Daddy's house, they had to fight to keep their hands off each other, at least until they were inside. Then there was no stopping them as they tore at their clothes and made it as far as the bedroom door before collapsing to the floor and fucking for all they were worth. Raw and primal, Thierry relished in Alex's hunger. They spent the afternoon making love like they had centuries to make up for. And when they rested, they talked.

Alex had told of his estranged family on the other side of the country. He spoke of how his power had manifested at an early age, when he'd broken an arm in a fight at school, and since then his ability had grown in strength. Asked why he didn't use it on others, he simply said that it caused more problems than it was worth.

And then there was the hustling. Thierry tried not to feel jealous, but slime oozed through his body. It had been a choice, a chance to earn extra money while he figured out what he wanted to do with his life. While other kids worked shitty after-school jobs for five bucks an hour, he tried something that paid better. And it hadn't been all bad—or so he said. There was no sparkle in his eye when he talked of it.

"Slaves and submissives are paid well." Then he stopped speaking.

For Thierry's part, he talked more than he had in centuries, but it was a fragmented history that jumped through times and places he only just remembered. He wasn't ready to talk too openly about Etienne or Reiner. He would eventually. Alex was content to hear of the past, even if it was edited of so much madness and murder.

"Tell me more about Carcassonne."

"It's hard to explain to someone who—" He slammed his eyes shut as his thoughts were swept away. He curled into a ball.

Olivier burned, and even when Thierry opened his eyes and his blurred sight sharpened, it continued to beat at him. This was not the Duke. That affliction was well known now. His weapons delivered crisp sears to his insides. Olivier had fallen into a witch's hands and there was no sign of the pain ebbing.

"Thierry, what's wrong?" Alex shouted, his hands squeezing Thierry's shoulder. He didn't dare move for fear of a second wave. If it came as strong, he might not be able to stop himself from lashing out at Alex.

"It'll pass. Just give me some time."

Alex placed both hands on Thierry's skin, and he could feel the healing energy enter his body.

"Stop! You can't heal this, and I don't know what will happen if you try." Olivier might feel it. His mouth went dry. What had Olivier felt *before*? No, he couldn't. Olivier was still glutted from all that blood. Nothing could have gotten through. *Could it?*

Grinding his jaw, Thierry's strength faded. He lay crippled, while somewhere in the city Olivier writhed beneath the onslaught. He twisted to find a way out, his body fought the attack, and he snarled.

The veil shimmered. He could almost see what was happening. Christ, he could feel the wall behind his brother's body and make out shapes in the dim light. He scrunched his eyes shut, desperate to block Olivier. His mind was on other things, but he was unpredictable at the best of times, and there was no telling if his attention would swing to the bond and what he could learn through it.

"Turn out the lights. Close the curtains. Get out of the room and shut the door," he whispered hoarsely and rapidly.

"But—"

"Just do it! Quick!" There was no time for soft words. Danger was closer than he thought.

Alex leapt off the bed, closed the curtains and shut the door. Thierry opened one eye and the room was pitch. It soothed him. The pain rippled and flared. He swore but slowly he mastered it. Then he could think.

If Olivier survived, he had to feed. Thierry would hold his face to an endless row of jugulars if he had to. The bond had to be smothered, and soon. That meant leaving Alex alone for a time.

A knock at the front door came as another blast racked his body and he was swept into the grunts of his brother and the roaring of flames in his ears. The darkness weighed on him, and he tried to keep from shouting out. That had gotten Alex into trouble before. He panted when the pain subsided and hugged his knees closer to him.

Once he was aware of his own body, he turned his ear to whatever was happening in the rest of the apartment. Had Alex answered the door? He heard no voices. No movement came from outside the bedroom. Olivier forgotten, and the agony now worn down to a mere irritation, he slid off the bed and crept to the door. He cracked it an inch. His eye landed on the open front door, and the note pinned to it. He ran to it, snatching the knife from the splintering wood and read the scrap of paper.

Without stopping to dress, he sprinted out of the apartment and hunted around the building, invisibility cloaking him. With Alex's scent locked in his nostrils, he found a lead and raced after it. He followed until the trail ran out suddenly in the midst of city streets. He sniffed the air desperately. He couldn't have lost him. The Duke couldn't have taken him.

But he had.

With Alex's path gone, he didn't know which way to turn. His naked feet stomped through dirt. He slicked his hand through his hair and pulled at it, hard enough to make his scalp cry. The Duke had Alex, and the note said there was only one way to get him back.

*Bring Olivier and I'll let him live. Come alone and he dies.*

There was an address, a time. That was it. He was stuck. Bringing Olivier to the Duke meant revealing Alex. Not bringing him meant...

There had to be a way this could work. Possibilities streamed through his head, each one beating him down and tearing a chunk out of him. He had been so close to happiness but now Alex had been forced into their feud. Thierry only hoped he could get him out of this alive.

# XVII

Olivier loved abattoirs, especially the old abandoned ones with rusty hooks hanging from the roof. Had the Duke chosen this location knowing this? He and Thierry crept in through a broken window, silently stepping over the detritus littered across the floor. Here and there were discarded and dirty clothes, ratty sleeping bags and soiled pillows, broken cardboard boxes and empty cans and bottles. Dim streetlights barely broke through the smeared half-cracked glass but they could see fine. The killing floor was large, the ceiling high, with a few holes that went up into the roof, and a few into the basement. Thick pillars held the whole thing up. Wherever the Duke was, there were plenty of places to hide. Not that he could hide forever.

The night had turned out better than planned. After he'd overpowered Oberon, Thierry, barely dressed but wearing a face of granite, assaulted him in the streets and insisted he'd found the Duke's lair. Envy skewered his entrails at not having found the Duke himself, but Thierry didn't gloat. Prickly, that's how he looked. And that's what it felt like to be near him, too, to sense him coursing through his veins. However weak. Oberon's blood had done wonders.

Olivier tried to coerce Thierry into waiting a day—whatever was wrong with him might make their attack more fragile than was safe—but Thierry wouldn't be swayed. His hand locked around Olivier's wrist and they were committed. The way Thierry looked, like a thunderstorm meeting an earthquake, Olivier couldn't resist. When Olivier asked why the rush, Thierry rounded on him with his fists clenched.

"He's lived too long."

It seemed a good enough answer. And the rage that churned through his brother was a marked improvement.

As they slipped through the run-down building, Thierry growled at something to their right. He cut off midway, but Olivier saw it. A human, bare to the waist, hung suspended from the ceiling with chains around his wrists. He breathed. Tape covered his mouth, but his wide eyes called to them and he rattled his shackles.

*Bait.*

Olivier almost brushed off Thierry's growl for annoyance, the cheap temptation to drink and distract him while on his mission. But the quick way he avoided Olivier's gaze and the twitching of his jaw was enough for Olivier to realize this human meant something.

And there could only ever be one person who meant something to Thierry.

And the way the bait looked at them...

Olivier bared his fangs and raised his fist, striking his brother's face. Thierry fell, spinning out of Olivier's reach, then jumped to his feet. Olivier charged. Thierry struck, and Olivier skidded back.

"You lying whore!"

He ignored his throbbing chin and ran at Thierry again, but his twin was prepared, and punched him square in the nose. Thierry didn't relent, again and again striking him, pummeling his face, his torso. He swiped at his legs to knock him off balance, but Olivier jumped up and kicked Thierry in the head. Spinning around, he met Olivier's jab with his right hand, blocked him and delivered a powerful punch to the center of his chest.

Olivier soared across the abattoir and skidded into the wall with a thud. Thierry didn't waste any time. He ran towards the human. Olivier scrambled to his feet. No way could Thierry be allowed to leave with that whore. Olivier would never see him again, and he'd be left to face the Duke alone, wherever he was in this crumbling wreck.

But Thierry didn't make it.

A shadow burst from the darkness and barreled into him, shooting him away from the human, pushing him back into the shadows and against a wall.

Olivier's chest exploded like he'd been stabbed with a freshly fired sword. He roared from the agony and crumpled to his knees. His cries matched Thierry's. When he looked up, he saw Thierry pinned to the wall, a sword sticking half out of him, holding him in place like a beetle on a collector's board. Two more fired into his shoulders, and his arms couldn't move to dislodge them.

The Duke fled into the shadows.

Thierry struggled, but that only made it burn more.

"Stop," Olivier whispered harshly but Thierry didn't follow his command.

Olivier forced himself to stand. The Duke could come

at him at any moment. Thierry's torment rippled through his body and threatened to bring him down again.

"If you don't keep still, we're both dead," he grunted through closed teeth.

Thierry shot him a look that would make a cobra retreat, but that was nothing to what Olivier felt for his *beloved* brother at that moment.

"You're dead anyway," said the voice from the darkness. It came from the shadows ahead of him.

Olivier straightened. The Duke wasn't going to see him cower. A shift in the wind signaled the Duke had moved. A second later, and a voice from behind confirmed it.

"Thierry gets to watch me kill you. And then his lover."

Olivier couldn't halt his growl, but as soon as it was out, he clamped his jaw shut. The Duke laughed. Him knowing about Thierry's *lover* was worse than any of the pain the Duke had rained down on him. It was an admission that Thierry's affections were always for someone else. Olivier could have lived with that knowledge gnawing away at the core of his soul so long as no one voiced it. He focused on that maniac's laugh. He was going to enjoy ripping his face off and giving it to Thierry as an offering. That, and the heart of the human.

Olivier swept into the darkness towards the Duke's voice and pulled out the salvaged dagger from behind his back. The Duke met his mid-air assault, a knife in each hand, coming up to block Olivier's arms. The impact echoed around the slaughterhouse. They fell to the ground with Olivier on top. He struck with his fangs and attacked with the knife, going for anywhere that was exposed. The Duke defended himself too well, but that was all he could do. The daggers clutched in his hands were unable to make a cut. He weaved his head left and right, ducking out of the path of Olivier's fangs, wrestling to keep him away. In one quick movement, he freed his right arm, sweeping it across Olivier's chest and pushing him back far enough to bring in his knee and heave Olivier off.

Olivier didn't wait for the Duke to prepare himself. His blood raged at the mere scent of him on his clothes. He lunged at him again, kicked him in the chest, and sent the Duke flying across the open space to ram into a pillar. Olivier soared with him. He raised his boot and brought it down on the Duke's hand, held protectively in front of him. He crushed the wrist against the floor, drawing from the Duke a growl. He grabbed Olivier's ankle and flung him off. The Duke snorted like a dying buffalo, but despite his weakening, he staggered to his feet and steadied himself. He still held the dagger.

Olivier stepped back into the shadows. From his vantage point, he looked into eyes of flint and study that face of bitterness. Olivier had been the one to do that. When they'd first met in Saxony, there had been pride, certainly smugness. There had been confidence, and a certainty he possessed power beyond that of mere mortals.

*Just like Henri.*

"You are a coward, Olivier," the Duke hissed into the black. "I would have been ashamed to call you my son."

Olivier darted towards the Duke and wrestled him to the ground. The daggers flew from the Duke's hands and skittered across the concrete. With Olivier pressing down on him, the Duke struggled to fight, tried to punch and throw him off, but Olivier gripped his arms. The Duke bucked his hips and kicked, but Olivier bore down on him.

"It's time we ended this," Olivier said.

The Duke spat in Olivier's face.

Olivier smirked, pleased. This is what he'd wanted all along, ever since that castle and his beautiful son.

Olivier saw his father staring out at him, saw the hate that his father had for him, saw the unwillingness to accept, to love, to give. The Duke was not here because Wolf had died. The Duke was here because he'd been cheated, he'd lost, and he'd been bested. A man who was so used to winning can't bear to lose, and now he was about to lose everything.

Olivier bared his fangs and dove down, forcing the Duke's head aside and sought his jugular. He sank his teeth into the hot, pumping vein. The Duke struggled, but Olivier kept drinking. His blood had the taint of dusty magic, like air in a forgotten cellar. This was no ordinary blood and the taste was nothing to be savored.

The power left the Duke's body, giving up the fight, giving up the anger, giving up the will. Eventually his legs stopped kicking, his arms fell. The pressure from the Duke's head as it tried to protect his neck evaporated. The last drop of blood, for Olivier had sought it all, wanting to make sure there was nothing left of the Duke to return, slid down Olivier's throat, and he moaned like a man blessed by God. He rested against the Duke and was still.

The corpse began to desiccate. He sat up and watched the skin thinning like old yellowing lace. It tightened against his skeleton. Before too long, Olivier straddled a papery skeleton. He stood and looked on the dried vessel. In a childish fit he jumped up and down on the body, crushing it until there was nothing but clothes. The dust dissipated and turned the air stale. Olivier sighed.

He looked up and into the eyes of his brother. They narrowed, and both of them snarled. He knew Thierry wouldn't ask for freedom. He took up his struggle again to break loose, and the blades scored Olivier's body. There was only one thing left to do.

He turned to the whore. He hung from the chains binding his wrists. Dried blood ran in rivers down his forehead and his chest, soaking his clothes. The whore watched him. Olivier advanced. This time, Thierry would see how much he was willing to do to make him stay. He would see how much Olivier loved him, and how much he would sacrifice to keep what he owned.

Thierry twisted on the blades, not caring about the damage he did to himself. Olivier flinched but did his best to steel his mind and focus on what had to be done. Thierry had to learn.

The whore was level with him, easy to bite, and tried to fight, swinging and kicking, but it wouldn't stop what had to happen.

Olivier gripped his head, pulled it back to expose the throat, then bit into his flesh.

Thierry screamed.

The whore whined.

Olivier drank. It tasted sourer than the Duke's blood.

"Wait! Oli, stop," Thierry called out. He was still. Finally.

Olivier drank.

"Please. Please, enough."

He drank.

"He can't die. He can't. Not again. Please."

He drank.

"I'll give you what you've always wanted. I will be yours to do with as you will. I'll succumb to you, and I'll love you and forget Etienne."

He bit harder at the mention of the whore's name.

"Please, Oli. If he dies, that's it. There will never be

another chance. I promise I will give myself to you completely. Like I always should have. Please, don't kill him."

Did he dare trust his brother again? Olivier stopped drinking but he didn't withdraw. The weak throbbing around his fangs told him the whore still lived but not for long. Not that Thierry would ever be allowed to find out whether he lived or died. Not after tonight.

"Release me, and I'll show you I mean it."

Olivier's teeth pulled out of the holes, and the whore slumped.

*How I hate to leave you alive.*

He walked over to his twin. He felt the desperation and the truth. Thierry meant what he'd said. He believed he could trade his whore for spending the rest of his immortal existence in the arms of his brother. That was all Olivier ever wanted, and now it was offered. Could he accept Thierry at his word? A love and a plea came through the bond. He wanted to believe it more than anything.

"I am yours, Olivier."

Olivier's chest tightened. He leaned forward slowly and touched his lips to his brother's. Thierry returned the kiss but with greater intensity. Their mouths opened and tongues touched. Thierry licked the coating of blood from inside his mouth. Olivier's knees shook. Centuries of longing and waiting, hoping that one day his brother would see the love he held in his heart. Thierry would know all Olivier ever needed was him. He could have wept with the relief.

The pain still carried on underneath, adding to Olivier's desire. It buzzed as Thierry moved, touched him, smoothed his fingers over his neck, pulled him as close as he could with the sword still protruding from his stomach.

The hurt in his shoulder intensified, but Thierry kissed deeper, holding him, forcing him to keep contact. Thierry broke the kiss momentarily, held his eyes, and pushed him back a few inches. A smile brightened his face, and Olivier was safe.

He was home.

# XVIII

THIERRY SHOVED THE KNIFE THROUGH THE SIDE OF HIS brother's neck. Olivier's eyes bulged, and his screams against the hellfire mixed with Thierry's own. Thierry pulled out the other blade from his shoulder and drove it into his brother's chest. He staggered back, and Thierry wrenched the sword from his stomach. He was free.

And Olivier was going to pay.

Thierry fought the pain, easier now that he'd become accustomed to it, and stumbled, but his purpose was pure, and nothing would sway him.

Olivier inched towards Alex. Even in this state, he was still a threat. He reached for the blade in his neck, but Thierry knocked Olivier off his feet and speared him with the sword. Thrusting the blade through the concrete, he buried it up to the hilt. Olivier's hands fell away from the sudden pain. Misery washed through him; Thierry quickly dammed his psyche. He might be weakened, but he wouldn't allow Olivier to attack him from the inside. He pulled the knives from Olivier's neck and chest and stabbed them through his twin's hands.

He glanced at Alex, his head slumped forward, fresh rivers of blood running down his bare chest. He breathed still, but slowly. Just. *Why hadn't he healed? Had too much been taken?*

"Alex?" he called.

Olivier bucked at the name and shouted at him, mad incoherent raving. Despite the pain, despite the magic and his growing weakness, Thierry didn't believe Olivier would stay down for long. He'd tear his hands off before too much time passed. Though there was one way to make sure Olivier wouldn't retaliate.

He rushed to Alex and unhooked him. He carried him in his arms and laid his head on Olivier's chest. Thierry bared his fangs and bit into his brother's flesh. Olivier screamed, but Thierry sliced open his skin, and when the hole was big enough, held Alex's mouth to the opening.

"Drink," he whispered.

Olivier thrashed, but Thierry held him down.

At first Alex didn't do anything, and Thierry thought he was too late. He was about to bring his own wrist to his mouth, to feed Alex himself, but then his tongue lapped at the liquid. His mouth moved and he took more. When the wound closed, Thierry leant forward and reopened it. Alex drank again.

The more Olivier struggled, the weaker he became. And the more Alex took in. Thierry repeated the ritual with about the same composure as he would have slaughtered pigs in the abattoir. He couldn't think that it was Olivier he cut into.

*My brother no more.*

Keeping Alex alive—and making him immortal and invincible—was all that mattered. He ignored the sickness swishing in his stomach and put it down to hunger. As Alex fed, Olivier became as sallow as Rellius had. Alex moved, sucked harder, raised himself. He stopped. Turned to Thierry.

"More. Faster," Thierry encouraged.

Thierry leant forward and bit into the underside of Olivier's upper arm, opening arteries. Alex dove for them and drew hard. Olivier groaned for the betrayal, groaned for his loss. Thierry forced his ears to hear only the sound of Alex sucking blood.

When there was nothing left that came willingly, Alex's lips left Olivier's body. He wiped his mouth with the back of his hand and turned to Thierry. He stood, stared at his own body as if he were noticing it for the first time. He noticed the sensations that Thierry had felt so long ago, as the blood reached into every part of his body, to replenish it, to reinvigorate it, to make it whole, immortal, strong, beautiful.

*Look at what I've created. And isn't he divine?*

Alex opened his mouth and his fangs appeared. He touched them with his fingers, cut himself, drank the blood, sucked his finger, and smiled at Thierry and knelt next to him.

"I thought I was going to lose you again," Thierry whispered.

"Never. I've never gone anywhere." Alex kissed him with a force he hadn't known before, one that spoke of pure lust and animal hunger but also rediscovered love. Thierry had him now. Never again could Olivier separate them. They kissed, and it was the kiss of centuries of longing, of waiting, of needing and of relief.

A scream from Olivier made them stop. The tortured sound of the vampire on the floor reminded them that an enemy was still here.

302             DANIEL DE LORNE

"He's weak," Thierry said, his voice glacial, "but not for long. When we were first made, he said we only had one chance to kill our maker."

Olivier must die. Though he struggled with the idea, he knew he would have to take part. Alex squeezed his hand, and they neared his twin.

"I thank you, Olivier," Alex said. "Without you, I would have died."

Alex bared his fangs. Olivier's eyes defied him, but he was too weak to defend himself. Thierry looked at Alex. He was ready to exact his first kill, all too happy for it to be Olivier. Thierry felt only sadness for the inevitability that it had come to this. With a weak smile, they hastened forward.

Their teeth hadn't touched the skin when a force hit Alex and sent him hurtling across the giant space, smashing into the wall and sending dust cascading from the crumbling bricks. He slid to the ground, still for a moment before he regained his feet and snarled at someone behind Thierry. He turned.

"Stay away from him. Both of you," Aurelia commanded.

Thierry rose to his feet. "No, Aurelia. He is ours to do with as we wish."

"No!" Aurelia showed her palm as Alex leapt for Olivier's body. An invisible force around Olivier repelled them both. Alex railed against it. Thierry, too. He knew it would be futile, but he had to try. Their future depended on being free of Olivier, and now that his mind had been set on this righteous act, he wasn't going to be thwarted.

But the shield held firm.

He turned a scream on his sister. "Why?"

He demanded freedom from this monster, the one

who'd tortured him for more than six centuries. They would never be left alone otherwise. Ever.

"Why must you allow him to live? What kind of existence will that make for us? For him? Put us both out of our misery."

"He is needed."

He was so sick of hearing that. She spoke with all the sanctimonious authority of a pope presiding over an excommunication. He'd always felt more affection for his younger sister than for his twin. She'd nursed him through the first few decades after Reiner was killed, and then she'd filled him with hope of finding Etienne's soul again. But protecting Olivier was beyond comprehension.

"He's nothing!" His voice echoed around the building. "A cruel parasite. When you told me to return to him, you said I would get what I wanted, that Olivier would no longer be an issue. Is this just another one of your games?"

"Brother, please, there are things that need to happen. Olivier must live."

Thierry hissed at her, moved to Alex and took his cold hand.

"Let me explain." She bent over Olivier and removed one of the knives from his hands. She examined it, and her mouth twisted like she'd eaten maggots. "All this, the Duke, the knives, the hunt—it's all part of a bigger picture. Did you never wonder where the Duke came from? Who gave him his power? Surely you must understand that someone wouldn't go to such trouble just for petty vengeance?"

Thierry bristled.

"There's someone else out there. Someone who was only too happy for the Duke to be the weapon. And if you allow Alex to kill Olivier now, then it's over."

"But I'll never be free of him," Thierry roared. "I'll

always be able to feel him coursing through my veins. I want this monster banished."

A sad laugh came from Olivier.

"We're twins, Thierry," Olivier murmured. "If I'm a monster, you're one too."

Thierry ignored him, choosing to glare at his sister, waiting for her answer.

"I'm here to tell you that Olivier must live. You will find out why soon enough."

"But what about the feelings? It's not just me feeling him, it's him feeling me. I don't want him inside me ever again."

"You enjoy it, Thierry," Olivier chuckled. "Admit it."

Thierry clenched his jaw. He wouldn't respond. He wouldn't allow himself. Olivier wasn't trying to fight; he was trying to break through Thierry's hate for him.

"He lives," she said matter-of-factly.

"Then take away the connection."

"No!" Olivier screamed.

"I can't."

"Don't lie. You can."

For the first time tonight, she looked uncertain. Almost afraid. The hardness had gone from her eyes and was replaced with the compassion he remembered so fondly.

"I don't care how it's done. Dampen it. Make it one way. Anything. I just don't want to feel it ever again."

He locked eyes with his sister. Olivier whimpered, and tried to reason with them. He was scared now, pleading. Thierry knew this was right.

With a sigh, she beckoned to Thierry. "Come here."

Olivier lurched, his one pinned hand tethering him to the filthy floor. "Aurelia, no!"

Thierry walked towards her. She placed a palm on his

chest, and he stiffened from the flow of power pouring into him. She closed her eyes, breathed.

A heat spread from her hand and under his skin, through his body, to his head, his arms, down his legs. It brought up all the feelings he'd ever experienced that weren't his.

The first time Olivier fucked a guy.

The fear and hatred of his father when he caught Olivier staring with lust and love at Thierry.

The night they killed the maker, and Olivier's joy at being with Thierry so completely.

Everything was awakened briefly, flared like a struck match, and then just as suddenly snuffed. No, not snuffed. Wrenched. When she let go, he doubled over.

With his eyes closed, he searched himself. He concentrated, trying to find any trace, almost desperate to find that which had always been with him. Had he made the right choice? Alex's hand rested on his shoulder and Thierry felt only his love for this soul, nothing else. No jealousy, no anger, no hate.

Thierry was Thierry.

Olivier was Olivier.

They were separate.

*At last.*

His brother wailed. How many times had Thierry done the same over a loss such as this?

"Only for now," Aurelia said. "You will be re-joined when required."

"Until then?" Thierry asked.

"Olivier is coming with me."

"Like fuck I am," his brother spat.

"Olivier, you are now too important to leave running

around unchecked. Who knows what you'll do? Who knows what Thierry and Alex will do when you meet?"

"You intend to keep me locked up?"

Aurelia didn't answer, just turned to Thierry.

"You can't! I'll kill you, like I should have done you when you were born." Olivier reached for the sword sticking out of his gut and pulled it out. He was about to rise, but Aurelia flicked her hand, and he was forced back down.

She smiled sadly at Thierry. "Goodbye, brother."

Then, with an exaggerated flourish of her arms, Aurelia and Olivier disappeared.

The abattoir was silent.

Pain and anger were echoed in the dust.

"What now?" Alex asked.

Thierry looked around the abandoned building, the crumpled clothes, the holes in the walls and floors, the blasted concrete. They looked as if they'd always been there. But for all its signs of decay, the place smelled of oranges in sunshine, a bright summer full of promise. Olivier was Aurelia's problem now, and she could handle him better than Thierry ever had.

"We should leave," he said.

"Where are we going?"

"Anywhere you like just...let's get out of this city."

"Anywhere?" Alex asked. His eyes glowed, the new vampire filled with power. "But what about..." He half-laughed. "I just realized there isn't anything to say goodbye to."

Thierry embraced him. He had lost Etienne the night he was made. He remembered placing his body in the grave he'd dug with his own hands. The memory of blood-tears falling on the freshly turned soil made his throat clog.

"Let's go somewhere we can be alone."

Alex kissed him, gentler than before, his tongue still rich with the taste of blood. Thierry gripped him hard, unwilling to let go, glad that he was vampire now, that he was unbreakable and couldn't be taken from him.

"I like the sound of that."

Thierry took Alex's hand. "I've waited centuries for you, and I'm never letting go."

# EPILOGUE

OF ALL THE SCREAMS TEARING THROUGH THE WORLD that night, only two made Aurelia shiver. Olivier roared in the darkness, severed from his beloved twin brother, bound and living at the mercy of his sister. The other—older and far more pissed off—made the ether quiver. Aurelia steeled her heart against both, blocked them from her hearing, and continued with her plans.

# ABOUT THE AUTHOR

**Daniel de Lorne writes about men, monsters and magic.**

In love with writing since he wrote a story about a talking tree at age six, his first novel, the romantic horror *Beckoning Blood*, was published in 2014. At the heart of every book is a romance between two men, whether they're irresistible vampires, historical hotties, or professional paramours.

In his other life, Daniel is a professional writer and researcher in Perth, Australia, with a love of history and nature. All of which makes for great story fodder.

And when he's not working, he and his husband explore as much of this amazing world as they can, from the ruins of Welsh abbeys to trekking famous routes and swimming with whales.

You can contact Daniel through his website or sign up to his newsletter to receive all the latest news on releases, giveaways, cover reveals and more.

*Connect with Daniel*
www.danieldelorne.com

ALSO BY DANIEL DE LORNE

## URBAN FANTASY / PARANORMAL

*Bonds of Blood Trilogy*

Beckoning Blood

Burning Blood

Binding Blood

*Immortals of the Apocalypse Trilogy*

Soul Survivor

Soul Savior

Soul Surrender

The Heart and Soul of Ragnar the Red:

An Immortals of the Apocalypse Origins Novella

## ROMANTIC SUSPENSE

Embers and Echoes

## CONTEMPORARY ROMANCE

The Love Left Behind

Set the Stage

## CHRISTMAS SHORT STORIES

Christmas with the Lumberjack

# ACKNOWLEDGMENTS

*Beckoning Blood* was my first published novel and I'd like to thank Kate Cuthbert and Escape Publishing for taking a chance on my boys and giving me my start in the industry. It came out on 1 May 2014. I decided to take it further on my own so republished it in 2020 with minor edits.

Eternal gratitude goes to my dear friend and fellow author, Nikki Logan, for her belief in me, in this story and these characters. Without her free-and-frank advice, critical eye, red pen and support, I wouldn't have gotten far.

Thank you to family and friends for frequently asking how my writing was going so that really, there wasn't any choice but to forge ahead.

And finally, thanks to Glen, for the years of encouragement and for allowing me to push him out of the room before he had the chance to read anything over my shoulder.

Printed in Great Britain
by Amazon